"Megan Crane uses wit, style, and pizzazz to chronicle the often heartbreaking hilarity of turning friends into enemies, enemies into lovers, and lovers into friends."

—Heather Swain, author of *Luscious Lemon*

"Megan Crane captures the emotional angst of love and betrayal between friends in this heartfelt story about how your worst enemy might just be yourself."

—Stephanie Lehmann, author of *You Could Do Better*

"Funny, sharp, and poignant, like eavesdropping on a wonderfully intimate conversation between girlfriends at happy hour . . . Megan Crane expertly navigates the tangled path of college friendship in a grown-up world."

—Melanie Lynne Hauser, author of *Confessions of Super Mom*

"Perfectly captures the poignancy of a broken heart and betrayal, while simultaneously making the reader laugh out loud with dead-on observations and wit. I rooted for this heroine and was completely swept away by her too-real tale."

—Erica Orloff, author of *Mafia Chic*

"I've been a fan of Megan Crane's since day one! FRENEMIES touches on so many themes—friends who stab you in the back, loving the wrong guy, anxiety over turning 30 . . . I related on so many levels."

—Johanna Edwards, bestselling author of *The Next Big Thing*

"A warm and witty coming-of-age story. Before you open the cover, make sure you've got a good bit of time blocked out for nonstop reading, apologize in advance to your neighbors for the hysterical laughter, have a couple of tissues on stand-by, and go ahead and schedule a get-together with your best friends. This may be one of my favorite chick-lit novels, ever."

—Shanna Swendson, author of
Once Upon Stilettos and *Enchanted, Inc.*

"This is a book you won't be able to put down until you get to the last page. Megan Crane spins a compelling story about the hazards of life, love, and friendship."

—Cara Lockwood, national bestselling author of *I Do, But I Don't*

"With FRENEMIES, especially the trials and tribulations of its wonderful protagonist Gus, Megan Crane has scored a winner!"

—Julie Kenner, author of *California Demon*

"Adorable! Megan Crane perfectly captures an underlying truth about the complexities of female friendships."

—Diana Peterfreund, author of *Secret Society Girl*

"A laugh-out-loud look at female friendships and the men who come between them."

—Lynda Curnyn, author of *Bombshell* and
Confessions of an Ex-Girlfriend

"With heart, humor, and rare honesty, Megan Crane creates a story that every woman should share with her BFF."

—Jennifer O'Connell, author of *Bachelorette #1*

"Megan Crane is a delicious writer, and FRENEMIES is another treat to savor."

—Laura Caldwell, author of *The Rome Affair*
and *The Night I Got Lucky*

everyone else's girl

english as a second language

ALSO BY MEGAN CRANE

English as a Second Language
Everyone Else's Girl

frenemies

MEGAN CRANE

NEW YORK   BOSTON

Copyright © 2007 by Megan Crane

5 Spot
Hachette Book Group USA
237 Park Avenue
New York, NY 10169

Visit our Web site at www.5-spot.com.

5 Spot is an imprint of Warner Books. The 5 Spot name and logo are trademarks of Warner Books.

Printed in the United States of America

First Edition: June 2007
10 9 8 7 6 5 4 3 2

Library of Congress Cataloging-in-Publication Data
Crane, Megan
    Frenemies / Megan Crane — 1st ed.
        p. cm.
    ISBN-13: 978-0-446-69855-9
    ISBN-10: 0-446-69855-5
    1. Female friendship—Fiction. 2. Love stories. gsafd I. Title.
    PS3603.R385F75 2007
    813'.6—dc22   2006024553

Because I knew you
I have been changed
for good.

        —Wicked

I am lucky enough to have been given the gift of very good friends, whom I hope someday to deserve. I am who I am thanks in large part to the phenomenal women and men who share, support, and enhance my life every day in their own peculiar and often marvelous ways.

This book is for you.

acknowledgments

A million thanks to Julie Barer for finding A-plots, explaining everything, talking me off ledges, being so effortlessly wonderful, and being the best teammate anyone could wish for. All while also being the greatest agent in the world!

If I hadn't already adored my fabulous editor, Karen Kosztolnyik, for her keen insights and ability to shape my stories so beautifully, I would certainly worship her for being a *Veronica Mars* fan and for comparing Henry to the delicious Logan Echolls. High praise, indeed!

Thanks to everyone at Warner Books (past and present) who help me in so many ways, especially Michele Bidelspach, Elly Weisenberg, Brigid Pearson, Mari Okuda, and Keri Friedman. Thanks also to Kim Dower and Allison Hunter at Kim-from-LA for so much help out on this coast!

Thanks to Michelle Kennedy Lower for answering so many Boston questions, and Charley Lower for chauffeuring me around on the hottest, most miserably humid day possible while Michelle gave me the insider's tour. Any

egregious Boston mistakes are entirely my fault and the
less egregious mistakes are, let's hope, creative license at
work.

Thanks to Anna Marsh Schroeder for living in that apartment all those years ago. (I just added a room!)

Thanks to Ani Matosian of the Getty Research Institute
for answering my questions about librarians, libraries, and
library degrees—all mistakes or exaggerations are mine!

To all of you who send me e-mail or comment on my
blog: thank you. You make my day.

I love (and owe a huge debt to) everyone who read
this novel in one of its (many!) drafts. Especially Kim
McCreight, who has read it almost as many times as I have
by this point. You deserve a medal!

To the marvelous Liza Palmer. And all the other aston-
ishingly talented authors I've been lucky enough to get to
know.

But most of all, thanks to and for Jeff Johnson.

chapter one

I blame it on Janis Joplin.

Because until that song came on, I was fine. *Fine.*

So what if I hadn't seen Nate since the memorable night I'd walked in on him kissing someone else two and a half weeks ago, which was seventeen total days, not that I was counting?

So what if he was supposed to be my boyfriend?

And so what if the girl he was kissing was none other than Helen Fairchild, my freshman-year roommate way back when?

Who, until that night, I'd thought valued our shared history and mutual exasperation enough to consider me a close friend—the sort of close friend who would find my boyfriend to be off-limits?

Seriously, I was *fine.*

I took a deep breath, and told myself that I didn't care *in the slightest* that Nate and Helen had just swept inside the bar together, looking flushed and giddy and bringing with them a swirl of cold weather from the fall night beyond. I didn't care that every single one of our mutual friends, all of whom were gathered together to celebrate a birthday, looked from the two of them to me to gauge my reaction. I didn't care that my heart—which I would have told you had broken into pieces too small to be seen with the naked eye and thus couldn't possibly break any further—thumped painfully in my chest, clearly whole enough to keep hurting.

If I burst into tears, I would never forgive myself.

I was so busy trying to look as if I didn't care and wasn't close to tears, in fact, that Amy Lee had to kick me under the table to get me to notice that she and her husband had returned from the bar, bearing armfuls of drinks.

"Stop staring at them," Amy Lee ordered.

"It's *fine*," I told her, which was surprisingly hard to do through a clenched jaw. "After all, who cares that we were together for almost four months after knowing each other since college? Who cares about *history*? I'm *perfectly fine* with this."

Amy Lee sighed and exchanged what I could only describe as a *significant look* with Oscar. Then, she and Oscar settled themselves on either side of me on the plush banquette. In support.

Or, possibly, to restrain me.

The two of them were a perfect example of the whole *opposites attract* thing, I thought, looking at them through the big mirror on the far wall. Amy Lee looked crisp and pulled together at all times, while Oscar always looked as if he'd just stepped off a skateboard. They'd met in dental school and fallen in love, apparently over molars. It was to their credit that I found that story romantic despite my long-held dental phobia.

Amy Lee slid a beer in front of me.

"Listen up, Augusta," she ordered me. Her use of my full, legal name—which I hated and therefore generally responded to only in places like the DMV—earned her a baleful glare.

But I listened.

"I get why you want him," she said. "Everyone adores Nate. He's practically made a career out of being adorable."

"I don't think he's adorable," Oscar said from my other side. "Not that he's *not* adorable, of course. I just don't think about it."

"I think even I had a crush on him for like fifteen seconds in college," Amy Lee continued, ignoring her husband. "How could you not? He was like the college version of the captain of the football team. All puppy-dog eyes and that bashful smile."

"Yeah, that's really adorable," Oscar retorted. "Let's talk more about his rugged good looks, so maybe I can have a crush on him, too."

Amy Lee had all the delicacy of a steamroller. I assumed this served her well in dentistry, but tonight it made me want to upend a drink over her head.

"'Puppy-dog eyes and that bashful smile'?" I echoed. I glared at her. "Why do you want to hurt me?"

"But here's the thing," Amy Lee said as if I hadn't spoken. "You've known the guy since we were all eighteen and only hooked up with him this summer. That's hardly raging-hot chemistry, now is it?"

"He hasn't been girlfriend-free since college!" I protested. "He was with that horrible Lisa for years!"

"I'm just saying it took you an awfully long time to get together with him," Amy Lee said. "Okay, sure, you liked him more than the weirdos you usually date, but still." She took a sip of her drink, which, unaccountably, appeared to be a Coke. I scowled at it, and she muttered something about designated driving.

As that was normally Oscar's job, I looked at him.

"I plan to drink a lot tonight," Oscar told me, his eyes across the bar on the Happy Couple. "I might toast Nate's *bashful smile* a few times, too."

Since he was staring at Nate, I gave myself permission to do the same. I watched as Nate peeled off his winter coat and exchanged manly handshakes with his buddies. I watched as Helen floated merrily on the end of his arm like a particularly well-tweezed balloon.

Seventeen days had not dimmed the pain even a little bit, it turned out, despite several bold proclamations to the contrary I'd made in the shower earlier that evening. If Gretchen, the birthday girl, hadn't called me personally and begged me to come, there was no way I would have attended this party. It had been bad enough to stand there that night two and a half weeks ago, face-to-face with the evidence that he and Helen were on kissing terms. Sitting in a crowded bar with half of Boston looking on as I was humiliated with every snuggle and simper was, it turned out, worse.

Much worse.

Nate and I first met years ago when we both attended Boston University. We became members of a wider group of friends who fell into two rough and interwoven groups themselves: those who had originally gone to BU together and others who had met thanks to summers spent on Cape Cod. We all became one big group of people who were loosely connected and spread out across the greater Boston metropolitan area, leading to a rollicking social life with competing parties almost every weekend.

And in this big group, Nate was the favorite. Everyone loved Nate. He was so good-looking and sweet-faced at eighteen that some women (who will remain nameless) had been known to lurk around the bushes to take pictures of him on the sly. He was also nice, which was so surprising it often stopped people in their tracks. He was sweet to everyone, universally considered cute, and, unfortunately, taken. Girls mooned over him and treasured the intimate conversations they had with him every now and again over beers when his girlfriend was somewhere else. Guys pounded him about the shoulders when they met him and thereafter, inevitably, called him "solid." Everyone loved Nate from afar until he'd finally broken up with Longtime Lisa (as she was known) for the last time in April.

The month of May was like the first season of *Desperate Housewives*, with all the girls playing Edie and Susan to Nate's Mike the Plumber, in a pitched battle to soothe his broken heart. Amy Lee and our other best friend, Georgia, took bets and predicted—accurately—that it would all end in rebound tears.

By the time Nate and I hooked up at a Fourth of July party, I figured we were out of his rebound woods. I'd been waiting for Nate for a long time. Amy Lee had a point about the kind of guys I'd dated throughout my twenties—commitment-allergic "musicians" and banker boys had been my specialties, and I was over them. More than that, Nate and I were a good match. Even an obvious match. I might not have the kind of irritating (to other women) bland attractiveness that girls like Longtime Lisa had, but I felt I was cute enough. More to the point, we had all the same friends. We liked the same things. We'd even lived in the same freshman dorm. I liked the story we could tell about how, once upon a time back in college before he'd fully committed to Longtime Lisa, he and I had almost kissed outside Sicilia's Pizza at 3:30 a.m.

Getting together with Nate *made sense.* It was the third part of my three-part plan for my twenty-ninth year, the one I'd come up with shortly after turning twenty-nine the previous January. The key to being a well-adjusted adult, I'd decided, involved three things: good friends, a good job, and a good boyfriend. I already knew that Amy Lee and Georgia were the best friends anyone could want—we'd been friends for over ten years and were practically family, and yet we had a much wider, active social group too, so no one had to feel claustrophobic. I was a librarian in a small museum near Boston Common, and I loved it. So what could be better than a boyfriend so perfect that other women plotted ways to impress him? A boyfriend who I'd actually been friends with for years? With Nate, finally, everything was as it should be. I could see our future stretch before us, one perfect fantasy after the next. I had nothing to fear from thirty. I was a *complete* adult, life was going along *as planned*, and there would be no need for the stereotypical I'm-about-to-turn-thirty breakdown.

And the fact that Nate was so cute that even Amy Lee sighed over him was just a bonus.

Across the room, Nate shifted position on his bar stool, so I could see his puppy-dog eyes for myself. And also the person those eyes were focused on: Helen.

I felt rage sweep through me, prickling along my scalp and then shooting along my skin to the tips of my toes.

The thing about Helen was that she was *that girl*, I thought as I knocked back my beer, and then helped myself to the rest of Oscar's. He didn't complain, he just raised his brow at Amy Lee and then launched himself toward the bar for refills.

You could say that I'd conducted a study of Helen, I thought then. It began the day she sauntered into the tiny, concrete-walled room we would be sharing for our freshman year, smiled at me and the remains of my high school hair, and claimed the bed beneath the windows. The better bed. I didn't even put up a fight. I was dazzled.

Helen, with her fashionably ratty jeans and casual assumption that everyone wanted to hang out with her, was cool. Impossibly cool. Even the fact that she had one of those jarring donkey laughs like Janice on *Friends* just made her interesting, when on anyone else, a laugh like that would be dorky beyond belief. Nothing about Helen was dorky.

Helen had no qualms about walking up to the cutest boy in our dorm and asking him what was going on that terrifying first night at college, and then inviting herself along. She didn't care if the more insecure girls hated her. She intimidated our RA simply by turning up and draping herself across a chair in that boneless way she had. She didn't seem to notice any of the tension or envy she kicked up in her wake.

Helen was a guy's girl. She never met a guy, in fact, who didn't want to be her friend. She never met a girl who did. I, meanwhile, was very much the opposite. My knowledge of boys at eighteen came entirely from fantasy novels and certain classic WB shows. I was a girl's girl. The moment I met Georgia and Amy Lee, I knew I would be friends with them, because we were all the same beneath the skin. Living with Helen was like seeing behind a curtain. I got to see what it was like to be everything I couldn't be.

She was *that girl*. The one I had believed for eighteen years existed only in the imaginations of Hollywood screenwriters. And the fact that she was my roommate meant that I got to be *that girl* along with her, if only in my own mind.

Between worshiping her at eighteen and wanting to leap across a crowded bar to strangle her at twenty-nine, however, there was the entire span of our friendship. There were the random nights out we'd had in those chaotic years after college, just the two of us, where I would marvel at her near-superhuman ability to attract cute boys and she would tell me how much she relied on my friendship. There were the phone conversations when she'd tell me long, hilarious stories about her romantic exploits that always ended with some guy begging for another chance while Helen tried to extricate herself. These were the things that made me roll my eyes when I saw her number on caller ID, and they were also the things that made me smile when I thought about her. There was no one quite like Helen. I'd known that even as a teenager.

When she'd started playing her little games with Nate over the summer—all those sidelong glances and overly intimate smiles she was so good at—I'd just gritted my teeth and ignored it. That was just Helen being Helen, I'd thought. That was the sort of thing she did, it didn't mean anything, she couldn't help herself. I'd spent long hours on the phone assuring Georgia and Amy Lee that *of course* it was annoying that Helen had no boundaries, but that *of course* nothing would *happen*, because even though she drove me crazy most of the time, she and I were *friends*. Having lived directly across the hall from us freshman year and having been less enamored of Helen than I was, Amy Lee and Georgia were understandably skeptical. But they both loved me too much to actually come out and say *I told you so* now.

"Here's a shot of Jägermeister," Amy Lee announced, slapping the shot down in front of me. I blinked, unaware until that moment how far inside my head I'd gone. "I think you should view it as an anesthetic. Numb the pain, sing 'Happy Birthday,' and when you go home tonight, you'll at least never have to face the two of them *for the first time* ever again."

I was already feeling blurry around the edges, but I took the shot.

"Let's stop staring," Amy Lee suggested. I realized it wasn't the first time she'd said it. "Let's talk about how Georgia's job is ridiculous. I'll start. It's ridiculous."

Georgia was a lawyer and, like tonight, was forever traveling for work. When particularly morose—which usually meant she'd over-served herself vodka without the Red Bull—she could sketch the layouts of most major domestic airports on cocktail napkins. This time she was in Cleveland. Or possibly Cincinnati. Somewhere out there in the middle. She had left me several supportive voice mails and a largely profane text message, encouraging me to ignore Nate and remember that Helen wasn't worth being upset about.

Though she didn't use those words.

With Jägermeister, I decided, that should be no problem whatsoever.

Later, I felt blurred right through to the core when I ran into Nate outside the bathrooms.

We stared at each other in the tiny little alcove, festooned with flyers for local bands and supposedly hip postcards.

For a moment we were completely alone. Helen was nowhere near. I wouldn't have chosen a noisy bar to finally have a moment to ourselves, but it was the first one we'd had in seventeen days. I couldn't be choosy.

But then, with only the slightest lingering glance, Nate slid past me.

It took another whole breath for me to realize that he actually, seriously, *really* wasn't planning to speak to me.

"Are you kidding?" I demanded. "You're giving me the silent treatment? *You* have the audacity to give *me* the *silent treatment?*"

"Gus." Nate sighed and shook his head. His silky brown hair tumbled across his forehead, and he shoved it back with one hand. His voice matched his eyes: sweet, rich chocolate. His hand rose as if he wanted to touch me, then dropped. "You seem so upset."

"Weird," I said through the tightness of my throat. "I wonder why? I guess that obnoxious *single* phone call failed to make me feel better about stuff like you lying to me and—"

"When you're calmer, and maybe not as drunk, we can talk," Nate said. As if he were being generous. "If you want." As if he were doing me a favor.

"Or maybe you can go to hell," I countered, hurt and furious. "How *could* you, Nate? How could you *do* something—"

I would have kept going. I might even have started to yell. But he reached out and put his hand on my arm.

I went mute.

"Gus," he said fiercely, his eyes darker than usual and sad, too. "You don't know how much I wish I hadn't hurt you."

"Then why did you?" I had to fight to get the question out, past the emotion clogging my throat.

"You want things I can't give," he said in that same hushed, hard tone, never breaking eye contact. "You're sweet and smart and funny and . . . I'm not who you think I am. The thing with Helen just proved that. I'm just not . . ." He broke off then, and ducked his head. When he looked up, his expression made me feel sad.

"You're just not what?" I prompted him, although everything felt precarious and I wasn't sure I wanted to hear his answer.

"I'm just not who you want me to be," he whispered. "I wanted to be. I really did. More than you'll know." He dropped his hand and stepped back. "It's better this way, trust me."

As I said, I blame Janis Joplin. And Amy Lee for introducing the Jägermeister, as well as the thought of singing, into the night. Mix Janis with a few too many beers and unnecessary anesthetic shots, roast it all on the flames of a broken heart, betrayal, and *It's better this way* and what did anyone expect?

It started with Bon Jovi. When I was growing up, no one admitted to listening to Bon Jovi, and now that we were almost thirty everyone seemed to know every line of "You Give Love A Bad Name." The bar erupted in sound, as everyone indulged in air guitar and the birthday girl herself rocked out in the middle of what was, on some nights, a makeshift dance floor.

This was probably what made me believe that I, too, should take to the floor.

The guitar kicked in.

Janis started to wail, "*Come* on, *come* on, *come* on—"

What happened next was probably inevitable.

Which didn't make it any less embarrassing.

I started off just singing. Then, right around the second chorus, something flipped inside me and I thought, *what the hell?*

This was always, I had discovered through years of trial and error, the moment at which I should stop whatever it was I was doing and take deep breaths until the *what the hell* feeling passed. The *what the hell* feeling was not my friend.

So, obviously, I ignored every lesson I'd ever learned in the span of my twenties and kept right on singing. Even louder than before.

Janis Joplin lured me on, with her scratchy voice and obvious pain. I thought, *Janis and I have a bond.* Then I thought *what the hell* again, and the next thing I knew I was shouting out the lyrics.

Directly to Nate and Helen.

Into their faces, to be precise.

My memory got a little foggy on the details, whether from Jägermeister or shame I would never know for sure, but I retained a crystal-clear recollection of myself *standing on a chair* as I towered above the two of them, shrieking out my extremely drunken version of "Piece of My Heart."

I didn't know which was worse: the appalled look on Nate's face, Helen's frozen smirk, or the sympathetic expressions both Amy Lee and Oscar wore as they drove me home to my little apartment around the corner from Fenway Park. All I knew was, I'd be seeing them play inside my head for the foreseeable future.

Outside my apartment building, I waved the car away and paused to take a deep breath while I reviewed the wreckage. I didn't feel blurry any longer, just slightly sick. The late October night was so cold and dark, however, that it was hard to take a deep breath. I was reduced to taking a few shallow ones instead. Somehow, that made it all seem worse.

I was turning thirty years old on the second of January, my perfect boyfriend had cheated on me with my freshman year roommate and then dumped me, and I had just humiliated myself in front of every single one of our mutual friends.

The good news was, it couldn't get worse.

chapter two

It was clear to just about everyone that I was meant to be a librarian when, in the fourth grade, I spent my winter vacation alphabetizing, arranging, and cataloging all the books in my parents' house. For fun.

It wasn't clear to me, however. My plan was to take the Broadway stage by storm (which, perhaps, puts the Janis Joplin horror into perspective). When I wasn't sorting my books into appropriate stacks, I was belting out show tunes. *Evita, Joseph and the Amazing Technicolor Dreamcoat, Phantom of the Opera, Miss Saigon, Les Misérables, Anything Goes*, and so on. If it had been up to me, I would have sung all day. I took voice lessons, sang in the school choir as well as the church choir, and often gave impromptu concerts to my collection of stuffed animals.

I'd always had a thing for *The Music Man*, so when Broadway mysteriously failed to come calling for me in Boston, I went with my second choice and got my master's in Library and Information Science. I soon discovered that Marion the

Librarian was expected to do a little bit more than sing and wear spectacles these days, however. While I was in grad school, I happened upon a part-time job in a tiny museum no one had ever heard of—the Choate Downey Museum, just a few streets off the Common. The Choate Downey Museum boasted the mediocre art and mediocre collections of the Downey family, of which Minerva Choate Downey was the current heir and curator.

She was also a complete lunatic.

When I graduated from Simmons with my master's in hand, I had big dreams of, say, a cushy job at Harvard or (during a brief, giddy spring fever in which relocation seemed crucial) the New York Public Library. But Minerva sat me down and offered me a full-time salary, excellent benefits, and the impressive title of head librarian. I was also the only librarian—the only employee, in fact—but at just twenty-five, who was I to argue?

Four years later, I was still head librarian of the Choate Downey Museum, and while from time to time I dreamed about a *really* exciting job—being a superspy like Sydney Bristow on *Alias*, for example—I was fairly content. The fact was, I loved what I did. I got paid to search for information, then to arrange it so others could experience the same voyage of discovery. I got to charter trips through knowledge. I spent my days researching questions no one in the world but me might ask—but if I decided the answer needed to be known, as head librarian I got to decide to search for it.

True, I had to deal with Minerva and her many delusions, but I tended to chalk that up in the "entertainment" column.

After all, Georgia had the theoretically more exciting job, being a big-time lawyer, but I was the one who got to spend whole mornings seriously debating whether or not it was appropriate for Minerva to identify herself as One of the Blood to the hapless fools who got lost on their tours of Revolutionary War Boston and wandered into our front hall. I doubted Georgia had that kind of fun while filing documents and typing out briefs.

Then again, Georgia lived for corporate law. Who knew what she found fun?

"I thought we had an anti-karaoke pact," Georgia said when she appeared before me that afternoon in the wide foyer that also served as my office. "It was my first year of law school, we chose to sing that 4 Non Blondes song about sixty times, and the next morning we *made vows*." She was shivering, and let the heavy door slam shut behind her, but not before a blast of frigid air rushed in from the street so I could shiver too. I wrapped the scarf I used to combat the Museum's inevitable drafts tighter around my neck.

"Hi, Georgia," I said from behind my desk, tucked at the foot of the stairs. On good days, that desk made me feel powerful and in control. I faced the day—and the door—with confidence. On other days, I felt lost and somewhat exposed behind it. Today I was still too embarrassed from the night before to care.

"I think that if we were breaking vows around here, I should have been consulted," Georgia continued. "That's all I'm saying."

"Next time I accidentally humiliate myself in front of my ex and his new skank who happens to be my ex-friend—"

"Are you sure you were *actually* friends with Helen? I mean, you were, but was she? Does she even know how to be friends with someone who doesn't want to sleep with her?"

"—I'll be sure to interrupt your depositions so you can race to my side and, hopefully, stop it." I slumped down in my chair. "I just can't understand how, in the space of two and a half weeks, I went from feeling totally grown-up to feeling about seventeen. Seventeen and *surly*."

Georgia clomped around the side of the desk in her knee-high court boots and collapsed into my visitor's chair, pushing her long legs out in front of her. I took the opportunity to study her. Georgia looked grown-up because she looked corporate and hot all at the same time. Georgia was tall and had wild, curly, unprofessional hair. It was a mix of reds, auburns, and blonds—all of it completely natural. She claimed she used the hair as a weapon. It was ditz hair, so no one saw her coming. She liked to pair the hair with very austere, severe suits, which confused everyone.

The Museum was thoughtfully located within walking distance of Georgia's firm. This triumph of coincidental geography meant that I saw Georgia more than anyone else outside her law firm. Whenever she was in town and she could sneak away from her piles of documents for a few minutes, we had coffee at the Starbucks around the corner or the occasional dinner. Sometimes I thought I was the only thing tethering Georgia to the life she was no longer living outside office hours.

She looked around, taking in the lazy afternoon stillness of the Museum, which was marred only by Minerva's latest obsession: operatic arias. Extremely dramatic music floated down from her quarters, which took over the entire top floor of the building. Georgia raised her brow toward the staircase.

"It's been arias for almost a month." I shrugged. "I'm expecting a change any day now. Care to place a bet?"

"I'm still recovering from her brief flirtation with grunge rock, a decade late," Georgia said darkly. "I'm not betting anymore."

In case I failed to mention it—Minerva sang. Very badly. Unlike me, she had never relinquished her dreams of stardom, and were it not for her Simon Cowell phobia, I had no doubt she would audition for *American Idol* in a heartbeat. Tuesdays and Thursdays, she was that scary woman who nipped into the karaoke bar (alone) and belted out five or six songs over the course of the evening to the horror of the assembled birthday and going-away partiers. Don't ask me how I knew this—I was still emotionally scarred and, as Georgia had pointed out, vows had been made.

"Court date?" I asked as Georgia glanced at her watch.

"Soon," she said. "I just wanted to make sure I was actually back on East Coast time, in Boston. I've been traveling so long, I'm never really sure where I am."

"Home sweet Beantown," I assured her. "Do you have time for coffee?"

"Not today," Georgia said, and stood up again. "I'll see you at the Halloween party tomorrow. We will look fabulous, we will be intimidating, and we will make sure no one remembers any singing incidents."

"I'm not going to the Halloween party."

"Of course you are."

"Georgia, please." I glared at her. "I wasn't going to the Halloween party as of two and a half weeks ago. If you concentrate, I bet you can remember why."

"The Halloween party is tradition," Georgia argued. "There's no reason you should give up long-term traditions just because one or two things have changed recently."

"You must be jet-lagged. Or maybe you're just insane." I held up a hand when she started to speak. "*Even if* I could somehow overlook the fact that Nate is *hosting* the freaking party *in the very house* where I discovered him *sucking face* with Helen—and who could overlook something like that, Georgia? Seriously?"

"But it's not like it's actually *his—*"

"*Even if* I could lobotomize myself so that I no longer cared about these things, the fact remains that I made a total ass of myself last night. I can't walk in there and pretend that I don't care that Nate's with her *of all people* when forty-eight hours earlier I was belting out Janis Joplin three inches away from their faces. And it's not like I can pretend it didn't happen, either, because everyone we know *watched me do it!*"

"First of all," Georgia replied, looking down at me, "I need you to breathe."

She had a point. I took a deep breath and relaxed my spine into my chair.

"If you don't want to go to a stupid Halloween party, then you shouldn't go," Georgia said. "Nobody would blame you if you wanted to hide away somewhere and lick your wounds, letting Nate, Helen, and everyone else realize exactly how much all of this is hurting you."

"Okay, good-bye. Reverse psychology is the last thing I need right now." I debated telling her what Nate had said about things being better this way, because he couldn't be who I wanted him to be. But I was still mulling it over, and just waved my hand in her direction. "Go to court."

"I'm just saying—"

"Are you wearing fake eyelashes?" The best defense was a good offense. "To the *courtroom?*"

"There's no reason not to accentuate the positive." Georgia smiled serenely, batting those fake eyelashes at me so I could better appreciate their length. "Cosmetics are just shrewd marketing."

"You sound like your mother," I accused her. Fighting words. Georgia winced.

"That serves me right for talking about your wounds," she said. Then shook her head. "Do you know, the woman called me on my cell phone while I was on my way to trial to let me know that she'd had a dream. And do you know what she dreamed?"

"Grandchildren?" I guessed. With Georgia's mother it always came down to grandchildren, one way or another.

"That I died alone and unloved, because I was too picky," Georgia said. "This is what she says to me, five seconds before a trial. What am I supposed to do with that?"

"Date a nice guy for a change?" I suggested, and laughed when Georgia just made a face. Because she and I both knew that Georgia's fatal weakness was for hot guys with commitment issues, the younger and more feckless the better. If they were actively mean to her, well, hell! She'd fall in love.

"I can hardly stomach the dates I have," she muttered. "I'm going to be late—I'll see you later."

I watched her haul open the heavy Museum door and stride back out into the cold, congratulating myself on avoiding further talk of the Halloween party. And also for being lucky enough not to have a mother who called me to ask when I was getting married, as Georgia's did several times a day.

Georgia's mother was Greek and had very clear ideas about the kind of man she envisioned her only child with: a Greek. Everything else was subject to interpretation but the Greek part was ironclad. Georgia wasn't permitted the luxury of choosing, say, a big American mutt of indeterminate ethnic origin like her own father. Georgia had been enthusiastic about her destiny until the dark day she discovered George Michael's true sexuality—having somehow believed he was heterosexual for most of the eighties.

These days Georgia's mother had subsided into a sort of dull hysteria that she expressed via dramatic voice mails. You didn't have to speak Greek to get the gist of them: *hurry up and give me my grandchildren before I die.*

My mother, happily, wasn't prone to the *my daughter is about to cross over into her thirties and is thus about to be a spinster* panic. Though she didn't necessarily *get* me, she never overtly interfered, which I figured was the better deal. Because Georgia's mother was just *scary.*

The moment that cemented my lifelong fear of the woman came while we were still in college. We'd all been out to dinner with Georgia's parents and were sitting in the car outside our dorm. In the throes of my collegiate self-absorption, I'd chosen to whine about how I would obviously never find love because I was twenty or some such unbelievably young age, which of course I thought was old as the hills, and blah blah blah. This, naturally, led to a withering self-analysis in which I concluded that I didn't actually *deserve* love because of the width of my thighs. Georgia's mother reached over and grabbed me high on the leg, startling me so much I actually jumped.

"You listen to me, Augusta," she said, startling me with her invocation of *the name* as well as her weird, creepy voice. "You will breed strong children with these thighs."

Needless to say, that ended the conversation. I slunk off into the dorm, embraced the post-traumatic stress along with my friends' hysterics, and contemplated my thighs with horror ever after. Not enough, then, that they were the first part of me to register the ingestion of chocolate. Not enough that my ass, at twenty-nine, now covered more parts of my upper thighs than I had ever imagined possible when I was sixteen. No, my thighs were *breeding thighs*. How delightful. How enticing and sexy. Perhaps I should trot that one out on the off chance I ever dated again, which seemed unlikely unless the gentleman in question had an unusual affinity for interpretive classic rock—

"And have you noticed my thighs?" I could say brightly, between the appetizer and the musical number. "A Greek woman assures me I'll breed strong children with them, you know. Very Oracle of Delphi, it's true. Just FYI."

*　*　*

When I got home from work that night, I was exhausted. It had been a long day of sending falsely cheerful e-mails around to my extended group of friends, as a form of damage control that of course fooled no one, all the while swearing to my inner circle that I was never leaving my small one-bedroom apartment again.

It was the same one-bedroom I'd been living in since I left college, for anyone keeping score on their "she's a loser" card. It was the one-bedroom that had been considered flashy and high-end by my friends back then, as they huddled in studios or shared places with the hygienically challenged while I got my master's degree at Simmons. The very same one-bedroom that was now considered a breath above squalor by these same friends, who had moved on to Real Adult Homes now that we were all about to hit the Big Three Oh. I would have liked to move on myself, and would have, were it not for the whole *mortgage* issue. But then, no one was a librarian for the money. (I repeated that phrase to myself sometimes as often as seventy times a day.)

And anyway, I had my dog and my books, so what more did I need?

When I pushed my way through my front door, my silly dog was jubilant at the sight of me. Linus leapt into the air and wriggled madly, which he would keep doing until I stopped everything and concentrated on saying hello.

I tossed my mail across the counter in my little galley kitchen—a selection of credit-card and utility bills along with two large, brightly colored square envelopes I suspected contained more holiday invitations. It had been suggested to me that deciding to become a recluse just as the holiday season was swinging into gear was like shooting myself in the foot, and I had to admit Amy Lee had a point. We had a big group of friends, all of whom believed in throwing parties. People who could barely afford to pay rent went all out to send engraved invitations. Every party was an opportunity to one-up the previous one, and we were nothing if not competitive. It wasn't as if I thought Nate and Helen were likely to keep themselves in seclusion to spare my feelings. So why should I hide myself away, as if I were the one who'd done something wrong?

I looked at my silly dog instead of following thoughts of Nate and Helen to their usual depressing conclusion, as he cavorted around in circles—a completely unapologetic spaz from his black-and-tan head to his oversize paws. I held his furry head between my hands and kissed him on his doggy forehead until he was calm and I was smiling.

Dogs: better for what ails you than the latest pharmaceuticals.

When the phone rang, I was feeling better. So much better, in fact, that I failed to check my caller ID before picking up the receiver.

I was a dumbass.

"Gus?" drawled the familiar voice. I froze. There was a pause, and I was sure I could hear him smirk. "It's Henry. It's been a while."

Several consecutive life sentences would not be long

enough to have not seen or heard from him, I thought. Several consecutive life sentences spent burning alive, in fact, would not even begin to be long enough.

And anyway, it had been about a week. Hardly long enough to qualify as "a while."

I wasn't exactly rational when it came to Henry. I could admit it. Even thinking about him made my stomach hurt. Hearing his voice made me break out in a sweat. He was like the flu.

"Henry," I bit out, by way of a greeting. It wasn't actually rude, I told myself. It was just his name.

To say that I disliked Henry Benedict Farland IV, known more simply as Henry and/or Beelzebub, was to so vastly understate my feelings that it was almost funny. Among other things, he was Nate's roommate and one of the people in my extended group of friends I'd known without knowing well for years.

Nate, naturally enough, adored Henry. I'd long suspected this had something to do with the fact that Henry was tall and in phenomenal shape, while Nate was shorter, stockier, and was obsessed with the size of his biceps in comparison to Henry's. It was a guy thing.

But the most important thing about Henry was that he was the one who had let me into the house that night eighteen days ago. If he hadn't opened the door, I would never have seen Nate and Helen together in the kitchen. If it hadn't been for Henry, I would still have Nate.

I just couldn't forgive him.

"So this is the situation," Henry said in that overconfident, lazy voice of his, the one I figured they taught on the beaches of Cape Cod. "Nate's convinced that you'd rather be dead than seen in the same room as him. Tell me that's just Nate being dramatic."

"Help me out here," I said, ignoring him. Along with the sickening image of Nate and him sitting down for a cozy chat about me. Because why shouldn't they? They lived together, after all. What a nightmare. "You're calling me why, exactly? To explore my emotional terrain?"

"I'm not much for exploring," Henry said. And why should he be? With ancestors who partied it up on the *Mayflower*, the "explorer" gene had probably been bred out sometime around the Boston Tea Party. The only thing Henry ever explored, as far as I knew, was the number of little floozies he could hook up with in a single evening. (And he could hook up with quite a few.)

"Thanks for calling—" I began in an overly chipper tone, meaning to hang up on him as quickly as possible.

"Here's the thing," Henry said smoothly before I could slam the phone back into the cradle and pretend he didn't exist. "You never RSVPed to the invitation for the party tomorrow."

That was because I'd received the invitation the day after discovering Nate and Helen in that house. The day after Henry had made sure I'd discovered them. I'd shredded it into bitty pieces and laughed at the very idea of entering that place again. I opened my mouth to tell him so.

"And I don't blame you," Henry continued. "But I think you should come. So what if Nate and Helen are there? Why should you care about them?"

"I can't think of a single reason," I said. Very snidely, because I was slightly surprised that he sounded . . . nice.

"I'd like to see you myself," he replied as if he hadn't heard the snideness.

I didn't know how to process that statement. I told myself I didn't *want* to know how to process it, because I didn't *want* to know why he wanted to see me. There was a whole part of the night after I discovered Nate and Helen together that I was actively repressing. Which was the other, equally compelling reason I didn't want to go to the Halloween party.

"I don't know what my plans are," I told him, through my teeth. I was clenching them tight together once again, a habit that made Amy Lee cringe.

"Of course you don't," Henry practically purred. Like he knew I was almost lying outright. "Well, you know where we live, so by all means, drop by. If you aren't too busy."

And then he hung up, because he was the Prince of Darkness and had to have the last word.

I stared at the phone in my hand. I had actually managed to shove Henry Farland and his part of the night I'd found out about Nate and Helen out of my mind.

Okay, that was a big lie. I *wanted* to forget about the Henry part. I was so upset and horrified by the Henry part, and by the worry that Nate knew about the Henry part (even if, technically, Nate had no grounds to complain, having, at that point, literally *just* dumped me), that my mind veered away from it in a panic every time a stray thought crept in.

But blame Henry I could. And did.

Henry's problem was that he had the great fortune to be both rich and good-looking, and he'd used those attributes to cut a wide swath through the female population of Boston, to say nothing of the Cape and Islands. He could be quite charming, and even entertaining, but only to those who weren't foolish enough to fall for him. He could be hilarious, particularly when standing in corners offering social commentary at large gatherings. The girls who fawned over him (and, just as often, his wealth) didn't think so. They adored Henry right up to the point where he stomped on their hearts and discarded them, at which point they loathed him, usually while crying. He, naturally, never seemed to be affected one way or the other by the women who loved him. He was womanizing scum, no matter how amusing he might occasionally be in between inflicting heartbreaks.

I knew all this from near-personal experience, thanks to the epic crush Georgia had had on Henry for years back when we first met him. (This would be yet another reason I was working so hard to repress.) She didn't just see Henry somewhere and think he was hot, either. She *pined*. She constructed elaborate plans to spend time in his vicinity, even if it meant befriending his various floozies. We once drove all the way out to his parents' summer place on the water in Dennis so that Georgia could monitor his comings and goings one memorable Memorial Day weekend. It was like Henry was Georgia's ex, except without his own side of the story, because the thing about epic crushes was that they had nothing to do with the crush*ee* and everything to do with the crush*er*. Nonetheless, I was still mad at him, years later, on behalf of Georgia's yearning, unrequited heart.

It just made his actions that night eighteen days ago all the more hideous, in my opinion. And would make the Halloween party equally awful.

I wasn't prepared to deal with Nate, who I was still an emotional wreck over. I wasn't prepared to deal with Helen, who I wanted very badly to harm—preferably in a permanent, disfiguring manner. And I certainly wasn't prepared to deal with Henry, who of the three of them I hated in the most uncomplicated fashion, because he was the easiest to despise.

None of which I could really talk about to my friends. They had never liked Helen, had expressed doubts about Nate the moment Helen started cozying up to him, and had maxed out on insightful conversations about Henry years ago. (Slurs and mean-spirited rumors about him, however, were always welcomed.)

That was fine, I thought then, collapsing onto my couch. *I* was fine. I told myself to breathe. There was no need to get confused about the objectives here. I was going to attend the party because I needed to be seen having a carefree, marvelous time. Last night's spectacle had to be erased. Or, anyway, mitigated. I would have to perform this same act no matter where the party was being held. The fact that I'd have to face Henry, too, just meant that I would have to prepare for the—

"Good God," I told Linus. He thumped his tail against the floor. "This party is going to suck."

chapter three

The fact that Henry lived in his own brownstone in the
same neighborhood as certain unsuccessful presidential
candidates with ketchup-heiress wives just added fuel to
my dislike, I told myself as we approached Henry's house
on Friday night. I couldn't imagine *renting* in Henry's neighborhood, much less *owning*. I couldn't imagine owning anything, including nice furniture. Much less an entire house
that was so spacious he rented out the top half to "friends"
like Nate. It wasn't that Henry went out of his way to rub his
wealth in other people's faces—it was more the fact that he
didn't *have* to do any rubbing. It was already right there, in
your face, in the form of a brownstone in Beacon Hill.

We trudged up the front stairs and squared our shoulders. Or I did, anyway. I'd been to so many parties here,
one more shouldn't matter much one way or the other.
Deep inside, however, I was thinking of the last time I'd
been here, and my subsequent vow never to return.

"No one prepared me," drawled a voice from above us,

rich with sarcastic glee. "Gus Curtis? At my house? They said it wasn't possible!"

I looked up and there was Henry Farland himself, lounging in the open doorway before us.

There was something mesmerizing about him, with his bright blue eyes, honey-blond hair, and a smirk that could draw blood. He looked dressed to kill. In his case, probably literally.

"Henry," Amy Lee bit out in an abrupt tone. "A pleasure, thanks for the invite, beautiful home."

Without bothering to wait for a response, or express her solidarity with me by—I don't know—punching Henry in the stomach, Amy Lee barreled past him. Headed, I assumed, for the bar. Amy Lee had been tired of Henry when it was Georgia who wanted to rant about him all the time. This probably felt like déjà vu to her. Oscar shot me an apologetic look and hurried after her, just doing that manly head-bob thing with Henry as he passed.

"Great to see you," Georgia murmured insincerely, sweeping inside. She, too, had better things to do than wait for Henry's reply. After all, she'd spent years waiting for Henry.

Not that Henry cared. His eyes were on me, glowing. With malice, obviously. Later, I would have to check for scorch marks.

"I'm not sure I deserved all that hostility," Henry said mildly. "But how are *you*, Gus?"

He glided forward to kiss me on the cheek, the treacherous snake, and I smiled as if delighted beyond words and did the same, because I was nothing if not fake in awkward social situations.

"You look great," I told him, trying not to think about the fact I was touching him. Anyway, it was true, he really did look great. But then, you would expect Lucifer to be hot. I felt a flash of anger and something like guilt, and ruthlessly repressed it.

Henry leaned back and just looked at me for a moment, as if waiting for me to say something. As if *daring* me to say something.

"Stop looking at me," I ordered.

Henry didn't take orders very well.

"This is supposed to be a party," he said. "Do you think you can keep things friendly?" He flashed me as patronizing a smile as I'd ever seen. "Didn't I hear something about an incident at Gretchen's party the other night? Another little piece of your heart, I believe?"

"You're scum," I said through a fake smile.

"It's good to see you too, Gus," Henry continued, his eyes especially bright, which always boded ill. "The last time you showed up at my house—"

"I bet you've been waiting at the door all night, hoping you could throw that in my face," I said. It felt as if he'd sucker punched me. Which I assumed was his goal.

"Don't worry." His eyes felt electric when they swept over me. "I haven't told anyone."

The *yet* was implied.

I didn't wait for more, I just pushed past him and into the house. I had to remind myself to unclench my jaw before something shattered or Amy Lee diagnosed me with Henry-caused lockjaw.

I risked a glance back anyway and, sure enough, Henry was watching me with that little crook of his mouth that managed somehow to be hotter than a smile. Not that I wanted to notice his hotness, however omnipresent it seemed. I was glad he found himself so funny. Somebody had to.

I moved carefully through the crowd, which was divided into three different sorts of people:

There were the Halloween diehards, who painted themselves blue or sported elaborate costumes involving much thought and papier-mâché. These people could often be seen sneering at each other, or saying things like, "Um, I think you'll find that *season four* Buffy had the curly hair, which means your *season three* leather with that hair is *totally* inappropriate."

Then there were the *cutely costumed.* These were almost all girls—the long-legged, bored-eyed girls Henry collected, for example. They had names like Eleanor or Maggie, and they liked to tell incomprehensible stories about their prep schools, their East Coast elite colleges, and their summers on the Cape or in Maine. And for Halloween, they liked to dress in pretty or slutty outfits that accentuated their bodies, so they could flaunt themselves in front of anyone who cared to look.

The other group—the majority I was pleased to be a part of, as I had no desire to attract any further attention to myself—had foregone costumes altogether.

I found my friends huddled in a corner about three feet from the bar. Georgia handed me a martini without comment. I made a face and handed it back to her.

"Please," I scoffed. "After my last outing? I'll have water, thanks."

Georgia rolled her eyes, and poured my drink into hers without a word. Amy Lee waved her hand at the room and sighed.

"This is lame," she said. "I don't know anyone. And if I were almost thirty years old and wearing Quidditch robes, I don't think I'd laugh *way* too loud like those guys by the window."

"I hate Henry," I said, without sparing a glance for the fully dressed and decorated Gryffindor Quidditch team, complete with broomsticks and goggles. "It's like someone showed him *Pretty in Pink* at an impressionable age and he's been channeling James Spader ever since."

"Oh, good movie," Georgia murmured from behind her drink. Because it truly was a great movie and also because, as a redhead, she viewed early Molly Ringwald films as a personal shout-out.

"Henry wanted to know if I could keep stuff on a happy, party level and not throw any scenes." I couldn't let it go. "As if having public dramas is something I really enjoy."

"As if you cause the public dramas!" Georgia retorted, scandalized. "And as if Henry, who is himself a public drama, should comment!"

I was more than prepared to throw myself into an orgy of trash-talking, as usual, but Amy Lee had other ideas.

"There was a really cool restaurant in DailyCandy today, did you guys see it?" she asked. "Some Asian fusion thing, very hip, apparently. I think we should check it out."

I couldn't process the change in subject. I drank my water in a big gulp and put my glass back on the bar.

"I feel oppressed by DailyCandy," Georgia confessed with a sigh. "Isn't that terrible? Every morning my in-box is swamped with a level of coolness I can't attain. Restaurants I will never eat at, clothes I will never buy—I can't take the pressure!"

"You could—I don't know—cancel your subscription," I suggested. "No one's forcing you to read it."

"And then what? Accept that I'm intimidated by daily e-mails?" Georgia shook her head.

"I think you're overthinking the DailyCandy," Amy Lee said. "And I'm making reservations for us because I don't care if we're almost thirty—we *are* that cool."

"If you say so," Georgia said, but her expression said something else. "But I'm warning you right now, I'm not dressing up like one of those Simpson chicks just to blend in."

The image of Georgia dressed as Ashlee Simpson was one I knew I would treasure for years to come. I could feel myself grinning.

"Because normally, you blend so well?" Amy Lee eyed her. "Since six-foot redheads are so common here in Boston?"

"I'm five-ten, thank you," Georgia retorted. "And don't pretend you're not jealous. You dream of reaching five feet, and that's when you have heels on!"

"I'm five-two!" Amy Lee cried. Georgia just looked at her. "Fine. Five-one and seven-eighths."

"And those seven-eighths make a huge difference," I added, and laughed. "They elevate Amy Lee far above the usual short person."

So it made sense that just then, just as Amy Lee made a rude gesture and I was beginning to think it was safe to be back in that house, something caught my eye from across the room.

Sure enough, there was Nate, standing at the foot of the stairs that led up to his rooms on the top floor. He scanned the crowd, and then turned back to take the arm of the woman behind him—as if precious Helen couldn't be expected to maintain her own balance without his assistance.

I watched as Helen whispered something into Nate's ear, something that made him smile and noticeably squeeze her hand oh-so-supportively. I racked my brain, and couldn't think of a single time Nate ever squeezed *my* hand. He liked to hold hands, though—and play with my fingers as he did so, as if each curve of each fingerprint was individually fascinating to him.

I must have had some of my feelings on that subject plastered across my face, because when Helen's gaze drifted to mine, she blinked. And then she smiled.

Directly at me.

"What was *that*?" I demanded out of the corner of my mouth.

"Ignore it," Amy Lee advised at once.

"Seriously," Georgia agreed. "Fuck her and her sweet little *smiles*—"

"Yeah, but . . . guys?" I was at a complete loss. "She's *coming over here.*"

Impossible, but true. I watched as Helen detached herself from Nate and made her way through the party. Okay, I told myself, I was standing right next to the bar. Maybe Helen had as much interest in talking to me as I did in talking to her—which was to say, none at all. Maybe the bitch was just thirsty.

That sinking feeling in my stomach, however, knew better.

"You have to hand it to her," Oscar said then. "She has balls."

"My ex-boyfriend's balls, to be precise," I snapped.

From across the room, I could see that Henry's smirk had sharpened as he watched the show. Terrific, I thought. Another drama for him to witness and then use to mock me.

And then Helen Fairchild, *that girl* in all her glory, was standing directly in front of me. Close enough so I could notice that her peach camisole top really suited her. I also noticed that she'd attached wispy little fairy wings to her back, the better to look ethereal and fetching. I wanted to smack her.

"Gus!" she said in her sweet, almost breathy voice, the one that inspired otherwise perfectly normal men to spring to her aid like some kind of modern-day white knights. The idiots. "I'm *so* glad you came!"

I heard what sounded suspiciously like a guffaw from Amy Lee, and I could feel the chill emanating from Georgia, but I knew better than to look at either of them. Despite some behavior that might suggest otherwise, this wasn't *actually* the seventh grade.

"Hey, Helen," I managed, with what I thought was extraordinary calm. Given the circumstances.

She reached over and grabbed my hands in hers, and I had to order myself not to leap back in fright. It was a close call. I *really* didn't like her touching me. For all sorts of reasons, but not least because she had her usual perfect manicure and I knew my own nails were in their perpetual state of scraggly disrepair. Like I needed further reasons to feel inadequate.

"Come on," she said.

At that point, I went into what I can only describe as an out-of-body experience. Because I didn't jerk away from her, or tell her where she could go. I just let her lead me away from the party, to a secluded little corner of the unused sewing room—once Henry's grandmother's refuge, if I remembered the story correctly. And if Henry's grandfather was anything like Henry, I could definitely see the need for refuge.

I stopped contemplating Henry's family tree and shifted my gaze to Helen, who sat down uncomfortably close to me on the rigid little settee. Her wing scraped against my shoulder.

"What was the other night all about?" Helen asked, gazing at me with what looked like pity. Of all horrible things. "Gus." She shook her head. "I don't want to scare you, or make you angry, but I wanted you to know I'm a little worried about you. A lot worried, to be honest."

Oh my God.

She wasn't trying to apologize, which I'd sort of assumed

she'd been planning. Because she had to at least pretend to be sorry, didn't she? This, however, sounded much more like tough love than the tearful appeal to my tender sensibilities I'd had every intention of throwing back in her face.

This wasn't going to be tearful at all, at least not on Helen's part. Not if I read that tone of hers correctly.

This was an intervention.

chapter four

An impromptu Janis Joplin karaoke intervention, for God's sake.

My life was a sad, sad farce.

"Worried about me?" I echoed her stupidly. "What?"

"Worried," Helen said firmly. She reached over and took my hand. I stared down at her pale, manicured fingers as they closed over my scraggly ones. "I *know you*, Gus. I know it's just not like you to make such a fool of yourself in public."

The clincher was the tone she used, the one that suggested we were such close, deep friends that she felt comfortable saying these potentially hurtful things.

"If you know me so well," I managed to get out past my brain's inability to accept that this conversation was happening, "I'm curious why you didn't foresee the fact that I wouldn't react too well to you *stealing* my *boyfriend.*"

To my surprise, and eternal horror, my eyes welled up

when I said it. I looked away. I would scratch my eyes out with my own scraggly fingers before I'd let her see me cry.

"Oh, Gus." She sighed. "I don't think 'steal' is the right word, but you can use it if you need to."

I wanted very much to stand up then. I wanted to leap to my feet, actually, and scream at her. But I was afraid that if I moved—even just a jerk of the hand to make her stop touching me—I wouldn't stop at screaming.

I breathed in, and then out. I forced myself to count, very slowly, to twenty. Then thirty. Then, hell, fifty—

"You can't say I didn't try," Helen said, getting to her feet. She finally let go of my hand and I cradled it with my other, uncontaminated one. "We're too good friends for me to let something as crazy as that performance just slide by. I hope you know, both Nate and I were scared for you. You should think about that."

I wanted to tell her that Nate hadn't sounded too thrilled with her when he'd spoken to me that night. In fact, the more I thought about it, the more it seemed as if what Nate had been saying was that I was too good for him, which meant Helen was just dirty enough. I would have told her all that—happily—except there was still too much moisture around my eyes and I didn't want her to get the wrong idea.

"Fine," Helen said. "Be this way, if you need to." She shrugged—audibly, thanks to her wings—and then flounced out the door.

I just sat there for a moment and tried not to scream.

The fact was, I'd been concentrating a whole lot on Nate's part of this mess. How my boyfriend could have left me, how I hadn't noticed that he was cheating on me, etc. The usual stuff. I was hurt and confused, sure. But really? It was Helen I wanted to kill.

It didn't matter that on occasion she drove me insane. *We were friends.* It didn't matter that it wasn't the kind of friendship I had with Amy Lee and Georgia, or that no one seemed to understand that, even if it was different, it was real. Helen and I had lived in the same room for ten months. We'd been eighteen and away from home for the first time together. She taught me the secrets of applying eyeliner and mascara, and I taught her how to cook pancakes and make chocolate chip cookies from scratch. We lived on ramen noodles and microwave popcorn for the entire month of March that year. I knew that she had bad dreams sometimes and that she'd regretted losing her virginity to that guy in high school because she'd really liked his best friend better. How could all of those things be true? How could she have done something so horrible to me when she was part of that history?

And more to the point, how dare she talk to me as if she were on some moral high ground here? Was she *completely* insane?

Quivering with fury, and that slippery emotion that had brought tears to my eyes, the one I refused to name, I surged to my feet and headed for the party. I wanted that freaking martini, and I wanted to kill Helen. Not necessarily in that order.

I was brought up short by the immovable wall of Henry that appeared before me as I walked into the living room. This was evidently not my night.

"Don't look at me like that," Henry said, laughing. "I didn't say a word."

"Your nonverbal communication is deafening," I retorted.

"I knew Helen wanted to reach out to you," Henry said, watching me so closely that I was forced to look away. I concentrated on his ever-present selection of bimbos, two of whom hovered just behind him, each dressed as some form of leotard-wearing cat. It was fun to watch them snarl at each other from behind masses of thick, blown-out hair and identical fake smiles.

Then Henry's actual words penetrated.

"Reach out to me?" I echoed. "Are you kidding?"

"I knew she wanted to," Henry clarified. "I didn't realize she wanted to drag you out of the room and be such a drama about it."

"Because if you had, you would have leapt right in there and helped me out?" I was as incredulous as I was sarcastic. "Because you're such a Good Samaritan?"

"The last time I tried to help you—"

"Good call, Henry," I snapped. "After a moment of sharing and growing with Helen, what I really want to do is revisit *that* nightmare. Thanks."

There was a moment of silence. His eyes seemed particularly blue, but that could have been the lack of oxygen I was taking in as I fought off hysterics.

"If you'll excuse me," I managed to say after the moment dragged on and became, if possible, even more uncomfortable, "I'll gather what's left of my dignity and we can return to our regularly scheduled program of hating each other."

"I think you're a strange one, and I have no clue what goes on in your head," Henry said, as if he'd given the matter some thought. "But I wouldn't go so far as to say I *hate* you. That's just one of those girl games you like to play."

Several feminist enclaves in Cambridge and out in Northampton keeled over and died at that one. I wasn't sure what it said about me and my commitment to the sisterhood that all I could muster up was an eye roll.

"Whatever." I felt surly and ungracious, a feeling I associated with being near Henry.

He didn't say another word as I stepped around him, but I was sure I could feel his eyes on me long after I thought he should have looked away.

This time, when Georgia handed me a drink, I took it.

I could only hope she was no longer monitoring Henry's conversations with other women—a reflex she'd maintained for a long time after the worst of the crush had ended—because I felt far too unsettled to discuss it. Especially with Georgia.

So I told her what Helen had said—and even reenacted the hand-grabbing—and then we stood there in silence for a long moment. Georgia scowled across the room in the general direction of Helen—whose horrible donkey laugh could just be heard now and again, braying above the music.

"I'm finishing this drink and then I'm out of here" was what I said when I could finally speak.

"Right after your private moment with Helen? As if she wounded you in some way? As if she was *right*?" Georgia's eyes flashed. "No way are we leaving."

"Fine." My snippy tone made it clear it wasn't fine at all. "Where are Amy Lee and Oscar?" To be honest, I was slightly hurt that they weren't standing by to see what Helen had wanted.

"I think they're having marital relations in one of the bathrooms," Georgia said.

"They are not!" I replied. Although I hoped it was true. At least that would mean *someone* was enjoying the evening.

"No, they're really not," Georgia said with a sigh. "I assume they're having one of those boring conversations about property values with other assorted married people in the kitchen. Although wouldn't that be funny if they *were* bathroom boinking?"

"Sure." I raised my eyebrows at her. "If we were seventeen."

"I refuse to participate in those discussions, fascinating as I'm sure it is to consider the market in Natick," Georgia said. She gave me a benevolent sort of smile. "I felt it was my duty as your friend to maintain my vigil. What if you needed someone to race to your side at a moment's notice and pry Helen's claws from your face?"

"And the fact that you're standing next to the bar is, I'm sure, purely coincidental."

"Purely."

"We actually can't talk about Helen," I said after considering it. "It might tip me over the edge." Besides that very valid fear, I knew that Georgia had never made any secret of the fact that she considered me a lunatic to waste a second on Helen once freshman year ended. She and Amy Lee both thought I should have excised Helen from my life years ago. Neither was moved when I ranted on about what friendship meant and how it wasn't always pillow fights and sleepovers, as shown on TV.

"Okay." Georgia considered her glass for a moment, then looked up. "I think Chris Starling was flirting with me."

"Chris Starling is your boss!" I was scandalized. Being that scandalized made my head throb, and I rubbed at my temples. "He's married! He's practically twice your age! And—hello—*bald*!"

"Yes, I'm aware of that. The true horror is that I was so lonely, I actually flirted back," Georgia confessed.

"*No!*"

"It was only for about thirty seconds, but it was a scary thirty seconds." Georgia shuddered. "I blame Des Moines, or wherever the hell I was. It was so boring that I actually considered the idea. I *actually* considered sleeping with him."

I blinked, but then thought about it for a moment.

"I bet he would be surprisingly good in bed," I said. "I mean, there's something to be said for men who can't coast by on their looks, right?"

"How would I know?" Georgia asked wryly. "The only men I ever meet are entirely too good-looking, know it, and are complete assholes."

"You have to get over that," I told her. "I mean, where does it end?"

"Please don't tell me you're suggesting . . ." She couldn't finish. She looked at me. "What exactly are you suggesting?"

I looked at my gorgeous friend, who spent all of her emotional energy on the kind of career-driven, flashy guys who had already maxed out their emotional energy banks on themselves. They all talked the same high-power, adrenaline-infused game, and they all left Georgia sobbing in her empty apartment when they were through with her.

"If you don't have the whole young-and-pretty thing going for you, you have to make up for it," I theorized. "Guys like Chris Starling are almost *forced* to develop other skills." I frowned. "Although not actually Chris Starling *himself*, because he's married. Ew."

"What are you talking about? Relationship skills?" Georgia smirked. "The kind where you learn how to say, 'My needs aren't being met' in words, not in suddenly moving to Jacksonville?" I winced. Georgia's last breakup had been particularly harsh.

"Among other things," I said.

Georgia shifted from one foot to the other. "I think Chris Starling might be one of those average, older guys who thinks of himself as hot just because he has money. One of those guys who thinks, okay, maybe he's not Brad Pitt, but he's rich, so that makes up for it."

"Presumably missing the key point about Brad Pitt," I said. "That being that he's hot *and* rich."

"It's a guy thing," Georgia said. "They truly believe that

money makes them good-looking. It's such a strange delusion. Because let's be honest—it makes them rich, which
isn't the same as good-looking, although it will garner you
the same results. That being a hot chick."

"A money-grubbing hot chick," I amended.

"Yes, but what do you care? You get to sleep with a hot
chick." Georgia ran her hand through her dramatic hair
and rolled her eyes as she scrunched a handful of it in her
palm. "We shouldn't talk. Women do nutty things, too."

"Like what?" I asked. "Women don't think a good job
makes them a supermodel."

"No, but let's say you had sex and it was lame." Georgia
looked speculative. "You would absolutely do that girl
thing where you tell yourself that, you know, he was just
nervous and then you keep trying but it's still lame and then
you just shut up about it, because sex isn't *that* important
and there are so many other facets to a relationship, and it's
not like it's *bad*, exactly—"

I glared at her. "Why would I do that?"

"I'm using the general *you*." Georgia made a face at me.
"I think that women are always putting up with a whole
lot less than they should. It's like a reverse delusion. Men
think they deserve better, women think they deserve less.
That's just how it goes."

"With that kind of attitude, I'm not surprised you're still
single!" singsonged Helen, rearing back up in front of us.
I jumped about five feet in the air, while Georgia looked as
if she'd turned to stone.

"What?" I asked, not even pretending to be polite.

"Nate and I were just talking, and we have the best idea!" Helen continued blissfully.

"I very much doubt that," Georgia snapped at her.

"What you two need to do is *get in the game!*" Helen exclaimed. "And lucky for you, I have a surprise. Two guys you *will not*—"

"If you're leading where I think you're leading," I told her, "I think I might actually—"

"Helen." Georgia interrupted me and leaned in. She towered over Helen, and looked as if she might reach over and pluck off Helen's wings. "Whatever you think is happening here, you need to stop. Back off."

"They're brothers," Helen continued as if she hadn't heard us. "And okay—not exactly Luke and Owen Wilson, but who is? It's not like we girls can afford to care that much about looks once we cross the Big Three Oh!"

"Excuse me?" Georgia was even more appalled. "No one here is thirty yet, for the love of God!" Helen ignored her.

Once again, it was like I was trapped on a train, and there was no getting off. There was only the inevitable horror.

"HEY!" Helen shouted across the room, completely at odds with her supposed daintiness. The woman was like a cockroach. A nuclear winter wouldn't slow her down at all.

"Helen, I swear to God—" I began, but it was too late. Sensing another drama—another one involving the same players as the other night—the room fell quiet in anticipation. I plastered my polite smile across my face, but it felt more like a grimace. I couldn't imagine what it looked like.

"You will pay for this," Georgia promised her, quietly.

Helen, of course, just waved her hand in the air, in the direction of two men who appeared, from across the room, to actually *be* Abbott and Costello. Or maybe that was the hysteria, taking over my sight.

"Robert and Jerry, get over here!" she cried out. "I have two single girls you *must* meet! They're absolutely *gagging* for dates!"

chapter five

It took me until my third bathroom break on Monday morning to even think about getting over it.

It being Helen, mostly, with a generous side helping of fury for Henry to go along with it.

Henry I was furious with because he was always *right there* to make me feel worse. Only Henry would think letting someone in so that she could personally witness her boyfriend cheating was the right thing to do. Only Henry would call that *helping*, the jerk.

Helen, on the other hand, was a more complicated problem. Screaming that we needed dates had been plain old nasty, and had necessitated evasive maneuvers on Georgia's and my part, but was, in the end, just annoying. I'd spent the entire weekend stewing less about that and more about her unexpected intervention technique. At first, I'd just been stunned. And a little bit—okay, a lot—hurt. But then it had occurred to me that she was deliberately playing a game. If I could just figure out her goal, I too could play the game, and she'd better watch out because I was all kinds of competitive when I wanted to be.

I was just having some trouble figuring out *why* she'd chosen to drag me off into a private room so she could spout *obviously crazy* nonsense right to my face. She couldn't possibly believe that she was motivated by concern for me. So what was she up to?

When I returned to my desk, I amused myself by thinking up revenge scenarios, but then decided to go in a completely different direction and deal with my rage productively. I decided to act like an adult and not play any *girl games*. (Not that I gave any credence whatsoever to anything Henry said.)

And what was more adult than having a rational discussion about one's problems with one's peers?

"I'm not sure I will ever be able to talk about Helen, *that bitch*, but I definitely can't talk about it today," Georgia snarled. "This is because I am about to board a plane to some godawful town with a name I swear to you is deliberately unpronounceable, in the company of Chris Starling."

"Married, balding, lecherous Chris Starling?"

"The very one. Although it turns out he's *separated*. Somehow, his telling me this didn't present the green light I think he hoped for."

"You have fun out there," I said, rather wanly.

She made a noise that could only be described as a growl, and hung up. I told myself the pounding in my temples had more to do with what sounded like African tribal chants floating down from Minerva's quarters—and if arias had given way to tribal chants, I might as well buy myself a month's supply of Excedrin at once—than with any urges toward homicide.

I thought about calling Amy Lee, but that would mean coming up with excuses to make it past the formidable Beatrice, the receptionist/hygienist in the dental practice Amy Lee and Oscar shared, who didn't believe in personal phone calls during the workday. I was exhausted by the very idea, and Beatrice, I knew, would pounce on any hint of weakness.

I made a few gestures toward actual work, and then spent the rest of my day with my earplugs in (I'd bought them during Minerva's particularly trying Scottish-bagpipe phase and couldn't imagine how I'd managed without them), Googling people I held grudges against.

For example: the name Henry Farland, it turned out, was etched on a large selection of gravestones in the greater Amherst area, every one of which had been photo-shopped online by some industrious amateur genealogist. None of those long-buried relatives, however, had been discovered to be the incarnation of evil during their lives, at least not so far as I could tell from the blurry headstones.

I found myself brooding ever so slightly on my way home from work that night, as I pretended to read my book on the T. I could see my reflection in the foggy glass of the windows of the Green Line car, and tried to remove the frown that seemed permanently lodged on my face with a few deep, cleansing breaths. It didn't work.

Girl games. What an obnoxious phrase. There had been

something in the way Henry had said it that—days later—
made me feel immature and a little bit sullen.

The fact of the matter was, I felt I was neither immature *nor* sullen. I was twenty-nine, and soon to be free of
the madness of my twenties altogether. I was practically
in my thirties already, and once I was I would *exude* calm.
I would be an adult. At last.

Not that there was anything *wrong* with the madness,
I thought when I got off the T at the Hynes Convention
Center/ICA stop. I headed toward home through the pre-
maturely dark Boston night, crossing Mass Ave to march
down Boylston—after all, who wasn't a little melodramatic
when they were in their twenties? Being unapologetically
histrionic was, as far as I could tell, the entire *point* of
being in your twenties. Just about everyone I knew who'd
crossed the Great Divide into their thirties talked about
their twenties like they'd escaped the gulag of drama simply by celebrating their thirtieth birthday. My birthday was
January second and I *couldn't wait.*

For some reason, I thought, looking down the street
to where the Victory Gardens began and the public allot-
ments spread out along the Muddy River, Henry Farland
had been placed on this earth to challenge my claims to
impending adulthood. If I concentrated hard enough, I
was sure I could blame him for the Janis Joplin tragedy,
too, even if he hadn't actually been there. Around Henry,
I behaved like the overwrought twentysomething I wanted
to leave behind, forever one emotion away from hurling
a cocktail across a room or bursting into inappropriately

public tears. But the key difference was that I was *not*, in fact, that twentysomething for very much longer. I could *choose* not to behave like her. After all, I couldn't change Henry. I could only change my *reaction* to Henry. And once I became the Zen goddess of social situations, I could shove my enlightenment directly down his smug—

I literally stopped in my tracks when I saw the figure outside my building—unmistakable even from this distance.

Although—happily—faced in the opposite direction, so that I could admire her delicate, pretty profile.

Helen.

One of the major benefits of living in the same apartment throughout my histrionic twenties was that I had been forced to develop numerous strategies for the avoidance of unwanted guests over the years. So while the horror of Helen's appearance outside my door was extreme, and I planned to rant about it at length when I was safely inside my apartment, alone, and could make the necessary phone calls, she didn't stand a chance.

I banked to the right before she turned and saw me, and then froze for a moment or so, convinced that God hated me and that at any second I'd hear Helen calling my name. But there was only the blare of road rage from the passing commuters and the far-off sound of a dog barking in the Fens. I made my way along the narrow alley between my building and the neighboring one, around the back to the freezing-cold and architecturally sketchy fire escape. As the smells of fried dinners and excess garlic wafted all around me, complete with the soothing, homey sounds of electric guitar music from the fourth floor (Berklee College of Music students) and the loud argument from the second floor (newlyweds, the rumor was), I hauled myself up to my third-floor windowsill. Rung by frigid, wobbly rung.

Another thing I learned in the madness of my twenties: don't look down.

Once outside my apartment, I wrestled with one of the two ancient, heavy windows that offered me a stellar view of the chipped brick building across the way and stained concrete "patio" below. I knew from experience that if I could jiggle the left window long enough and in exactly the right way, I could get the lock to fall open, allowing me to crawl through it into the corner of my bedroom where I kept the pile of not-quite-dirty-enough-to-merit-the-use-of-my-laundry-quarters clothes. Sometimes they were on top of an old leather chair Amy Lee and I had found on the street during college, sometimes they beat the chair into submission.

I jiggled, and then I jiggled some more. I'd forgotten how long it took, and how loud it was. Not to mention how cold and dark it was outside on the fire escape. The last time I'd done this, I'd been basking in the warmth of entirely too many White Russians—the reason Georgia and I gained about fifteen pounds the year we were obsessed with them—and might even have been humming a merry tune. I was rather unfortunately sober tonight, however.

I sent a fresh batch of hatred Helen's way, and scowled at the window. This close, I also noticed that it was in serious need of Windex.

There was a cough from behind me and I froze—convinced that somehow Helen had chased me back around the building and, who knew, maybe even up the rickety fire-escape ladder. She was a wily one. But when I sneaked a look around, there was only my next-door neighbor, leaning out his window to glare at me from behind huge tortoise-rimmed glasses. It wasn't that he was unattractive—it was just hard to tell where he could be hiding his hotness behind that bright blue robe and the wild wisps of hair not quite covering his head.

In any event, the message I was receiving was this: my next-door neighbor did not approve of me.

Which was fine. He'd moved in months before and I'd barely seen him. I didn't even know his name.

"Oh," I said. As if it was perfectly normal to find me hanging about on the fire escape. "Hi! Don't call the police or anything. I actually live here, I just—"

"I know you live here," he snapped at me. "Augusta Curtis, apartment 309. I'm well acquainted with your habits."

"That's me!" I agreed with a broad, fake smile. *Freakazoid stalker*, I thought. The guy looked older than me, and as my friends liked to point out to me, only freaks and weirdos chose to spend their adulthood in a dump like my apartment building. "Although I prefer 'Gus,' actually—"

"Well, *Gus*, I've been meaning to talk with you about the level of ambient noise for some time. Since I moved in five months ago I've kept a journal of noise violations." His brows collided over the top of his eyeglasses as he intensified that glare he had trained on me.

Amy Lee had been somewhat excited for me when he moved in, I remembered then, because he wasn't the usual college kid (the only sort of person who normally rented in the building) and she figured *bookish-looking* meant *smart and interesting.* Then he'd started pounding on the wall during movie nights, and she'd declared him an enemy of the state. We called him Irritating Irwin. I had never been interested enough to investigate his mailbox to find out his real name.

"Okay," I said, fake smile in place. "Well, you know, it's kind of cold out here and I really—"

"I have the journal right here," Irwin said, whipping out a black-and-white notebook and flipping it open. From where I stood, I could see incredibly small, shockingly tiny letters stretched to fill the entire page.

He had to be kidding.

"June 25. Laughter in hallway at 11:56 p.m. June 26. Coughing in bedroom at 2:33 a.m. June 29—"

He wasn't kidding.

I turned my attention back to my window, rattling the damned thing with increased desperation. Irwin had one of those nasal voices that was really more like a whine, and for the love of all that was holy, he was still droning on about the first week of July.

I gave the stubborn window one last, mighty shove and—thank the heavens!—it fell open.

"Freezing cold!" I singsonged at Irwin. "Hypothermia, must run!"

I heaved the window open and hurled myself through it, more or less belly flopping on my pile of clothes and bodysurfing my way to an undignified heap on my bedroom floor.

Moments after this, my ace watchdog, Linus, skittered into the room and barked a combined alarm and greeting.

Behind me, I could hear Irwin's nasal whine. I had the horrifying thought that he might just stand there at the window all night, regaling the entire building with a minute-by-minute re-creation of my every movement during the past few months.

Out in the living room, I heard my old-school answering machine click on.

"Hi, you've reached Gus. Please leave a message." My disembodied, oddly robotic voice floated through the room, sounding far more cheerful than I felt. I shoved Linus off of me and began struggling to my feet.

"Hi, Gus," came Helen's sad, sad voice. "It's me again. I guess . . . I guess I'm going to give up now. Um. I still think we should, you know, talk."

Click.

What does she mean, "again"? I wondered.

I staggered over to the machine as it blinked and reset, and had to take a moment to believe what I was seeing.

Ten new messages.

Ten.

I stood there for a moment, feeling almost dizzy. I wasn't Miss Popular, but neither was I a troll beneath a bridge. Telemarketers didn't leave messages, of course. But even if Georgia, Amy Lee, my mother, *and* my sister all called me in the same evening (which was highly unlikely) that still left six. Six messages that would be quite enough to frighten me, and that was without the personal appearance at the front door.

It was official. Helen was stalking me.

chapter six

When Georgia sauntered into the glitzy, primarily gold lobby of the Park Plaza Hotel two weeks later, she was looking particularly fabulous. We had an engagement party to attend and she had her glorious hair swept up into one of those impossible hair creations that I was eternally baffled by. She was showcasing the entire length of her ridiculously long legs beneath the simple and elegant shift dress she wore, which looked to rival the cost of the shoes on her feet. Christian Louboutin, if I wasn't mistaken. (And I was never mistaken about shoes.)

Why was I so interested in Georgia's outfit? A valid question.

While she was dressed for an elegant affair, I was dressed for the prom. The prom circa 1985, that was. I was sporting a royal blue taffeta gown complete with puffy cap sleeves and matching royal blue *pumps*—which, attention shoe manufacturers, was there an uglier word?—as well as a matching royal blue clutch. It was one of the least attractive ensembles I owned. In it, I looked like a royal blueberry.

The engagement party invitation had specified formal-wear. And what, Georgia and I had asked each other, was more formal than an old bridemaid's dress?

"You know perfectly well that you're supposed to be in this dress," I snapped at Georgia when she came to a stop in front of me. "I don't think I'm speaking to you. Maybe not ever again."

"This is the thing," Georgia said, settling herself beside me on the plush settee. If she was impressed by my threat, she failed to show it. "When I wear that dress, people flip out and start calling me a giant Smurfette—"

"Exactly one person called you a giant Smurfette, and he was wasted the *single time* you ever wore this dress," I interrupted. "And how is that any worse than rolling around looking like a royal blueberry?"

"I feel bad," Georgia confessed, meeting my eyes. "But not bad enough to change."

"This was your idea!" I shrieked at her, completely forgetting where we were.

My own voice, in a screech like a fishwife (as my mother used to say, not that she had ever explained—to my satisfaction—what a fishwife *was*, other than loud) at top volume, reminded me.

Georgia and I assumed meek smiles and fell quiet, as, all around us, the opulence of the Park Plaza registered its disapproval. The Park Plaza Hotel was not the sort of place where screeching was tolerated. It was swanky, historic, and filled with impressive flower arrangements. Tourists clumped together and gazed about in awe, while businessmen oozed expense-account nonchalance and headed for the bar.

"Did you just make that noise?" Amy Lee demanded, striding up to stand in front of us. "My ears are still ringing."

"It was some girl," Georgia lied vaguely, waving her hand in the approximate direction of the elevators.

Amy Lee glanced over and then looked back at me. She frowned. She was suitably attired in the same black dress she trotted out to every single semiformal and/or formal occasion she'd attended since sophomore year in college. The only things she ever changed were her accessories. She claimed she'd learned this trick from Coco Chanel, and when she made that claim she liked to make it sound as if she'd learned it from Coco *personally*, instead of reading the same selection of quotations in fashion magazines everyone else had.

"What the hell are you wearing, Gus?" she asked. "Is that *taffeta*?"

"Oh," I said blandly. "Why? You don't like it?"

Next to me, I saw Georgia hide a smile behind her hand.

"It's hideous," Amy Lee said flatly.

"You always claimed we could wear them again," I told her sweetly, "and check it out, you were right!"

There was an extended silence, as Amy Lee took a long, hard look at the atrocity she'd foisted upon her closest friends, all in the name of her Day of Love.

"Doesn't look so good outside the wedding madness, does it?" Georgia asked in an arch tone.

"Once again," Amy Lee said, "I saved you from the chartreuse chiffon my mother fell in love with. How come no one remembers that?"

"You have a picture of your special day on your wall, Amy Lee, in which you and Oscar seem to be beaming amid a sea of blueberries," I pointed out. "A sea of puffy, taffeta blueberries. I have to spend eternity as one of those blueberries."

"What sucks for you," Amy Lee retorted, "is that you are just a lone blueberry tonight. Bet this was a whole lot funnier when you were getting dressed, wasn't it?"

I glared at Georgia, who had the grace to look slightly ashamed. In truth, it was difficult to maintain my righteous indignation when I knew I looked like a righteously indignant *blueberry*.

Then I looked back at Amy Lee and shrugged. "That's pretty much the story of my life," I told her.

"If it helps," she said then, "I never liked those dresses as much as I pretended to."

Some hours later, I was taking a break from the blueberry fun at the table we'd been assigned with a selection of other BU graduates who were also friends with the Happy Couple. Everyone I knew was off dancing, while I took the opportunity to wonder why, exactly, I always found it necessary to take things just that extra bit too far. It was amusing to stand in one's own apartment, imagining the reaction a best friend might have when one turned up to a formal event kitted out in the dress she'd foisted upon her bridesmaids. So amusing, in fact, that I'd told myself I *didn't care at all* that Nate and Helen would be present to see me in said bridesmaid dress, and that my wearing it *knowing* they would see me looking absurd was a *power move*. It was proving far less amusing, and not at all empowering, however, to parade around a party all decked out as a blueberry. Because all of my friends might have known why I was dressed up like a refugee from an eighties movie, but the rest of Chloe and Sam's extended family thought I was just a pathetic creature with an unusual and/ or alarming fondness for royal blue taffeta.

I stared across the crowded banquet room toward the main table and located Georgia easily enough. She was right where I'd left her: flirting shamelessly with a very hot consultant who worked with the groom-to-be. His name was Justin or Jordan or something like that, and he had *ambitious corporate shark* tattooed all over his excellently maintained body.

"That's an accident waiting to happen," Amy Lee said with a sigh, sitting next to me and also looking at Georgia.

"I'll collect the chocolate and the Aimee Mann CDs," I agreed. "You work on the speech."

"I've been telling her to look for a different type of guy for the past ten years!" Amy Lee protested.

"Which is why the speech needs work."

We sat there for a moment. I tried to send positive thoughts Georgia's way, on the off chance Jonah or Jesse (or whoever) was just a lamb in shark's clothing. But it was unlikely. As a rule of thumb, if Georgia was attracted to him, the guy had to be a jackass. Witness Henry, the ultimate case in point.

"I have to say, I was looking for a little more excitement," Amy Lee said. "If I have to put on formalwear, there should at least be something to gossip about." She shook her head when I nodded over at Georgia. "I can't bring myself to gossip about something we both know we'll end up dealing with when it all goes horribly wrong."

"I agree. I expected someone to be swinging from a chandelier, or falling down drunk on the dance floor," I complained, looking around at the sedate gathering. People laughed and sipped drinks on all sides, looking as perfectly well-behaved and about as likely to throw down and get rowdy as a Junior League convention.

"Henry was panting all over some stick figure with boobs," Amy Lee threw out there. "But I guess that's not exactly interesting or new, is it?"

"He is Satan, after all," I agreed, without the slightest pang of guilt. The other pang, I ignored. Fostering my friends' dislike of my enemies was a responsibility I took seriously. There was no time for inconvenient pangs. I sighed. "This party is way too . . . civilized."

Usually when a group of such size was convened by a member of our wider group, you could count on scandal and intrigue. Someone was always kissing drastically above or below their station, and at a different engagement party last winter someone had actually spiked the punch.

"The night is young," Amy Lee said, sounding hopeful. She looked around. "I have to get some mandatory mingling in. Oscar thinks we need to expand our practice." She grinned at me. "I'm assuming you're not that interested in trolling for patients with me?"

"You're assuming right," I agreed. I made a shooing motion with my hand. "Go schmooze."

"Oscar's much better at it than I am," Amy Lee said, getting to her feet and smoothing her dress. "He makes people *want* to come get a root canal. But strangely, he thinks we both have a responsibility to our livelihood."

"Men are so crazy!" I commiserated, shaking my head. We grinned at each other.

"What are you going to do? Sit here, feeling blue?" She cracked herself up with that one. I ignored it.

"I'm avoiding my stalker," I told her primly.

"Which we need to talk about."

"After you drum up business," I said, and shooed her away again, for good this time.

So far, I'd been doing a pretty good job of avoiding both Nate and Helen, both of whom I could see from across the room. (Helen, as it happened, was not wearing a gown that made her look like a gargantuan blueberry. She'd opted for a somewhat more flattering silver dress.) The fact that Nate's eyes lit up when he saw me as if he'd never ripped my heart from my chest led me to conclude that he had no idea his girlfriend had called me not just eight times that night (yes, eight—and the other two were hang-ups, so draw your own conclusions), but a number of other times throughout the past two weeks.

Here's what I'd pieced together from various answering machine messages and a few cell phone voice mails: Helen wanted to talk. She wanted to talk to me so badly, in fact, that she didn't mind coming over all *Fatal Attraction* to do it. I knew Helen well enough to know that normally, her self-absorption prevented her from wanting to talk to anyone else. Much less *needing to talk*, as she'd repeatedly claimed. She could sit for hours and just sort of stare off into space, doing nothing. Not reading a book. Not daydreaming. Not thinking about anything. Just sitting there. It used to drive me up the wall when I would look up from my reading to find her *just sitting*, like an android someone turned off and left propped up on the cot across the room.

This was not someone who *needed to talk* to anyone, about anything. Which meant she had to have a reason.

I'd had some time to wonder what that reason might be, and I'd narrowed it down to two possible motivations. Either a) she was plain old batshit crazy or b) she felt guilty for her behavior. And the phrase "her behavior" could, in this case, encompass anything and everything, from flirting shamelessly with Nate at the Labor Day party with her boobs pressed up against his arm, to the actual theft of Nate to her intervention-speak at Henry's house. She was guilty of so many sins, really, that it was impossible to pick *just one* she might feel guilty about.

If our interaction at Henry's house had been a preview, however, I was planning to miss the show, thanks. I didn't want to talk to Helen—I wanted to scream at her, and possibly resort to fisticuffs. Being all delicate and waifish wouldn't help her if I went all Courtney Love on her ass.

The previous weekend there had been an unexpected gap in my social calendar, which had meant I got to spend the entirety of the weekend lounging around my apartment, catching up on my TiVo and meaning to clean. It had been nice to spend some time *not* contending with my failed relationships and the problem of Henry. It had been even nicer *not* making an ass of myself all around Boston. It was like a deep breath of a weekend.

And now that it was November, the holiday season was in full swing. I had one party or another to attend every single weekend for the remainder of the year, up to and including a huge New Year's eve bash a friend of ours was throwing out on the Cape.

On the one hand, it was exciting to have a vital and energetic social schedule. On the other hand, I was going to have to deal with the post-traumatic stress of my breakup with Nate at almost every single one of those parties, and by *post-traumatic stress* I meant not just my emotions but Helen.

I was exhausted just thinking about it. I certainly didn't need to discuss it with the person who caused it all.

Across the room, Helen let out one of her donkey laughs and then looked up. Our eyes met. Hers narrowed, and I felt a flush of panic.

Realizing that sitting still made me a big royal blue target, I jumped to my feet and headed out of the banquet room. I was looking around at the grandeur, should anyone ask—which meant, obviously, that I was hiding. I had exhausted the lobby after a few turns around the perimeter, had eyed every piece of Boston and/or Red Sox paraphernalia in the gift shop, and was resigning myself to reentering the party when the elevator directly in front of me opened.

Inside, Henry pushed a skinny brunette away from his body and looked up. Our eyes met.

The fact that he was evil made him hotter than the sum of his actual body parts, I thought in that brief, searing moment, like Sark on *Alias*. And maybe he wouldn't even be *quite* so evil if he weren't *quite* so delectable.

I would have to think about that. Later.

"Hello, Gus," Henry said. It was the *way* he said my name that I objected to, I thought. As if it meant something else entirely in his language.

He stepped from the elevator, tugging the leggy brunette in his wake. *She* looked lazy and postcoital, not that you could tell that anything had gone on from the state of her sleek blowout, which remained perfect. Henry looked the way he always did: gorgeous. And, when looking at me, also secretly amused.

"My God," he said, his eyes raking me from head to royal blue toe. "You dressed as Violet Beauregarde. I didn't realize this was a *Charlie and the Chocolate Factory* costume party."

The worst part was that I was, in fact, dressed like a blueberry. This meant I had to stand there and take it.

"This is Ashley," Henry told me, continuing on happily. "Ash, this is my friend Gus."

My automatic fake smile made my cheeks ache. I didn't know why I bothered with it. Except something about Henry made me feel that I had to at least *pretend* to be polite.

"So nice to meet you," I murmured at his . . . whatever she was. For her part, Ashley kept running her skinny, manicured fingers up and down Henry's arm instead of answering me.

"I need a drink," she whined at him.

"There's a bar inside," he told her in an indulgent and yet dismissive tone that set my teeth on edge. He launched her on her way with a light smack on the ass.

"What a terrific way to treat your girlfriend," I said, sniffing.

"She's not my girlfriend," he responded. Henry, I knew very well, preferred a constant stream of interchangeable bimbos to anything resembling a relationship. While Oscar felt this ought to be celebrated as a valid lifestyle choice—*a man who* can *date empty-headed yet gorgeous twenty-three-year-olds is unlikely* not *to date them just because they annoy you, folks*—the rest of us felt it was evidence of a deeper personality flaw. Namely:

"You're disgusting," I told him, as the girl tottered a few steps down the hall.

"You only think so when it's convenient for you," Henry replied. "Poor Gus, so conflicted."

"I would tell you to go to hell," I said with a sweet smile, "but that would be redundant, wouldn't it?"

"We keep glossing over a point here," Henry said. "I have secret information I'm guessing you don't want made public. Shouldn't you be a little bit nicer to me?"

"Are you threatening me?" I hissed at him.

"Easy there, drama queen. I was kidding."

"That didn't sound like kidding. It sounded like a threat."

Henry shook his head at me.

"Are you coming?" Ashley demanded. I'd forgotten about her. "These shoes are killing me."

Henry aimed a smile her way, and then looked at me. "Well? Are you coming?" he asked, his eyebrows rising. "Or are you waiting around for the rest of the fruit salad?"

"I hate you."

"You've mentioned that." He grinned. "Well?"

It was a dare.

So I sniffed, and walked next to him as if he didn't bother me at all.

We made our way back into the party like we were one big, happy trio. I had the Prince of Darkness on one side of me, making sure I was aware of his presence. Silly, whiny Ashley was on the other, oblivious to both Henry's sharp red horns and my own discomfort. In front of us, the scrum around the bar was getting louder by the second as just about every person I knew in Boston jostled for another drink.

And I, ever the clown, had chosen to dress myself as an oversize blueberry.

Obviously, I had absolutely no recourse but to dive right in and get wildly, embarrassingly drunk. After all, that strategy had worked before. I might be humiliated *forevermore* about my rendition of "Piece of My Heart," but at least I could take comfort in the knowledge I'd given people something else to talk about. Something other than the original humiliation of Nate's defection. The greater the spectacle I made of myself, the more attention I could divert from the real issue.

It almost sounded reasonable.

I left Henry and his bimbette without a backward glance. I kept my eyes on the bar. I had an involved fantasy about drinking myself into a state of collapse, wherein I would be unable to care what I looked like and could furthermore be unable to sing a note. I could hardly wait.

I was so focused on the first martini I planned to order that my sense of self-preservation completely deserted me.

It came back to me in a flash when I realized I'd walked within grabbing distance of Helen. She blinked at me, and opened her mouth to speak.

Absolutely not, I thought.

Without consulting my brain, my body made an executive decision. I dove into a passing crowd of matronly types—all out-complimenting one another with a passive-aggressiveness that put me and mine to shame. I snuck out of the banquet room again—using the sniping ladies as cover—and made for the bathroom as if pursued by the hounds of hell. The bathroom was always a safety zone. Every teenage girl who'd ever wept over some zit-faced adolescent boy knew the comfort of a quiet bathroom stall.

Once inside the bathroom, I dove into the nearest stall, locked the door behind me, and perched there on the toilet seat, breathing heavily.

Surely I would be safe. Surely even Helen wouldn't—

I heard the door creak open.

I held my breath.

"Gus?" She was right outside my stall. She even knocked. Once. Twice. "Gus? I know it's you, I can see those blue shoes."

I flushed the toilet in the hope it would shame Helen into running away, but no, she was still there when I swung open the door. Like, *right there.* I couldn't even exit the stall.

"Can we talk?" Helen asked, leaning way over into my personal space. The only place to go was back into the actual toilet, which, while appealing, was hardly dignified. I chose to stand where I was and suffer her closeness.

"Well . . ." I hedged.

I couldn't imagine what Helen wanted to talk about this time, but I was betting I wouldn't like it. It was unlikely to be something I might care to discuss—like, to pick a subject at random, the ethics of boyfriend-poaching from women you were supposedly long-term friends with.

"Please," Helen pleaded with those anime eyes of hers that turned men into fools. I wasn't immune, either, and it made me cranky.

"Um, I guess so," I said, because what else could I do?

Helen sighed then. Heavily. Signaling that this time, she wasn't planning an intervention.

Again, I felt the dizzying urge to slap her, so I looked

away—toward the far more dizzying reflection of my vast blueberryness in the mirrors behind her.

I dragged my attention back to Helen, and waited. She had about three more seconds, and then I was breaking for the door. One. Two—

"The thing is," she said, staring at the hands she'd folded in front of her, "I thought we were friends. I just . . . I wish . . ."

Again, she turned her eyes on me.

"What?" I asked, a little alarmed.

"Gus," she said, as if saying my name made her sad. "Why do you hate me?"

No, really.

She meant it, too.

chapter seven

Why did I hate her?

Because when we were eighteen years old you grabbed my hand the first time either one of us got drunk at Freshman Week and swore you would never forget that I held your hair back, I could have said. *Because when we were twenty-five you announced you were having a quarter-life crisis and demanded I drive with you overnight to Acadia National Park, where you were sure the first rays of summer sunshine to hit the United States on Cadillac Mountain would show you what to do with your life. Because neither of these memories mean anything to you. Because it turns out you are all of the things I have spent years telling people you are not.*

But I didn't say anything like that.

The desire to punch her in the face got tangled up in the desire to behave like a grown-up, somehow, and I choked.

I turned red in the face and let out a strangled sort of cough.

"Um . . . what?" I asked. As if I misheard her. It was pathetic.

"Why do you hate me?" she repeated, her eyes trained on me. I avoided looking at them directly—the way you avoid looking into the sun—and looked to the side instead, where her frilly bra strap had worked its way down over her shoulder.

"I—uh—I don't hate you," I stammered. I couldn't believe she had the nerve. I mean, *of course* she had the nerve, but it was still *unbelievable*.

Helen sighed.

"We used to be friends," she said. "Good friends, or anyway, that's what I thought."

And for some reason, I found I was unable to open my mouth and let Helen know what I thought of her, or point out that this woe-is-me act was at odds with her I'm-telling-you-this-as-tough-love act from the Halloween party. I wasn't afraid of what I might say, I was afraid I'd start crying again, and even though Helen seemed to have just remembered that we were friends once I still thought I'd rather maim myself than let her see how much that hurt me. I suspected this sort of conflict-avoidance spoke to flaws in my character, but mostly I just wanted to escape her and those wide eyes of hers that tugged so expertly at the heartstrings. Even mine.

I looked around for a way out, but there was nothing. Only a row of sinks, my ugly dress in the mirror, and the party beyond. In a pinch, I supposed I could hurl myself back through the stall door and bar myself inside, but that seemed overly dramatic even for me.

"Well," I said, because she seemed to want some kind of response from me and I couldn't stand the silence. "Things certainly got a little awkward."

If by *awkward* I meant *painful*, *uncomfortable*, and *fodder for years of therapy*.

"I just don't understand you," Helen said softly. "I thought maybe if I could introduce you to some nice guys at the Halloween party, you wouldn't feel like you had to act out again. It was supposed to be a gift."

Was that how she was spinning her little act of aggression? She had to be kidding me. Some of my outrage must have shown through, because she hurried on.

"I was just trying to be nice by introducing you to Robert and Jerry," she said, her eyes so very big and full of shit. "Georgia didn't have to *threaten* me."

"The thing is, Helen," I bit out, "it's hard to see how publicly humiliating me was actually you trying to be nice."

"Henry said you were mad," Helen said. Sadly. As if Henry had advanced the theory and Helen had dismissed it as impossible until this very moment, when I'd confirmed her worst fears.

Why did everything always have to involve Henry? Why couldn't I get away from him?

"The problem is that you're dating Nate now," I pointed out, shoving the Henry issue aside. "It makes things difficult."

Talk about understating the obvious.

Helen blew out a breath. "Yes," she said. She let out a knowing sort of chuckle. "But you know Nate. He doesn't know how to do anything the easy way."

This wasn't happening. I was in hell. Or in an alternate reality in which current girlfriends had overly familiar conversations about their boyfriends with the ex they'd helped kick to the curb. Or maybe I was on a reality television show in which, at any moment, some has-been celebrity would leap out from behind a potted plant and explain that *of course* this conversation wasn't actually happening *for real*—and *of course* I was being set up while millions of viewers tittered at my predicament from the safety of their living rooms.

"Sometimes," Helen continued in that same musing sort of tone, seemingly oblivious to my horror, "I think that he goes out of his way to make things as difficult as possible. I totally believe it's because of his issues with his mom. What do you think?"

It was definitely time for the hidden cameras to make themselves known. Before I was forced to take matters into my own hands or—more frightening—actually engage in some sort of in-depth analysis of the man we'd both slept with. I shuddered at the prospect.

"I don't . . ." I was at a loss. Also, there was a building hysteria spreading out from my gut, which I definitely wanted to keep inside. Hysteria, in my experience, opened doors best left sealed tight and padlocked shut. I coughed, and started again. "I'm not sure I really . . ."

"You know, because with that kind of mother, it's not surprising Nate has intimacy issues," Helen blathered on. I watched in a sort of distant amazement as Helen slid her soft pink bra strap back up over her delicate shoulder.

I was afraid that I would be frozen somewhere between discomfort and horror for the rest of my life, forced to contemplate such unknowables as: if Helen couldn't find a bra to fit her properly, who could?

I was definitely getting hysterical.

Helen aimed a tremulous smile my way. "I mean, you know Nate's mom," she said. "Every time we have lunch, I have to remind myself that she's just a lonely woman who doesn't know any better, you know?"

All right. Hold up.

Here was what I knew about Nate's mother:

She had *disapproved* of me. Not because of anything concrete, let me hasten to add. I'd never disrupted a family outing, let loose with obscenities on the telephone, or dressed like a hooker for Sunday church.

No, Mrs. Manning had, on principle, disapproved of any woman she felt usurped her position in Nate's life. Textbook stuff, really. Because of this, I'd never met the woman during my tenure as Nate's girlfriend (a term he hadn't used himself until near the end, but don't get me started). We certainly didn't engage in any cozy Mom-and-Usurper lunches.

Helen, I was quite certain, knew this.

Not only did she know it—she was rubbing it in. This was typical Helen shenanigans, because if I called her on it, she could very easily bat those big eyes at me and claim she'd just been trying to bond with me, the way she'd been *being nice* when she'd opened the bidding on me as a date. It was passive aggression at its finest: walking that line between inappropriate and friendly, and using it to plant the knife.

And all this from the woman who had *stolen her friend's boyfriend.*

She was good.

God, I hated her.

"You know what, Helen?" I asked with the suppressed rage I'd thus far saved for rants to Amy Lee or Georgia. "I think it's time you and I—"

But I never got to tell Helen what it was time for, because the door to the bathroom swung open and bride-to-be Chloe charged inside with her bridesmaids-to-be, all of them chattering excitedly.

Helen and I were immediately swept up in the commotion. I had to crack a smile and clamp down on my anger, which was never the easiest thing in the world to do anyway, and certainly not when you were dressed like a royal blue clown.

Helen simpered and leaned close to my ear. "I do still want to talk," she told me in her saddest voice.

And then she sailed into the stall I'd vacated and shut it in my face.

Outside the bathroom, Nate was leaning against the balcony railing, looking down at the bustle of the lobby below. I watched him for a moment, feeling the hysteria in my chest settle into something else. Something that ached and brought a sort of heat to my face.

He turned and looked at me.

The fact was, I didn't understand. I didn't understand how he could have cheated on me. I didn't understand how he could care so little for my feelings. How he could dismiss me so easily. How he could smile at me as if he was still delighted to see me, but think he wasn't exactly what I'd wanted.

What I still wanted.

I didn't understand why I still could see how cute he was. How dark his eyes were against his rosy cheeks. I remembered the scratch of his jaw against my skin, and the way he stretched when he was sleepy. More than that, I knew we were perfect for each other. He was a smart guy. He deserved better than a manipulative queen bee bitch like Helen. How could he possibly want her? The only way he could—I knew in my bones—was if he didn't realize how evil she was.

Looking at him made me feel lonely.

"Is Helen in there?" he asked finally.

"Yeah." I searched his face for some sign that all of this was a result of Helen's mind control. Helen had to have planted those strange words in his head. Because none of it made sense otherwise.

"You might try telling Georgia that it's not cool to tell someone she's going to 'make them pay' when they're only trying to be nice, by the way," Nate said, making the sort of face you make when you're sharing a joke. Not that I thought anything was funny.

"You can't possibly believe that Helen was trying to be nice." My voice was flat.

"Helen has a different approach to things," Nate said, but with that same conspiratorial smile. *We know what a handful Helen can be*, that smile said. It confused me, even as it invited me to share. "And what did you say to Henry? I know you weren't exactly a member of his fan club, but when did you start hating his guts?"

"What?" I couldn't possibly have a discussion about Henry with Nate. My mind actually blanked out at the very idea. "What are you talking about?"

"That Ashley girl doesn't like you much, anyway," Nate said with a laugh. "She wouldn't stop bitching about you. But I keep trying to tell him that's what happens when you date idiots."

This affable version of Nate was the one I'd fallen for, not the sad-eyed guy who'd said incomprehensible things on Janis Joplin night. I felt a rush of warmth. Maybe he wasn't as much a stranger to me as it had seemed.

"I thought you agreed with Oscar," I said, smiling back at him. "Those who can, do. When it comes to moronic bimbos, anyway."

"Sure," Nate said. "But after a while, if you actually have a personality, you have to find a girl with a personality, too. Otherwise you're basically just masturbating."

We both laughed at that, and then a companionable sort of silence fell between us. The way it always had.

There was no way he and Helen talked like this. There was no way she *got* him the way I did. I opened my mouth to say so, but it was like he read my mind.

"Gus," he began in a softer tone, the one that matched the look he sent my way. "You know I never meant to hurt you, right? Tell me you know that."

"I know it," I said quietly, although I wasn't at all sure

I meant it. I just wanted to stay in that shared space of agreement with him.

"You're the kind of girl a guy takes home to his mother," Nate told me with that same sweet smile. With vaguely sad undertones. "I always knew I could count on you."

I smiled automatically, but then felt it falter. Because he'd kept me far away from his mother, and what had he counted on me for? To let him go?

"Wait," I started, confused.

"I'm so glad you guys can talk," Helen cooed from behind me. I jumped a little bit. Nate turned toward her but didn't smile.

I clung to that.

"Helen," I said, because for that single moment there, I'd forgotten about her. Or I'd wanted to.

"Seriously," Helen said, smiling at me with great benevolence. "I want you and Nate to be friends, Gus. It's really important to me."

"Of course we're friends," Nate told her. "We've all known each other way too long, right? I remember studying for finals with you guys freshman year. That's a long time."

I noticed no one consulted me about my feelings on the subject of our continuing friendships.

But "Of course!" I said brightly when they both looked at me. Helen's smile set my teeth on edge, but Nate looked so . . . hopeful. As if he and I were in on something. Together.

I couldn't believe how very much I wanted that to be true.

"You can always count on Gus," Nate told Helen, his eyes bright as they caught mine. He was repeating himself deliberately, I could tell. He was sending me a message. It made me feel hopeful, too.

"We'll always be friends," I promised like an idiot, and then stood there like a big, blue loser while Helen kissed my boyfriend.

Again.

chapter eight

Note to self: The next time you feel the need to prove just how funny you are, please endeavor to do so in a way that will not involve performing the Royal Blueberry Walk of Sartorial Shame across the Boston metropolitan area at two o'clock in the morning, to the delight of Boston's numerous drunks, one of whom you're pretty sure thought you were Pat Benatar. Furthermore, please recollect in future that the horrifying dress in question comes with a pair of shoes (pumps!) that are not only uglier than sin but desperately, blisteringly uncomfortable.

It was a week before Thanksgiving in Boston, and the gray Saturday was so cold the air practically shattered around me when I inhaled. I jammed my (embarrassingly ugly, yet warm) hat tighter on my head and wrapped my scarf around my neck an extra turn, and yanked Linus along on his leash. It was a short walk to the park at the Victory Gardens, where dogs romped around off leash and I could brood over my ridiculous life. Today the walk felt even longer than usual.

Half because of the bitter cold, and half because my brain refused to stop turning over the events of the night before.

Event one: Helen. And everything she'd said and/or insinuated, which seemed to be repeating on an unpleasantly loud loop in my brain.

Event two: it was perhaps time to realize that not all things that made me snicker had to be acted out—which was to say, it was one thing to cackle with Georgia about the idea of wearing the blueberry dresses out, and another thing entirely to *do* it. The blueberry dress—I could see now—was a metaphor. It was time to retire the blueberry dresses.

Event three: Nate. Thanks to that strange little moment we'd had at the party, and his repeated assertion that he could *count on me*, I was more hurt and confused than ever.

Event four: Henry. More specifically, knowing that Henry and Nate were roommates had started to panic me. Talk about too little, too late. The fact was, Henry could at any moment decide that he needed to come clean with Nate. He could be doing it *right now*. And yet, somehow, every time I saw him my brain vacated the premises and my mouth took over, and the next thing I knew I was exchanging insults with him. As plans went, mine needed some serious work.

I pulled my heavy coat tighter around me while I kept half my attention on Linus. I called him back from an overenthusiastic sprint toward some distant pedestrians, and then scowled. I was still hearing Henry's threat in my head, and I didn't like it.

Here was the story with Henry: I slept with him.

Georgia's epic crush. Boston's number-one male slut.

The roommate of the guy I had literally just found out was cheating on me. I still didn't understand how it had happened. It was an accident, and then it was embarrassing, and then he was a jerk.

Well, he was always a jerk. That was sort of his niche.

This was what happened that night, in its entirety:

Nate had called to tell me that he didn't feel well and couldn't come over as planned. *As planned* meaning *as decided after I all but begged in a humiliating conversation I could never tell my friends about; they'd disown me.* I had decided that I would be like the physical embodiment of chicken soup. I'd soothe him. And if he wasn't actually sick, as I was trying not to suspect—well, we could talk.

So, clearly, I kind of knew.

There was a moment, the way I guess there always is, when I second-guessed myself out there on the doorstep. I hadn't rung the doorbell yet. I could have gone back home and let things play out however they were going to play out. I didn't have to force the issue by showing up. I didn't have anything to prove, after all. Nate was my boyfriend. He'd actually said so himself to a third party (if Henry counted) a few weeks before. I had no reason to worry— except for the fact that I was already worried enough that I'd hauled myself over to his house to prove to myself that I had no reason to be worried.

I rang the doorbell and Henry answered. He lounged across the doorway in that lazy way he had, and smiled at me. I remembered it as a smirk, but I thought that was just retroactive editing.

That night, he was doing that thing guys do, with his hand against his belly so his T-shirt rose up and his six-pack peeked out. It was impossible not to look, so I did, even though the truth was, I never really permitted myself so much as a stray fantasy about Henry. He was hot, true, but he had always been Georgia's domain. End of story. He said hello, and told me that Nate was in the kitchen.

And then he just stood there for a minute, and looked at me.

"What?" I said. With absolutely no sense of foreboding of any kind.

"Nothing," he said, and then he stepped aside so I could walk into his kitchen and find my boyfriend kissing Helen in the shade of the copper cookware hanging from the ceiling.

It was a bad scene.

The thing no one ever told you about scenes like that was how completely unlike television and the movies they were. Because first of all, there was no soundtrack. That sounded like an unimportant detail, but trust me. Without a soundtrack, there was just you. Standing in a doorway, watching your boyfriend kiss a woman who was supposed to be a friend of yours. Just you. And the desire to walk back out, or blink, or do *something* to make it not real. No music as you spoke, and no writers to make you say something interesting when you did. I wanted to denounce them both—scream—demand explanations—

But I said, "Um."

They looked at me.

"Um," I said again, in a very high voice that sounded

nothing like me, and certainly didn't sound the way I wanted to sound, which was unaffected by what I was looking at. "What are you guys *doing*?"

As if I couldn't see what they were doing.

But my brain was already racing, constructing stories, making excuses, making it right. Making it not only okay, but *necessary* that Nate was kissing Helen.

Before I could come up with anything, Nate sighed. He shook his hair back from his forehead with a jerk of his head. He looked pained, as if he were the wounded party.

Helen touched her hand to her lips, and then squared her shoulders. She didn't look even slightly pained.

She looked me straight in the eye and said, "I told him to tell you."

And then everything went to pieces for a while.

When the smoke cleared—and I mean that literally, since the meal they were cooking got forgotten in the oven in all the yelling and started smoking right around the time Helen decided she was too fragile to handle all the drama so Nate (the scumbag) chased after her to make sure she was all right, leaving me to sob and rescue the charred remains of their illicit feast—I found myself sitting at the table in the kitchen, going drink for drink with Henry.

I wasn't sure when he'd turned up in all the commotion, but I didn't much care. I was stunned and angry. I was hurt. I couldn't believe either one of them could have betrayed me, and certainly not *together.* I cried, and Henry handed me a bottle of Jack Daniel's. I thought that he was a good listener. And that my nose was running. Things got a little bit blurry.

I'd like to claim that Henry took advantage of my emotional state, and part of me still thought he did. True gentlemen, it didn't need to be said, would not avail themselves of the weeping drunk girl they found in their kitchen, especially when they were the ones proffering the alcohol. But no one ever said Henry was a gentleman, and anyway, he was drunk himself. I'm not sure why drunk men were expected to be more responsible than drunk women—it seemed like further condescension toward women, quite frankly, but that was me avoiding the subject.

There was that other part of me. The part that remembered that it was me who leaned over and laid my mouth on his. Me who pulled him to his feet and then pushed him back onto the long oak table. Just as it was me who crawled up there on top of him. I had perfect frozen images of myself doing all of those things. Of the Celtic tattoo he had on his left shoulder blade. Of the sweet hollow between his pectoral muscles. And more.

What I didn't remember was how we got upstairs, or what else happened that night, although I had the faintest memory of talking, held up close to him in that huge bed of his. And I distinctly recalled waking up sometime before dawn, with the expected hideous headache and parched throat, in a state of horror and despair. I also remembered the actual Walk of Shame I undertook then, cursing myself all the way. When I got home, I commenced crying, which I did for a long, long time.

I never told anyone.

I mean, I told them about Nate and Helen, of course. But

as for Henry, I just told them that he'd let me in when he knew exactly what I was walking into, and let me walk on into it. I may have embellished his role. I may have added a smirk, and a tone, like he was enjoying himself. I may, in fact, have deliberately suggested that he'd enjoyed the whole spectacle at my expense.

And my friends had believed me, because it was easy enough to imagine Henry the Womanizing Scum also being Henry the Guy Who Finds It Amusing That His Roommate Is Cheating.

Not that Henry Farland was anyone's victim. Hardly. He turned up at yet another birthday get-together the Wednesday after that night. He had the gall to seem surprised that I was mad at him.

"What was I supposed to do?" he asked, his eyes registering something sharper than their usual lazy amusement. "I'm not his butler. I wasn't going to lie for him. Isn't it better that you know, though?"

"Thanks for your concern for my feelings," I snapped at him. "I suppose you're so disgusted with his behavior that you're kicking him out of your house, right?"

"Gus . . ." Henry shook his head. "I'm sorry that Nate treated you like that. I mean, the guy's a jackass. But I'm not sure I can evict him over it."

"Men." I glared at him. "Fucking typical."

"And anyway," he said. "I think we have other things to talk about, don't you?"

"We are never talking about that," I hissed at him.

He blinked. "What?"

"It never happened," I declared.

"Yeah, but it did."

"Which I'm certainly never admitting, and neither are you!" My voice sounded scathing. It was because my heart was pounding too hard. Even talking about what had happened between us made me feel weak and angry and kind of slutty.

He just looked at me.

"Promise me!"

He shook his head. "Fine. Whatever you want."

"What I *want*," I snarled at him, "is to live in a world where people don't break up with other people in such a horrible, *crappy* way. Where people are *grown-ups*."

"Oh," Henry said, his eyes narrowing. "You mean like where they talk about suddenly having sex with someone they've known for almost ten years? That kind of grown-up stuff?"

"I hate you," I told him, and stormed away.

Roughly ten days later, I was wasted and belting out classic rock. A week after that, I was back at the scene of the crime. The only thing that had changed in the interim was the fact I'd managed to rile up Amy Lee and Georgia on my behalf. Not that it took much riling, when it came to Henry.

Anyone would do the same, I thought then. In all the years I'd known him, I had never harbored any romantic feelings for Henry. Other than thinking he was incredibly good-looking in that smooth, blond way, which was sort of like noticing that the sunset was pretty. It was just a fact. And I'd had plenty of time to consider my feelings for Henry in detail during the long years of Georgia's obsession with him. There was no way I could admit that after years spent pointing out his numerous character flaws, all the ways in which he could never be worthy of Georgia, and the simple fact of his apparent disinterest in women over ninety pounds, I had accidentally slept with him. I wouldn't know how to begin to broach the subject. It was far better to pretend it had never happened.

Jack Daniel's had a lot to answer for.

Besides which, I knew perfectly well that Nate had a *thing* about Henry. You might even call it *jealousy*. If he found out, it wouldn't be pretty.

I braced myself against another rush of cold wind. Linus was oblivious to the temperature as he romped around the frozen ground with another creature of indeterminate breed. The sky looked like snow, all sullen and metallic, which only added to my unpleasant mood. Nothing like a New England winter to beat the will to live right out of you.

I smiled at the other dog owner, and whistled for Linus when I could no longer feel my toes. He surprised me by obeying immediately. (It was *really* cold.) We trudged back to the sidewalk, where I clipped his leash to the metal ring on his collar and tugged him with me across the street.

Back in the steamy warmth of my cozy little hovel, I collapsed on my couch (liberated from my parents' garage years ago, it boasted that black-and-white zigzag pattern that was now almost delightfully retro) and kicked at the blueberry dress. I'd left it crumpled in the middle of my puny living room when I'd arrived home last night. The blueberry pumps had gone to their maker via a quiet death in the garbage chute.

When the phone rang, I was so busy continuing to justify my hate-on for Henry that I didn't glance at the caller ID.

That was proving to be a costly mistake.

"Gus," Helen purred at me. "I took a chance that you'd be home. I'd love to see you, just for a quick chat. Would you mind if I dropped by?"

"Um . . ."

"Excellent!" she cried. "I'll be about a half hour."

Which was how the enemy found her way into my home.

chapter nine

First, though, I threw myself into one of those whirlwind cleaning frenzies, the sort you could only summon the energy to perform when someone was about to enter your house for the first time in years. (Or when your mother called to announce she was dropping by, but that was a whole different level of panic.) Having lived with me when I was eighteen, Helen knew that I had once been lackadaisical about housework, to the point of outright slovenliness from time to time. The fact that this was still true over ten years later was irrelevant. I just couldn't allow her to assume I was still my eighteen-year-old self, based on my continuing lack of housekeeping skills.

Helen, I was sure, would take one look at the dust bunnies cavorting about in the corners and assume they were stand-ins for deep-seated character flaws she'd long suspected lurked within me. Dust bunnies were *representational*, as every woman with a subscription to *Real Simple* knew full well. I refused to let Helen think she had some kind of shortcut into my psyche based on my inability to wield a Swiffer.

It wasn't only my house that needed cleaning, either. When you've had the bad luck to spend an evening with a collection of your nemeses in a Royal Blueberry Bridesmaid's Gown (with matching bag and shoes), you'll find that you *cannot bear* to let your number-one nemesis see you in all your Saturday morning glory. It wasn't just that I suspected I looked bad. It was that looking bad in front of Helen would *prove* that Nate had been right to dump me for her. That I deserved it because I was fat, ugly, and unlovable.

Sure, it was pathological. Welcome to neurotic womanhood. It wasn't like I was alone.

Every woman I knew had *specific* complaints about *that thing* that rendered her ugly and unlovable. I'd yet to meet a woman who didn't have her own secret shame hidden away in there somewhere, clutched in tight fists by her sulking twelve-year-old child within.

Georgia, for example, never seemed to care about her weight or her clothes size. She told me once she'd never in her life fit into clothes below the double digits and paid no attention to it anyway. She *enjoyed* being statuesque. And yet she hated her ankles. For years, she'd refused to wear short skirts because she felt her ankles were so thick that she ran the risk of having people point and laugh at them. It didn't matter how many times you told her they were fine, either, she still wept over those shoes with ankle loops and considered herself deformed.

Amy Lee, meanwhile, was obsessed with her thighs. The fact that she was tiny, had never worn a garment above a size four in her life, and had a flat stomach no matter what she ate or how little she exercised? She didn't care. She was forever railing against the *tyranny* of bikinis and rattling on about *minimizing* her *thunder thighs.*

For me, without question and despite certain Oracle of Delphi moments concerning my own thighs, it was my belly. The belly that refused to turn into abs no matter how many crunches I performed or how few carbs I ate. (This obviously led to alternating phases wherein there were no crunches and only carbs, to soothe the pain.) Either way, the belly hung there over the edge of my otherwise fabulous low-slung jeans, rounded and spiteful, despite my best efforts. I was convinced the belly made me a troll. That it was disfiguring. That it was the *outward evidence* of my true inner unlovableness. No one could convince me otherwise.

Helen knew about my belly issues. She would be able to glance at me, see the belly that damned me, and use it against me to play on my worst fears. And what could I use against her? She claimed to feel oppressed by her eyebrows, which was weak, to say the least. Eyebrows could be tweezed into submission. My belly just hung out for all to see.

A glance in the bathroom mirror confirmed it: I looked like the sea hag. (Not *a* sea hag—*the* sea hag.) It went without saying that I also looked fat. My hair was mushed into vaguely geometric shapes, and the less said about my half-hungover eyes, the better.

Of course Helen was on her way. *Of course* she, out of all the people I knew in Boston, should get to witness the haggishness.

It was just so unfair.

So I cleaned like a whirling dervish for about fifteen minutes, which involved flinging the contents of my living room into my bedroom and shutting the door, and then attacking particularly egregious problem areas with a Swiffer and some Windex. After that I dove into the shower, where I held my breath and stood under the hottest spray I could handle. Then the coldest spray. Then the hottest again. When I climbed out of the ancient, claw-footed tub (the sort of tub that was only cool when it came with a matching, painstakingly renovated country house—otherwise it was just old and you had to use one of those handheld things clipped to a pole as your showerhead) part of me was shivering and part of me was scalded, but the bags under my eyes were gone.

I just had time to twist my hair back and throw on a pair of jeans and a sweater that I would normally wear only to work but looked like the sort of thing I imagined Naomi Watts might lounge about in on a rustic weekend. I applied a strategic layer of cover-up to approximate the flush of health. I was arranging my magazines into piles—with the more intellectual ones on top, of course, and the weeks of *US Weekly* hidden below—when my buzzer went off.

As Linus reacted with his usual hysteria, I had a moment to consider just not letting her in. She couldn't actually *make* me open the door to her, after all.

Maybe I wanted to talk to her more than I wanted to admit to myself. I pressed the DOOR button.

Helen swept into my apartment moments later looking like an advertisement for Banana Republic's snazzy winter line. Those who were naturally slim, after all, looked adorable in puffy white winter coats with bulky scarves. It was the rest of us who looked blown up to five times our natural size, as if we were auditioning for the role of the Sta-Puft Marshmallow Man's girlfriend, not that I'd wanted to wear that coat. I tried not to hold it against her, but failed.

Once inside, Helen patted the very top of Linus's head in a manner that indicated that a) she didn't like dogs, b) she specifically didn't like *my* dog, c) she suspected Linus might attack her, and d) she would very much like to wash her hands. If it was calculated to get under my skin, it worked.

I watched Helen take in my apartment and tried to imagine the place through her eyes. The same rescued furniture and posters on the wall—although I had actually framed all the posters a few summers ago, after deciding that I could probably upgrade my walls from frat boy chic to something a bit more in line with what I felt my tastes ought to be. I'd only gotten as far as early dorm room, I noticed, having been sidetracked by laziness. Aside from the posters, wherever there was room, there were books. Stacks and stacks of books. Books crammed into mismatched shelves and towers of books up to the ceiling. I liked my books.

I was a sucker for libraries and book collections of any kind, in fact. Give me shelves piled high with books and I was set for days at a time. My favorite private library was the gorgeous little den in Henry's house, the one I'd spent some quality time in while Nate crashed out in front of ESPN. Henry's library, of course, was probably for show. No self-respecting member of the New England elite would dream of living in a home without an ostentatious display of intellect. But that didn't mean Henry had read any of the books himself. Nor did it detract from the gorgeous chocolate leather couches arrayed around the fireplace.

My apartment, needless to say, was not on par with Henry's house.

"Wow," Helen said after a moment, pursing her lips slightly and nodding to herself as she settled on the edge of my couch, her back perfectly straight. "I can't remember the last time I was over here, and it looks exactly the same. Didn't we have that Picasso poster on the wall at BU?"

She might as well have said, *You are still eighteen years old and a fool. My taking Nate was no more than you deserved.*

Maybe because what she *might as well have said* was echoing in my ears, it cleared my head of embarrassment and led me straight into my anger. My deep, cleansing, articulate anger.

"Why are you here?" I demanded without preamble. "Why do you keep calling me, and chasing me into bathrooms, and appearing at my door? Are you stalking me?"

That knocked the little holier-than-thou smile off her face.

"Of course I'm not *stalking* you!"

"And yet here you are." I opened my hands wide. "Why won't you leave me alone?"

"I wanted to clear the air," Helen said. She let out an

affronted sound. "That was all. Trust you to take a nice gesture and turn it into something awful."

"Which nice gesture is this, now?" I pretended not to understand. "The one when you were running around behind my back with Nate? Or the face-sucking that I walked in on?"

Helen crossed her arms beneath her chest and visibly bit back what I'd bet would have been a nasty comment. We looked at each other, while Linus rolled around on the floor between us, joyful and completely oblivious to the tension.

"You know, I understand that you're upset," Helen said coolly. "But *I* wasn't dating you. *I* didn't cheat on you."

I opened my mouth, and then shut it again.

Much as it hurt me to admit it, Helen had a point.

I just wanted Nate back. I wanted explanations and apologies from Helen. It turned out that she was the one I was *really* mad at.

On a philosophical level, I found this appalling. Way back in my college days, I'd concluded that there was nothing more pathetic and wrongheaded than a woman who opted to reserve her ire for the Other Woman. Not her misbehaving partner, who was the one doing the betraying, but the Other Woman, who had presumably never made any promises to the woman, or anyway, none like the ones the partner had made. We used to sit and watch daytime television on Amy Lee's crappy little set, rolling our eyes at all the betrayed girlfriends who catapulted themselves up and over the cheating body of their man to pummel the woman he'd cheated with. What was *that* all about, we demanded, waving fistfuls of SnackWells in the air. What does *she* have to do with the primary relationship? *She* was just a symptom. *He* was the problem.

And yet, all these years later, there I was doing the same old tired thing. I hardly knew what to make of myself.

Except the fact that the Other Woman in this scenario wasn't some faceless creature—she was my friend. Or I'd thought she was my friend. So while it was possible I was betraying the sisterhood by wanting to forgive Nate, I was angry with Helen all on her own merits.

"You're right," I snapped at her. "We weren't dating. But, correct me if I'm wrong here, you and I were supposed to be friends. Friends don't steal each other's boyfriends. It's like the number-one cardinal rule."

"You and Nate were never going to work out," Helen said dismissively. "It would have been like Lisa all over again. He would have dated you forever but believe me, nothing would've come of it. At least you found out what he was up to. You should thank me for that."

"Thank you?" I pressed my fingers against my temples because I couldn't process what she'd just said. It was too astounding. I plowed forward. "You knew how much I liked him! You *knew* how excited I was about him! And you decided that meant you should hang all over him for the rest of the summer!"

"I did you a favor!" Helen retorted. "You're supposed to be *my* friend, Gus. I can't believe how resistant you are to even the possibility that I might be happy!"

I blinked at her. "What am I supposed to say to that? Do

you want me to *apologize* that I'm not more supportive of the new relationship you have because *you stole it from me*?"

"Look," she said, "I'm sorry for my part in this. I just wanted to let you know that. Even though, once you get over being mad about stuff, I think you'll agree that this is for the best."

Why did they both keep saying that to me?

"I'm glad you think so," I replied. "But right now I'm pretty sure that's never going to happen."

"I know Nate," Helen said with a shrug. Then she smiled at me, a big, wide smile. It was alarming, to say the least. "And speaking of Nate, I'm *thrilled* that you and he are able to be friends again. I know he's relieved. He never meant to hurt you, Gus. And I'm just so pleased that you can look past your anger with him and remember the years of friendship—"

As was becoming usual around Helen, I found it hard to believe that what was happening was *actually* happening. And yet . . .

"—Because really what matters here is the friendship. We all need to make sure that no one forgets that, you know?" She seemed to want a response.

"Of course," I murmured. "Friendship is what counts. As I believe I've been trying to point out to you."

"I knew you'd understand!" she cried.

She went on like this for some time, extolling the virtues of Nate's and my *friendship*. How happy she was we were *friends*. How important it was not to let emotional upset destroy *friendships*, because everybody needed *friends*, especially if romantic relationships couldn't possibly have worked out anyway... And blah *friends* blah *friendship* blah. She wisely steered clear of our own supposed friendship.

I'm not sure when it dawned on me that she was doing damage control.

All I knew was that at some point, the more she used the word *friend*, the more I became certain that anyone who was genuinely interested in encouraging a healing sort of friendship between her current boyfriend and his ex would not haul her ass across town on a weekend to share this interest with said ex. In fact, there was only one reason I could imagine for anyone to invest this much energy in a friendship between two other people, and that reason had nothing to do with the goodness of Helen's heart or her finer motives. It did, however, have a lot to do with that look I'd seen on Nate's face the night before. As if there was something only we knew. Helen must have seen more of that exchange than I'd realized. It must have worried her.

Hallelujah.

Finally—*finally!*—Helen had overplayed her hand.

I couldn't help myself.

I gloated.

Because there was one thing I knew about dirty, underhanded girl politics, whether it involved *that girl* or not: nobody wanted another woman to be *friends* with her boyfriend to this degree, unless she was very worried indeed that *friends* wasn't what her boyfriend had in mind at all.

Which meant something glorious.

Nate still had feelings for me!

Nate still wanted me!

Enough, at least, to get Helen all up in a tizzy.

Gloating felt good. It felt, in fact, like summer in the middle of November gray. I let myself bask in it.

"I really hope you understand," she said at last, studying my expression as she wound down. "I just want what's best for everyone."

"Believe me," I told her, unable to hide my smile. "I understand you perfectly."

chapter ten

I would have liked nothing more than to spend the next week or so going over Helen's every word, movement, and facial expression with Amy Lee and Georgia, but I was foiled by the national holiday.

The fact that it was Thanksgiving week meant that Georgia was pulling twenty-three-and-a-half-hour shifts at the office in order to get some time off to see her mother, which was obviously nonnegotiable. She was also, she told me in hushed tones, planning to keep seeing Jethro or Jamie or whatever his name was, whom she'd met at the Park Plaza. I could tell by the way she told me that he was already getting slippery, some three days after they'd first met.

Thanksgiving week also meant that Amy Lee was consumed with her usual holiday rage over her mother-in-law's historic inability to say what she wanted, which inevitably resulted in her not getting it, which led directly to tears and recriminations when Amy Lee just wanted to eat turkey. Neither one of them had time to parse Helen's visit for clues. I had to pretend to be gracious about it.

The fact that it was Thanksgiving week also meant that I would have to wait until December—next week, sure, but it felt like forever—to see Nate at one of the many holiday parties I knew were coming. He couldn't actually call me, of course, not after everything that had happened, so I had to try to be patient and wait for a party. Once there, I was gleefully sure, things would fall back into place, Helen could chase someone else's boyfriend, and everything would be fine again.

I barely slept Tuesday night, because I had to go home and issue the usual holiday press releases about my life to my family. It wasn't that I felt I had to lie to them about anything—I'd simply learned over long years that it was better to wrap up the bullet points of my existence into easily digested sound bites. The more positive, the better. I usually spent most of November crafting the appropriate little nuggets of information to share when I headed home. Thanks to Nate, Helen, and Henry in equal measure, I'd left the crafting until too late, and had to cram it all in at the very last minute.

Which was another way of saying I had some wicked insomnia Tuesday night as I lay awake, coming up with perky nuggets to fling around the Thanksgiving table.

Examples: *Work is great! I'm so lucky to have such an advanced position so early in my career. Minerva's a dream to work for—I have complete autonomy to conduct whatever research I want and to organize the collection the way I like.* Or, because

I hadn't told them about dating Nate in the first place, so I hadn't told them about his defection, either: *No, I'm not seeing anyone special, but you know I have other things on my mind. Minerva's thinking of expanding the entire library . . .*

Toward dawn, I gave up my frustrated attempts to sleep and moved into the living room, where I sat with a comforter wrapped around me and channel-surfed until the clock hit nine and I could take Linus to the kennel. My sister had requested that Linus not join the family this year, since her youngest son was working on a fear of dogs—possibly the fear Linus had instilled in him the previous year with his version of "kisses." I'd reluctantly agreed, since Linus was a walking failure of obedience classes. He was also kind of psychic—wherever you least wanted him to go (like the baby's face), that was where he would head immediately. Like some kind of hairy homing missile.

Getting Linus to the kennel was a process. It involved tricking him into thinking he was going on an innocent morning walk, and then coercing him through the door to the vet's office with various bribes: bacon, pleading, and assorted dog biscuits. Or anyway, that was the plan.

Linus was no fool. He was having none of it.

He took one look at the vet's front door and hurled himself onto the ground where, every five seconds or so, he would twitch impressively as if undergoing electroshock therapy. No amount of tugging on his choke collar could move him—unless I wanted to actually hurt him, which I really didn't.

At least not at first.

"Come on, Linus," I tried to croon, as suspicious citizens

hurried by on their way to work, no doubt planning to call the ASPCA from the next block to report the obvious cruelty I was inflicting upon my poor, defenseless dog.

Yeah, right. I glared down at him. His gray-and-tan fur stuck out in all directions, making him look like a surly, canine Einstein. Linus was so ugly that he became cute—or at least, I'd always thought so—but one thing he wasn't was *defenseless*. I could see that cunning, defiant look in his eyes even if no one else could.

After about a half hour of this nonsense, when I was just about ready to hire the nearby, bemused homeless guy to lift Linus up and cart him inside for me, Linus condescended to rise from his protest position—which was completely prone, across the sidewalk, feigning death. And not because of anything I did, but because he was probably either cold or bored. I dragged him inside—ignoring his jaunty little trot, which was his version of flipping me the doggy bird—and filled out the necessary paperwork.

"Oh no," I assured the anxious-looking receptionist. "He's actually fine. That wasn't a seizure. He just likes to act up."

"Dogs aren't *people*, you know," she told me with a sniff. "They don't actually *perform* unless trained to do so."

You must be a bird person, I thought, *or possibly a fish person, whoever* they *are*. I showed her my teeth in an approximation of a smile.

"You don't know Linus," I told her.

"I know dogs," she retorted, crossing her arms over her scrubs. "They don't have agendas. They're *pets*."

I wanted to vent my spleen in the worst way possible, but I was already late for work, so I was forced to smile instead, and fume about her all the way to the Museum, where Minerva insisted upon celebrating her Puritan ancestors by dressing in period costume and forcing me to eat "harvest stew." (About which I refused to think, as I had some serious concerns about the ingredients.) Afterward, she served pumpkin muffins from the local bakery, which were at least edible.

After work, I raced home and commenced shoving things into a bag. Jeans—but only the pair without any tears or distressed patches, as my mother had made her feelings plain about torn clothing back in the eighties. (Not a fashion choice she'd supported, let's just say.) I piled in a few sweaters and was digging into the terrifying back of my closet for my ancient pair of Timberland boots when my buzzer rang. Early, as usual.

Narrowly avoiding death when an entire pile of bags tottered over and rained down on me, I lurched to my feet and through the living room toward the door.

"Yes?" I asked through the intercom. I braced myself as I pressed the LISTEN button.

"DOUBLE PARKED!" my father roared, knocking me back a few feet. I suspected that he didn't quite believe in the concept of intercoms, and that was why he always bellowed into mine. But I knew better than to make him wait too long, and hurried downstairs just as soon as I wrestled the zipper shut on my duffel.

"We'll catch up after I make it out of the city," Dad said after the obligatory cheek-kissing. "You wouldn't believe the traffic. Boston is a parking lot as far as I can tell." He frowned at my doorway. "Can't believe you still live in this place."

As this was a variation on the same theme he trotted out every time he was forced to taxi me about for holiday get-togethers, I only smiled and directed my attention out the window at the dark night settling all around us.

I ordered myself to relax. It was marginally successful.

Despite the dorm room decor of my apartment and my constant envy of Georgia's wardrobe, I thought as my father navigated the holiday traffic headed north out of the city, I had just about everything the average woman on the cusp of thirty could want. I lived where I wanted to live, had a job I loved, the two best friends in the world, a larger social circle that meant lots of invitations, and a romantic situation that, while complicated, was looking up. At least I hoped it was. As far as I could tell, I was back on track to having it all.

What I didn't have, I thought on Thanksgiving Day while recovering from a gravy overdose on my parents' couch, was a time machine that could catapult me forward to the next party.

I couldn't wait to see Nate. I couldn't wait to get him back.

And when I did, maybe I'd spend some time hanging around Helen's apartment, harassing her into awkward conversations. Maybe I'd embarrass her in public by throwing her at random men, the better to suggest that she was incapable of finding one on her own. Maybe I'd trap her in bathrooms and, when she asked how I could treat her so badly, maybe I'd act confused as to why she wasn't just a little bit more supportive of me and my needs.

Turnabout on Helen wouldn't just be fair play, it would be sheer delight.

I felt a searing sort of pang then, and remembered that hushed dawn on Cadillac Mountain, with the world still and dark everywhere around us. We'd huddled together in the early-morning cold—so cold I couldn't bring myself to imagine winters in Maine, if that was what June felt like—and giggled. It didn't feel like a personal memory—it was more like a movie I'd seen once. The kind of movie that made you believe that friendships that involved vision quests to Cadillac Mountain would last until the friends in question were old, quarrelsome women on a porch somewhere. Men should never come between those kinds of friends. Not even someone as golden and sweet as Nate Manning.

I curled myself into a ball and pulled the fleece throw up to my chin, tuning out the football game and my mother's chatter.

Cadillac Mountain hadn't mattered to Helen. It shouldn't matter to me, either. She'd showed me what our friendship meant to her.

Now it was my turn.

Back in Boston, I spent the first week of the last month of my twenties recovering from food overindulgence and trying to cope with Minerva's new affinity for the didgeridoo, traditional musical instrument of the Australian aborigines.

"The power!" Minerva warbled from halfway up the stairs. "The earthy *mysticism*, Gus!"

It was a long week.

And then, soon enough, it was Friday night and I was on my way to a party at a sprawling house out in Winchester that belonged to an old friend of ours who'd given in entirely to her Daughters of the American Revolution roots. We all assembled dutifully enough at Amy Lee and Oscar's place in Somerville so we could pile into Oscar's car. We'd even come bearing the hostess gift all the manners mavens insisted upon. Because we were grown-ups, damn it!

This time around I was dressed like a normal human being instead of a giant berry, which was doing wonders for my mood. Not to put too fine a point on it, I felt hot and sexy in the sparkly little dress I'd found on sale just that morning, during the shopping trip I'd felt compelled to take after a long contemplation of my blueberry appearance at the last event.

I'd put my hair up and created a little mascara magic. Everything was perfect. All I needed was to see Nate, and everything would fall into place. He would forget all about Helen and race to my side, and in a year or so we'd laugh about that strange gap of time when he'd been so confused.

I didn't consider Helen's feelings in this scenario.

Which concerned me for about as long as my feelings had concerned her—about three point five seconds.

I was sipping my white wine and feeling very nearly merry when there was a sudden pressure at my elbow.

An unpleasant pressure.

"Ouch," I said.

"We need to talk."

I looked up, and was somewhat confused to find Nate standing there, still grabbing me. Not to mention, looking as close to furious as I'd ever seen him. Nate didn't really get mad, as far as I knew. This had a lot to do with the fact that most people simply melted when he looked at them with those big brown eyes. Except tonight those eyes were narrowed with temper and aimed right at me.

This wasn't how I'd planned our reunion.

There was no knowing glance or secret smile. His eyes were darker than usual, the rose in his cheeks more pronounced. He was definitely worked up about something. Something that appeared to be me.

"What is wrong with you?" I demanded.

"What's wrong with *you*?" he retorted. "Helen told me all about the conversation she had with you. You are *out of control*, Gus!"

"I don't know what you're talking about. Helen—"

"Don't try to put this on her! I had to drag the story out of her! She was actually trying to protect you!"

"I bet she was." I glared at him. "I don't know what she told you, Nate, but she's playing you—*again*. This is what Helen does."

He glanced around then, which is when I noticed that we were attracting attention. Not in a Janis Joplin karaoke way, thank the gods, but attention nonetheless.

"I can't believe you would try to mess with me like this," Nate hissed at me. "But it stops now."

He propelled me across the well-appointed living room with its lush Oriental rug and huge blue-and-white china vases, into the drafty front hall laid with bricks and sporting a wrought-iron banister on the stairs. I was forced to concentrate on the decor, because the only other thing to concentrate on was the fact that Nate was *manhandling* me.

I let him do this mostly because I was determined that this time I would not cause a scene. I wouldn't cause one, and I wouldn't be *part* of one. The vision of me in the blueberry gown, reflected back to me in the Park Plaza bathroom mirrors, was with me still. Which meant Nate got off pretty lucky.

"Exactly what is it you think I'm doing?" I asked him when we were more or less alone.

"Like you don't know," he scoffed. "Helen refused to come tonight, by the way. She's mad at me because I forced her to break your confidence, but I'm glad she did."

"I still have no clue what you're talking about," I assured him. Although I wasn't that dim. I had an inkling.

"Stay away from Helen!" Nate ordered me, leaning closer for emphasis. "I'm glad that you want to be friends, Gus, but ranting on about what good friends we are in some weird attempt to make Helen jealous isn't going to make me anything but mad. Do you understand what I'm telling you?"

He wasn't making sense, of course, but I understood him anyway. I could see how it had gone. Realizing she'd overplayed her hand, Helen had no doubt taken advantage of the holiday week to let Nate drag this story out of her. She'd even gotten "mad" at him, the better to make him feel all self-righteous and furious with me.

"Let me guess," I said dryly. Because I could practically see the scene unfold in my head like a movie. "Helen stopped by to extend an olive branch, I ranted alarmingly about my *close friendship* with you, and she wasn't necessarily *threatened* but . . . ?"

Nate looked as if he pitied me.

"Yes," he said. "She told me everything."

It was genius, really. You had to appreciate the beautiful simplicity of it. She was so good, it was scary.

I almost regretted the fact that I was going to have to kill her.

Preferably with my bare hands.

chapter eleven

I let my extreme, focused outrage take charge, and the next thing I knew I was standing in front of the grand house in Winchester, watching my breath form huge clouds in the frigid night air. I tucked myself a little deeper into my coat and wished passionately for a car.

A few minutes later—when I was reconsidering my burning need to race back into the city and confront Helen in her lair, mostly because my feet were turning into ice, and not metaphorically—Henry's Jeep pulled into the driveway.

I was going to have to learn to be more specific about the wishes I made.

A million dollars in my pocket right now, I thought fervently, but nothing happened. There were only my hands in my pockets, curled up in their mittens. It was very disappointing, and then there was Henry to contend with, too.

"And what to my wondering eyes did appear," Henry intoned as he climbed the front steps toward me. He stopped on the step below mine and smirked. We were at eye level. "But Augusta Curtis, Boston's own Christmas cheer."

I wanted very much to fling something snarky right back at him, but I held myself in check. Not because I'd suddenly discovered my inner maturity, but because I'd had an idea. I looked at him for a long moment, considering it. It was flawed, that was for sure.

"What?" he asked, looking more amused than unnerved. "Is it because I said 'Augusta'? I don't know what your issue is with it, it's a great old name. Of course I could be biased—"

"Is there any possibility at all that you would do me a huge favor?" I asked him.

Henry smiled, and rocked back on his heels.

"Gus," he said, as if enjoying the shape of my name in his mouth. "There's always the *possibility*."

"How much of a possibility?"

"That would depend on a number of factors, obviously." He was enjoying himself. "How much you wanted the favor versus how much fun it would be for me to do it, versus—of course—how much *more* fun it might be for me *not* to do it. It's a tricky analysis that can only be performed on a case-by-case basis."

I frowned, thinking it over.

I had been *on fire* with self-righteous indignation after Nate stalked away from me, true, but this inferno had not managed to persuade Amy Lee to leave the party.

"You need to let go of this," she'd snapped, glaring at me. "Stalking your ex through his girlfriend is the kind of thing that never, ever ends well."

"She needs to be taken down as a matter of *liberty* and *justice*!" I replied, outraged. "This has nothing to do with *stalking*!"

"It has to do with Nate, and I'm not driving you back into Boston so you can make the whole situation worse," Amy Lee had told me. "End of discussion."

"Just see if I'm ever available again for one of *your* hours of need," I told her then, but she was already ignoring me.

In retrospect, I would have been better off concealing my motives. I could see that now. Amy Lee was very often prickly about the strangest things, and sometimes required careful handling.

It was too late now: I was freezing my ass off on a front porch in Winchester.

The front porch that now held Henry Farland. I gazed at him, thoughtfully.

"You're trying to figure the best way to work this, aren't you?" Henry asked.

"I might be."

"Because you think a specific approach will somehow make me forget or overlook the past few weeks?" He shook his head. "I can only think of one that might work." He considered. "No, two. But it's a little bit too cold for either of them."

I shook my head at him. "You're—"

Just in time, I caught myself. Henry smiled.

"If I were you," he advised me, "I'd just ask."

*   *   *

Which was how I found myself bundled up in the front of Henry's car, being chauffeured back into Boston. He had the heat turned up and the music low. I-93 spread out before us, the lights of Medford twinkling off to the right as we headed south toward home.

Henry drove like a benign lunatic—which was to say, he was better than most of the other drivers on the road. Massachusetts drivers weren't called "Massholes" by accident.

"Why are you so quiet?" Henry asked, shifting in his seat.

I was quiet because I was suspended in the dark with him, racing down the highway, with nothing to do but realize how intimate it could be to find yourself cocooned in a car with someone else. Intimate and awkward. Particularly someone else with whom you had *a history*. I hunched down in my seat and kept my eyes on the red taillights dotting the road in front of us, wishing he would speed up.

(That one didn't work, either. Apparently the wish thing was a one-shot deal.)

This was exactly why I'd gone to great lengths to keep from thinking about this situation in the first place. I avoided Henry for a reason.

I was so flushed in the face I was worried he might actually be able to see me glowing red in the darkness.

"I thought the point of this was for you to be more entertaining than that stupid party," Henry said when I still hadn't answered him. Because, obviously, despite his many nefarious powers, he still couldn't read my mind. "If I wanted to sit in uncomfortable silence, I'd find myself a girlfriend."

"Wow," I said, knocked out of my discomfort, which, it occurred to me belatedly, might have been his intention. "Was that sexist or misogynistic? Or both?"

"Just the voice of sad experience."

"I believe you," I told him. "Where's Ashley tonight?"

"I think we already talked about Ashley," Henry said reprovingly, although his mouth was twitching. He was trying not to laugh.

"Oh, right," I said. "Not your girlfriend, just your fuck-buddy."

He actually laughed then. "I think that's a glass house you're standing in, Gus."

He had a point. I felt myself flush again, even hotter and more ashamed, but for some reason he still seemed to be amused.

"Anyway," he said after a moment of silence. "Ashley's kind of crazy, it turns out."

"I would be surprised if she's even twenty—"

"She's twenty-two! I think."

"—So you shouldn't be surprised. You were crazy at that age yourself. I was there, I remember."

"I'll let you in on a secret," Henry said, looking over at me. "I don't know why or how, but I can pick out the raving lunatic lurking in a roomful of normal women. It's like I have this homing device. Usually you can't even tell when you look at her, but it's there. Waiting. Everything's fine for a while and then BOOM! She goes nuts."

I considered that for a moment. "Maybe it's you."

"I figured that might be your take on it."

"I don't mean because you're evil," I hastened to assure him. "Although, of course—"

"Of course." He let out a sound that was halfway between a sigh and a laugh. "Satan. Got it."

"I just mean, maybe there's something about the kind of boyfriend you are that lets the lunatic creep out." I was warming to my topic. "I think everyone walks around with the *possibility* of crazy lurking around in them, but it takes certain circumstances for it to burst free."

"Which you think I provide," Henry said. "I'm like the conduit for craziness."

"Maybe. It's like how Georgia will date only men who are, essentially, genetically predetermined to be assholes." This didn't qualify as sharing personal information with the enemy. Henry had known Georgia as long as he'd known me. He knew the guys Georgia dated.

"And what about you?" he asked.

"Me?" I shot him a look, but he didn't appear to notice. "I don't really date that much."

"Just disastrously," Henry said, and let out a laugh.

Ha ha.

He ignored the scowl I sent his way easily enough, and before I knew it we were sitting outside my building. I wanted to flounce out of the car, slam the door behind me, and have that action garner the sort of response it would if I were a girl like Helen. If I were Helen, the faintest *hint* of disapproval would have the man groveling. A slammed car door would guarantee weeks of flower deliveries, I was sure of it.

I didn't know what it said about me that I wanted that, but I suspected it was a moot point in any case, because I didn't do it, because I wouldn't *stoop* to Helen's *level*. (And also because my disapproval had so far inspired Henry only to match my level of snideness and immaturity whenever possible. There was a decided lack of blossoms.)

"Thank you for driving me home," I said very stiffly. "Um. Have a good night."

"Oh, come on." Henry had one arm propped up on the steering wheel, and leaned back against his door so he could face me. "What are you going to do now?"

I glared at him. He returned the glare mildly, with a hint of smile, as usual.

"Things," I said coldly.

"Like what things?" He grinned. "I'm not driving all the way back out to Winchester. It's Saturday night. You look like you want to kill somebody and I'm betting that's the most entertainment I'm likely to see tonight. Bring it on."

"I think, actually, that you're the raving lunatic. That exposure to you makes people *feel* like they're also crazy but, no, it's really just you."

"That's an interesting theory," Henry said. "Now are you going to tell me what this is all about?"

Which is how I found myself trudging up the stairs in my apartment building with Henry at my side. Not an eventuality I'd ever thought to plan for. I was actually struck dumb by the fact that it was happening.

"I just have to change," I said when we got to my door.

"I heard you the first time," he said, his eyes laughing at me as he stood over me. "I promise not to look."

"The *point* is that my apartment is a mess," I said. A little bit desperate.

"Because I care deeply about the state of your apartment?"

"I do!" Just flat-out desperate.

"Why does everything with you regress to the sixth grade?" Henry asked. Rhetorically, I assumed.

"Look, I don't live in a historic town house, okay? It's just the same crappy one-bedroom I've had for years," I said—still just as desperate and also a bit too loud. It reverberated up and down the hall. Henry looked incredulous.

But he didn't get a chance to respond, because the door next to mine flew open then, and Irwin the Irritating— clad, as ever, in that same tatty bathrobe—threw himself into the hall.

"Really, Miss Curtis!" he scolded me. "I must protest! Do you know what time it is?"

"It's eleven-thirty," Henry said. In an overly helpful sort of tone, as if he thought Irwin had ventured out to ask the time because he really wanted to know. I considered the fact that he was a wiseass for a moment, but then turned my attention to Irwin.

"It's actually *Ms.* Curtis," I interjected. Henry slid me a look that suggested he wished I would shut up.

"Your dog has been barking for hours!" Irwin snapped at me.

This was a complete lie. Linus the Wonder Watchdog

wasn't even barking as I stood there, talking, directly outside the door. The only things that Linus barked about were when he wanted to a) go outside while I was sleeping, b) eat while I was sleeping, or c) attack whoever was foolish enough to ring my buzzer. Otherwise, please. He was too lazy.

"He seems to have stopped," Henry pointed out. Helpfully.

Irwin brandished his notebook at me. "I'll be sending my complaints to the landlord! Just you wait!"

"Fine," I snapped at him. "Go right ahead! I'm sure you've been doing it for months. The landlord doesn't care what happens in this building unless it can turn into a lawsuit, though, just so you know."

"I'll be sure to note *that* remark as well," Irwin huffed, and sure enough, rooted around in his pocket until he found a pen. He extracted it with a flick of his wrist. As Henry and I watched, he stuck his tongue between his teeth, opened the notebook, and began to write in absurdly tiny letters across the page.

Next to this, having Henry in my apartment seemed by far the lesser of two evils.

"So," I said when the door had slammed behind us, Linus was leaping up to lick at Henry's face, and Irwin was left out in the hallway to scribble in his journal all night long for all I cared, "this is home sweet home." I eyed him as I flicked on the lights and saw him take in the towering mass of books. "Be careful. Some of the stacks are dangerous."

"That's what people used to say in college," Henry murmured.

I decided not to answer that, and made for the bedroom.

The bedroom door didn't really close any longer, thanks to the closet's worth of clothes on the wire rack that hung over it, but I tried to shove at it anyway.

I was aware of Henry inside my personal space in a way I really didn't like. For a long moment I just stood in the middle of my room, picturing him standing in the living room with that superior smirk on his face, and it made me a little bit breathless. Was he judging me by my books? Because that's what I would be doing. *Had done*, in fact, when in his library. He would be the sort to look down on romance novels, I fumed. And he would think I only had the latest eight-hundred-page literary tome out there to be trendy. Or maybe he would think the fat philosophy books were only displayed so guests would think I was an intellectual. I could practically *hear* his disparaging thoughts about my Nora Roberts hardcover collection, the snob!

I flung off my new dress and hurried into the nearest pair of clean jeans. It was way too cold out there, and I didn't think I'd be able to confront Helen while suffering from hypothermia. I pulled on a turtleneck sweater and pulled my hair back into a ponytail. A pair of boots and I was done.

I burst out through the door, prepared to deliver a stinging defense of my reading choices, and found Henry lounging on the couch with my ecstatic—and traitorous—dog lying next to him to receive his petting. He looked completely at ease and not at all snobby or superior. It stopped me in my tracks.

"That was fast," Henry observed.

"No need to linger." I frowned at Linus. So much for the

bond between dog and owner. Linus acted as if I wasn't in the room.

"Someday I'm going to have to come back here and go through all these books," Henry said in a tone I couldn't quite place. It sounded almost . . . reverent? Impossible.

"You're a big reader?" I realized that came out a tad too disbelieving, and widened my eyes innocently when he looked at me.

"Well, yes," he said as if I were extremely stupid. "You've seen my library. Let me guess—you thought it was all for show, right?"

"I never really thought about it one way or the other," I lied. In a lofty tone.

I thought it was probably as good a time as any to change the subject, particularly since I could *feel* the way he was looking at me. I wrapped my scarf around my neck. I picked up my coat.

"You ready?"

"Sure," Henry said with a soft drawl, but he didn't move.

We looked at each other across the postage-size space, which seemed smaller by the second. Suddenly it seemed as if he wasn't lying there on the couch so much as *waiting*. His clear eyes seemed to see right through me, and the more they saw, the hotter my cheeks grew.

So naturally, that was the moment I noticed how good he looked, which maybe I'd overlooked before in the dark. His blond hair gleamed against the deep brown of the coat he wore open over a gray sweater and black pants. That last, fateful night, he'd been in jeans and a T-shirt and he had smelled like rain and spice. I imagined I could smell him again, and it made my body feel like liquid. Or maybe that was just because I knew the killer six-pack was hidden away there, just out of sight.

"Are we going?" I asked, but something happened and instead of sounding annoyed and brisk, it came out breathy.

Henry smiled slightly and got to his feet. He never broke eye contact.

"Where are we going, exactly?" he asked, but his attention seemed to drift then. To my mouth.

"I have to go kill Helen," I told him, entranced as he moved across the small room and stood in front of me, his hands outstretched to rest on either side of the archway that led into my minuscule foyer. I felt crowded. And also mesmerized.

"Why don't you forget about Helen," Henry suggested.

"Well, I would," I replied, watching him warily. "But it's imperative that I punch her. Maybe in the face."

"Gus, Gus, Gus." He said it in a sigh. Almost like a song.

" . . . What?"

"You know I'm not going to let you punch Helen in the face," he said.

"Like you can stop me."

"I'm bigger than you," he pointed out, unnecessarily, since I had to tilt my head back to look at him. "Also," he almost whispered, "I'm the one with the car."

It was like everything went still. Like I tipped forward and got lost somewhere in the way he was looking at me.

I knew, in the back of my head, that this was wrong. It was

a betrayal of Georgia. It was Nate I wanted—Nate I missed. Wasn't it? Even if he had been a jackass at the party.

But nothing seemed to matter next to that knowing gleam in Henry Farland's eyes.

I didn't know what I was going to do until I did it.

I reached out and splayed my hands open across his chest, enjoying the kick of his heart and the feel of his sleek muscles beneath my fingers. I watched his eyes widen and then narrow as I traced my way down his glorious six-pack and beneath his sweater so I could feel his skin. I felt as well as heard him suck in a breath, but he still held on to the doorjamb. It was as if I'd tied him there.

This was definitely an image I enjoyed.

"I think," he said in a hushed voice, "that that smile should be illegal."

I smiled wider. Then:

"Kiss me," I ordered him, because there was no doubt at all in my mind that right then it was what he wanted more than anything else in the world. Because I did, too. "Make it good, too."

"I always do." Like he was warning me.

"Well?" I cocked my head to one side and dared him.

I saw a strange expression flit across his face. Second thoughts, maybe. But the hunger there won out, and without a word he leaned forward to press his mouth over mine. One of his hands slid around my back and pulled me closer, tighter.

It was revenge. It was getting back at Nate. I felt powerful and wicked and hot.

And he tasted like magic.

chapter twelve

I jolted awake.

Outside my window, the sky was turning that deep almost-blue that meant another day was coming, and Henry was in my bed.

I remembered the night before immediately and in full HDTV with surround sound.

Needless to say, I didn't feel anything magical any longer.

Something else, something hot and heavy, snaked its way down my throat and into my belly. Maybe it wasn't just shame. Maybe it was a little self-hate, too. Either way, it was bitter and left a trail.

Next to me, Henry slept with the same sort of easy arrogance with which he did everything else. He sprawled across my bed as if he belonged there, and murmured something not quite in English when I sat up. It sounded sweet.

I wanted to cry.

I shook that off—along with Henry's hand, which was

curled around my hip, and crawled out of the bed. I didn't look back at him—I made directly for the shower.

After some unnecessary thinking time under the hottest spray I could handle, I found myself in the living room once again, my hair wrapped in a towel and my mind reeling around as if the apartment's disarray was finally getting to me.

I sank down on the couch, shoving in next to Linus, who pretended to be asleep and immovable. I wedged myself in under his rump, and stared at the evidence spread out across my apartment. Henry's coat and sweater in a haphazard pile near the archway. My turtleneck a foot inside the living room. Various other items of clothing festooned about the couch and nearby floor. And sizzling, embarrassing memories to go with all of it. Apparently, there were some compensations that went along with being Satan. And this time I could remember each and every one of them.

I forced myself to swallow past the lump in my throat.

Then, a few moments later, I reached down to dislodge the lump under my butt.

It was my cell phone. I picked it up and frowned as I tried to make sense of the LCD screen.

Seven missed calls.

How could my phone have rung seven times without my noticing? Confused, I looked at the sound menu and saw that the ringer was turned off. I usually kept it on around the clock, the better to receive dramatic phone calls from friends at inappropriate hours.

But tonight it was off, in defiance of my entire history, and so, naturally, tonight was the night I'd missed seven calls.

I felt my stomach give way when I looked at the missed calls menu.

All of them were from Nate.

"Hey, Gus," he said the first time. "I'm really sorry that things got a little weird, that wasn't my plan at all. Amy Lee said you bailed, which I hope didn't have anything to do with me. Because the truth is, I kind of had a fight with Helen and saw you and blew stuff out of proportion . . . The fact is, she doesn't really see things—I mean, you would understand where I was coming from better. I don't want stuff to get messed up again with us, because I really do want us to stay friends. I really meant that. God, I'm rambling, aren't I? Call me and maybe I'll come have a drink with you wherever you are. Okay, later."

"It's me again," he said the second time, an hour later. "Where did you go? I'm back at my place and I was hoping we could talk. Call me."

"I think you're screening your calls," came the third message. A half hour later. "I know you love doing that. It's not going to work, though. I know where you live."

The fourth message, forty-five minutes later: "You're leaving me no choice here, Gus. I hope you realize that."

"Okay, I'm obviously too lame to be a stalker," he said in number five, in a whisper. It was a good hour later. "I'm standing outside your building and there's definitely

no light on in there. It occurred to me that you might not
have a sense of humor about me showing up like this, at
like 1 a.m., but then I figured it would be fine, and now
I just feel like kind of a jackass because it's colder than
balls out here and I think your freaky neighbor might have
called the cops. I'm calling you for bail."

"You thought this was a bail call, didn't you?" he asked
in his normal voice in the sixth message. "Don't worry, I'm
perfectly fine, just cold. I really wish you were home, or
answering your phone, Gus. I really need to talk to you.
I really think—" He broke off, and sighed. "I realize you're
just out or something. Maybe you don't even have your
phone with you, maybe you're just sick of my shit, and I
can't blame you. Please call me when you get this. I don't
care what time it is. Seriously. Just call."

The last call came in just before four. Nate's number, but no
message—just the phone hanging up. Like he'd given up.

My head spun, and it was suddenly hard to breathe. Nate
had called me, repeatedly. Had he and Helen broken up?
He would have said that, wouldn't he? No—they probably
weren't broken up, exactly, but things certainly couldn't be
good if he'd spent so many hours calling me, showing up at
my apartment, leaving me increasingly emotional messages.
I'd thought that Helen had outplayed me, but maybe not,
maybe Nate had finally seen the true Helen and realized—

"What's going on?"

Henry stood, clad only in his boxer-briefs, in the bedroom doorway. He looked rumpled and sexy and too good
to be true.

I'd forgotten all about him.

I looked down at my cell phone, and then, just like that, I knew.

Henry must have turned off my ringer. I didn't really understand why he would do that, but he must have. Nothing else made sense. I couldn't possibly have missed Nate's calls all on my own. Life couldn't be that cruel. Henry had to have done it.

"Did you turn off my ringer?" I demanded.

Henry rubbed a hand across his face, and then eyed me. Warily.

"It was good for me, too," he said. "I particularly like that thing you do with your—"

"My phone!" I brandished it at him. "It was on the couch. Did you do it? Did you maliciously turn off the ringer?"

"I'm very rarely malicious with phones, Gus. This is because they're inanimate objects."

"*Damn* you!" I shouted at him, and winged the phone at his head.

Luckily for Henry, I had about as much aim as I had maturity. Which was to say, none. The phone missed him entirely, hit the wall, and split apart. Linus barked in the direction of the battery case, but otherwise didn't move.

The moment the phone had left my fingers, I realized I was acting like a crazy person. Of course Henry hadn't messed with my cell phone. Why would he? I had probably sat on it. But it was too late to do anything about that now. I was just another one of his lunatic girls. I wasn't sure why that made me feel worse.

I hid my face in my hands, and wished that one of us would disappear. I didn't care who.

It was quiet for a long time.

"Do you want to tell me what's going on?" he asked eventually.

I really didn't.

"It has nothing to do with you," I mumbled.

"I know that," Henry bit out. Surprised, I looked up to see temper written all over his face. "Do you want to know how I know it has nothing to do with me? Because I was asleep."

I wanted to apologize, but I couldn't seem to form the words. He looked at me for a long moment, and when I couldn't take it any more I muttered something about my hair and fled to the bathroom.

When I came back out, the sun was up and he was gone.

I took a long nap on the couch and when I woke up, I still felt that heaviness, like I might cry at any moment.

I shouldn't have let things happen with Henry. Again. I could rationalize accidentally sleeping with Henry when out of my right mind with grief and Jack Daniel's. It had been a bad mistake, but understandable under the circumstances. But how could I rationalize last night? How could I possibly have done such a thing to Georgia?

It didn't matter that she had never touched Henry, that he had never thought about her *that way*, that she wasn't even a blip on his romantic radar. The fact that those things were true made what I had done worse. Cardinal rule number two was that you didn't touch the men who caused your friends emotional trauma. Ever. No matter what.

No wonder I felt bad about myself. What made it all hurt a little bit more was that there had been something sweet about everything that had happened with Henry. I could still see that look he'd had from time to time—if I hadn't known better, I might have thought it was tenderness.

But that was impossible. That wasn't who Henry was.

I shook it off and called Nate, which was what really mattered. Or anyway, was the only thing I had the tools to deal with. I would just file Henry away and forget about it. He and Helen were just a phase Nate and I once went through. Just a phase that didn't bear repeating, and one Georgia would never hear about.

Nate picked up on the third ring.

"Hey there," he said.

"Hi." I felt shy and giddy all at once.

"I think I owe you an apology," he said, his voice ripe with merriment. "I drank way too much last night and I have the terrible feeling I left some drunk, incoherent message for you. I did, didn't I?"

"Well," I said, taken aback. "There were *seven* messages, actually, and they weren't incoh—"

"I told Helen this is what happens when she's not around to keep me on a leash," Nate said with a chuckle. "Sorry, dude!"

He was with Helen *at that very moment*. And he was pretending I was a *guy*.

I was so stunned by this, I fell silent.

I could hear Helen laughing in the background. The familiar horsiness of that laughter made my stomach twist.

"Okay then," Nate said, as if I'd continued to joke about
the drunken message he'd left in some parallel reality
where this awful conversation wasn't breaking my heart.
Again. "Just delete it, and we'll pretend it never happened,
okay? Cool. Later."

And he hung up.

For the first few hours I rationalized, which I was clearly
getting good at. I figured he was mid-breakup with Helen
(her confusing laughter notwithstanding) and that as soon
as he could get away, he'd call or come over and explain
everything. Because otherwise, nothing made sense. He
couldn't call me *seven times in a row*, say the things he'd
said, *hint* the things he'd hinted, and then wake up the
next morning feeling . . . nothing. That wasn't possible.
That wasn't even within the realm of possible. Was it?

As the day wore on, though, other thoughts crept in.
This was the guy who'd cheated on me, after all. Why was
I so eager to forget that? Why did I hold it against Helen
instead? As if she were more responsible for betraying me?
Was it because deep down, I'd suspected that *of course* a
guy would leave me for her? Particularly a guy like Nate,
whom everyone wanted? Was I really that self-loathing?

When the phone rang with Nate's home ID, I practically
burst into tears of relief.

He hadn't played me (again). It was all okay. It was going to be all right.

"Hey, Gus," Henry said.

"Oh." I was crestfallen. Then I recollected myself and tried to rally. "Hey."

It wasn't much, but it was all I had.

"Listen," he said after a small sigh, "I wanted to call and apologize for my behavior this morning."

"You did? Why?"

"Because I ran out of there, and I'm not proud of it," he said. For all the world as if nothing had precipitated his leaving, and he was the crazy person who might at any moment fling electronic equipment around. "I'm sorry."

"Oh, well." I didn't know what to say. "I mean, I would have done the same thing."

"I shouldn't have."

There was a long silence.

"Anyway," I said. "I appreciate your call."

"You can tell me why you were so upset," Henry offered. I remembered that tender expression on his face and shook it off. "I kept you from committing a felony against Helen last night. I feel like I can be trusted."

"Thanks," I told him, oddly touched. "But I'm okay."

We didn't talk about what had happened between us. This time, I noticed, he didn't even ask. He just mouthed a few pleasantries and then hung up. It was all very civilized. Very calm.

I didn't realize I was crying until a tear splashed down

on my hand, and it took me a long moment to realize what it was.

I had to stay away from Henry, I told myself fiercely. I had enough on my plate without all these confusing and scary emotions to fend off. I didn't even *like* him.

Who was I kidding—like him or not, there was obviously enough of a something between us if I kept ending up naked with the guy. As long as it never happened again, and neither Nate nor Georgia ever found out it had happened at all, everything would be fine.

Fine.

I shuddered.

I slipped off to sleep sometime later, still waiting for the phone to ring.

But Nate never called.

If I hadn't saved all of his messages, I might have thought I'd dreamed them. But no—I listened to them again and again, parsing them for nuance and meaning. He had really called me. He just hadn't called me back. I spent all weekend with my cell phone clamped to my ear, listening to Nate, tracing his movements in my head, making myself sick over the fact I'd missed out on what might very well have been my one chance to get Nate back.

Missed out because I was doing something—again—I shouldn't have done in the first place. It was going to be difficult to make Nate pay for Helen after our inevitable reunion when I'd been up to the same thing with Henry, after all.

As far as Henry went, however, I'd decided that I *had*

dreamed it. I decided, in fact, that I had no option but to believe that it had been a particularly graphic creation inside my head. Because let's face it—there really wasn't any other possible explanation for my behavior.

Henry had *actually* just dropped me off after the party, I told myself, probably not even bothering to put the car into park. I'd had to leap and roll to make it out of the passenger seat. If I concentrated, I could hear the sound of his tires squealing as he peeled off, leaving me at the curb, all alone in the dark, with no tender moments that made zero sense. To say nothing of the sizzling moments that made even less sense than that.

Anyway, I had other things to obsess about.

Georgia called on Tuesday to announce that she was currently in Naples, Florida.

"What are you talking about?' I asked lazily, sitting back in my chair so I could peer up at the ceiling. It was afternoon in the empty Museum, and I'd spent the entire morning cataloguing a new shipment of reference books Minerva had found somewhere and wanted included in the library *immediately*. Because of the high volume of researchers we fielded daily, no doubt. I gazed around the empty Museum hall and sighed.

"I'm talking about my geographic location," Georgia retorted. "I'm like *Where's Waldo?* but with much better clothes."

"You were at brunch on Sunday, is what I'm saying," I replied, ignoring her tone. Her very bitchy tone.

"Well, now I am in Naples, Florida, and not in any fun, bikini-wearing, holiday-in-the-tropics way," she hastened to add. "Although no one told Chris Starling that. He just announced he's spending the afternoon by the pool, and who cares what the clients think."

"Good for Chris Starling," I said, propping my feet up on my desk, which would have given Minerva heart palpitations if she had seen me. Not because she cared about the desk, but because she felt feet on the desk was a *mannish* position and no woman ought to be *mannish* when she could be *womanly*. Happily, she was entirely too wrapped up in *mapping her song lines* to check up on my gender role today.

"I'm sure it's great," Georgia snapped, "but he's the senior associate. He's supposed to be handling the deposition. Whatever. I think he's losing his mind."

"I thought that happened a long time ago," I said. "Like when he propositioned you. Or almost did."

"Something's up with him, that's for sure," Georgia muttered. "But that's not why I called."

"I could analyze Chris Starling for days," I assured her. "It totally doesn't matter that I've never met him."

"You can change all that this Friday, as a matter of fact," Georgia said. That she was trying, suddenly, to sound enthusiastic was so alarming that it took a moment for the words themselves to sink in.

"No way!" I said then. "Why do you think I want to go to your office party every year?" More to the point, why did I let her talk me into it every year?

"Because I want you to go, obviously," Georgia said, dropping the scary enthusiastic voice. "Anyway, why not? The place is packed with young, reasonably attractive men. All of whom are gainfully employed. Any one of whom you could date."

"You hate everyone you work with, particularly the young, reasonably attractive men," I reminded her. "You refer to them as the Leeches, I believe, and that's when you're just being competitive. When you're mad, you get way more personal."

"Because I have to *contend* with them on a professional level," Georgia said, sounding exasperated. "I can't believe you're arguing with me! When's the last time you went out on a date, anyway?"

"A what?"

"Exactly." She sniffed. "The fact of the matter, Gus, is that you've been locked in your scary post-Nate phase for way too long. This past weekend just proves my point. Whatever he might have said to you—and please, of course it was heinous, I'm not even debating that—racing across Boston with *Henry fucking Farland* to go get in Helen's face in the middle of the night was just *insane*. Lunatic behavior."

"It's not like I *actually* got in Helen's face," I argued, stung. "And like I told you the first eight billion times, spending time with Henry actually turned out to be sort of illuminating."

That was the word I'd used repeatedly on Sunday, when I'd been forced to explain to my disbelieving friends what had gone on the night before.

Illuminating, I kept saying—*surprisingly illuminating!* But no matter how I tried to steer the conversation toward more interesting things, like what Nate was up to after I left Winchester—they kept getting stuck on the fact I'd chased after Helen in the first place. That I was stalking Nate through Helen. In the company of someone I hated. Someone we all hated, and had hated for years.

Needless to say, the version I'd told them of the end of the evening was edited to look a lot like the one I'd made up. As far as they knew, Henry dropped me off, I came to my senses, and decided not to go punch Helen in the face. The end. The part of me that felt badly about this was . . . very small indeed.

"It sure was illuminating," Georgia agreed now. "For example, it illuminated the fact that you've been acting like a crazy person. You're obsessed. But who cares, that's over and done with. Come to the holiday party, find a nice lawyer boy, and you can start a whole new relationship with a whole new set of things to be obsessive and weird about."

"Georgia—" I began, annoyed, but she cut me off.

"And anyway," she said, "I always have more fun when you're there. I have to go and kiss some asses, but I'm not taking no for an answer from you, Gus, so just prepare yourself."

"I'm not going," I told her.

"You have to," she said then. "I told Jared it wasn't a date thing. He wouldn't go if it was just him as my date because he thinks that's too much pressure and can you just do this for me, Gus? Please?"

"Georgia, that's crazy," I began.

"Like you're one to talk," she snapped, and then she hung up on me. Which happened to be one of my pet peeves, as she knew very well.

I returned to a more upright position, took my feet off my desk, and fumed, for two reasons. The first reason was that I knew I would end up going to Georgia's stupid party, because I couldn't withstand the guilt trip if I didn't. Please. I couldn't withstand a long, lawyerish look. More to the point, I already felt guilty for the crimes she didn't know I'd committed. The second reason was that I thought Georgia was insane to let some little shithead play games with her, and *she* thought *I* was equally insane—but she had faulty information.

Okay, sure, Georgia and Amy Lee had maybe had a point about the Nate and Helen thing. I had gone a tad overboard. Not so much in anything I'd *done*, I didn't think, but I could maybe tone down the rhetoric a bit—particularly, as Georgia had pointed out, since I was the one who kept bringing them up again and again.

But their major point—the thing, they'd said, that indicated I'd lost my freaking mind—was that I'd willingly gotten into a car with Henry who—as Amy Lee had reminded me—I'd been at pains to convince them was evil incarnate for weeks.

So I could hardly turn around now and announce that Henry really wasn't *that* bad.

What would I tell them, anyway? That I imagined he might have tender moments? I mean, I could try, but sooner or later someone (probably Georgia, who was predisposed to consider problems concerning Henry) would start wondering *why* I hated him so much if he *wasn't that bad*. I couldn't tell them that we'd slept together the night I'd walked in on Nate and Helen, and I certainly couldn't tell them about our more recent shenanigans, unless I was ready to explain how I'd managed to sleep with the major epic crush of Georgia's twenties without sparing her so much as a thought. Twice.

So I was basically screwed. Either Henry wasn't that bad and I would be outed as a liar and a betrayer, or he was evil as usual and I was just your garden variety psycho ex-girlfriend.

Frankly, I didn't much care for either option.

What a tangled web, indeed.

chapter thirteen

"You don't *really* think I'm crazy though," I said the day after next, encouraging Amy Lee to agree with me. Amy Lee had her Thursday morning free and had met me for an early lunch. She just stared at me now, over her mountainous turkey sandwich. Fresh turkey sliced from the newly-roasted bird in front of her eyes, because suddenly nothing prepackaged would suit her, yet I was the crazy person.

"Oh, come on!"

"Gus, I don't care if you're clinically psychotic," she replied. "Just to be clear."

"But you think I am."

"Oh, hell, yes," she said. "But the good news about that is, I've always thought you were crazy. Since the day we met. When you were ranting about your mix tapes and you had your hair in that . . ."

She gestured at her head, forcing us both to remember the hair I'd graduated from high school with.

"That *thing*," she finished vaguely.

"That's very reassuring." I stared glumly at my own sandwich—sun-dried tomatoes and brie, usually delicious and today practically tasteless as far as I was concerned. Revisiting hairstyles past didn't exactly help, either.

"It was actually sort of cute back then," Amy Lee lied, looking at my expression.

"I don't know that you should really be the one to talk, here," I sniped at her. "It's not like you're your usual pulled-together self today, are you?"

It was true. Amy Lee looked frazzled, and her cheeks were flushed. Two things about as un-Amy Lee-ish as could be.

"I'm fighting off the flu," she snapped at me. And apparently she was feeding that possible fever, because she practically inhaled a huge bite of her sandwich.

"Obviously," I said then, forgetting about her flu, "I want you to tell me that you think Georgia's just using my *supposed* insanity as a cover for the fact that Georgia's *own* situation with what's-his-name—"

"Jared," Amy Lee interjected. "I'm pretty sure. Or maybe Justin. Or no, that's the singer guy."

"Her own thing is precarious and bad and also insane, and that's what her issue is." I eyed her. "That's what's going on here, right? This isn't *actually* about me at all."

She smiled.

"If it makes you feel any better," she said, "I think Georgia is *also* crazy."

*   *   *

Friday night came despite my best efforts.

I didn't make the mistake of believing that Georgia might be put off by a display of surliness on my part or by my not being ready when she arrived. I'd tried that kind of thing before, with little result. If I was lolling around in sweats and an attitude when she arrived at my house to usher me to the Waterbury, Ellis and Reardon holiday party she would simply haul my butt into the shower, then into an outfit of her choosing, and then frog-march me off to make merry.

Much as *she* might enjoy that, I knew I certainly would not, so I was reluctantly dressed in all my finery when my buzzer rang. (I'd even applied a curling iron to my hair—an almost unheard-of event.) So much for my fervent prayers that the snow we'd been having would have caused interminable delays and she would remain stuck somewhere south. She buzzed again—and I could practically *hear* her impatience. I pressed the button to unlatch the door. Slowly.

"This is very disappointing," Georgia murmured when I opened the door for her. She had an evil spark in her eye. "I was really looking forward to dragging your ass off the couch and tossing you into the shower. Sometimes I think I would have made an excellent prison guard."

"It's nice to see you too, so glad your plane wasn't delayed," I said, with a wide, insincere smile. "And that's possibly the most terrifying thing I've ever heard come out of your mouth. Which is saying something."

"Whatever," Georgia retorted. "Let's go. Jared said he'll meet us there later." The "maybe" was implied.

"Great," I said, with an eye roll toward the back of her head as she walked out the door. "What a fun night. Lawyers and partners and Jared, oh my!"

"Don't start with me," Georgia warned as I locked the door.

"I wouldn't dare," I murmured. I waited for Irwin to emerge from his den, but apparently even he was cowed by Georgia in stilettos.

"I've just spent way too long in the exclusive company of Chris Starling and my boyfriend can't seem to return a voice mail message in under seventy-two hours," Georgia snarled. "I had to deal with Logan Airport on a Friday, don't get me *started* on the traffic, and I am not in the mood for any shit, okay?"

"Wait—what?" I zoomed in on the crucial bit of information in that little rant. "Your *boyfriend*? When did this guy become your *boyfriend* and why wasn't I informed?"

"We can talk about that later, at the party," Georgia said, "because what you're not hearing is that I need a cocktail." She pointed her finger at me. "Right now you just need to start thinking about your reasonably attractive, brand-new boyfriend, the one you're about to meet."

"The one who will save me from myself, like in all the fairy tales?" I asked in an over-the-top voice that suggested I was disgusted at the very idea. But I was a single female on the verge of thirty, so in the unlikely event that Prince Charming did pop up at Georgia's office party, it's not as if I would slap him down just to retain my feminist street cred. Tattered as it was. Though I would insist on saving myself, for sure.

"It's entirely possible that you might need saving tonight," Georgia barked at me. "And not from yourself."

"I can't wait," I lied, and we were on our way.

Georgia fetched us each a cocktail when we arrived, and I sipped mine as she did a few perfunctory rounds of Schmooze and Smile. The big conference hall on the top floor of the firm had been given over to the Waterbury, Ellis and Reardon version of holiday fun. Fir trees were topped with menorahs in a gesture toward inclusion, no doubt offending all parties. The main attractions were the bar and the buffet table, while a band played sedately in the background. Some in the crowd were glammed up, while others looked as if they'd just returned from court. Harried-looking paralegals appeared periodically—in suits that looked rumpled, possibly because they'd slept in them—and whispered into various partying ears. Despite the fact it was a work event, I knew from experience that it was only a matter of time before the liquor flowed just that little bit too freely. The dancing would start, some first-year (or tenth-year) associate would become delightfully inappropriate, and the real fun would begin. Until then, everyone was schmoozing their ambitious behinds off, and I half expected William Shatner and Candice Bergen to come waltzing out from behind the nearest potted plant.

"You must be Gus," a voice said in my ear, and I turned,

assuming it was Georgia's (apparent, and sure-to-be-odious) "boyfriend."

Instead of the sleek, toothy guy I remembered—very vaguely—from the Park Plaza, an older man stood in front of me. He was about Georgia's height, and had the liveliest pair of brown eyes I'd ever seen. It took me a moment to notice anything else about him—his eyes danced with merriment and cleverness, so that he seemed to be lit from within.

"Hi," I said, immediately charmed. I had no idea who he was.

"I'm a psychic," he said, very matter-of-factly. "I discerned your name from the ether."

I almost believed it, too.

"Or I told it to him," Georgia snapped in exasperation. She shook her head at the guy. "Why can't you just introduce yourself like a normal person?"

"It's hard to believe I'm her boss, I know," he said. Supposedly to me, but he was looking at Georgia. "Beneath all that bluster, she's really impressed with my authority."

"Gus," Georgia said, waving her hand at him. "This is Chris Starling."

"I know Georgia uses other names, most of them inappropriate, but you can call me Chris," he told me. I wasn't sure, but I thought my jaw might have dropped open in astonishment. Not that either one of them was paying me any mind. They were far too caught up in their banter.

"And again—hilarious," Georgia was saying, rolling her eyes.

"And there's Bob Young, giving me the 'come worship' eye," Chris Starling said, only grinning at her. "Off to the salt mines I go."

"My lord," Georgia said when he walked away. "Isn't he the most annoying man you've ever met?"

It took her a long moment to stop frowning after him, and to look at me.

I searched her face. "Georgia, you told me he was short, fat, balding, and horrible!"

Georgia's gaze was blank.

"He is," she said.

"Sure," I agreed. "Except for the part where he's not short at all, not fat at all, and has the most amazing eyes I've ever seen. He's got Gandalf eyes or something. It's like he *knows things*."

"What are you talking about?" Georgia asked. "Did you just say *Gandalf*? And what do you mean, he's not fat? Believe me, maybe it's hidden behind his jacket tonight, but the guy hardly has abs of steel."

"*Maybe* he has a stomach, which is very different from being *fat*." I enunciated each word carefully. "And maybe he's secretly the boss from hell, but he seemed *nice*. Charming, actually. Not horrible and nasty at all!"

Georgia stared at me for a moment, as if she couldn't quite understand what I was getting at. Then she let out a laugh.

"Absolutely not," she said. "I forbid it."

Now it was my turn to stare uncomprehendingly. "You forbid what?"

"You and Chris Starling," she said. "I didn't bring you here so you could hook up with my weird, *old* boss. That's like trading in *crazy* for an entire *asylum*. Forget it, you can't have him." She patted me on the arm. "You'll just have to find a nice guy your own age, and look! There's a whole pack of them by the bar."

"First of all, he's what? Forty-five at the most?"

"Old," Georgia repeated. "And off-limits. Seriously."

"I don't want him!" I snapped at her.

"Glad to hear it," she said. She frowned at me. "What is your problem?"

I shook my head to clear it, and frowned back at her.

"I don't know," I said. "I'm just kind of stunned that you created this whole version of him that isn't even remotely real!"

That hung there for a moment, taunting me. I felt as if I'd somehow ejected myself from my own body and was hovering outside it, watching myself say that out loud.

I almost wished Henry were there to witness it himself, since he'd be the one to enjoy it the most, given my daily assassinations of his character.

I was so taken back that it took me a moment to notice that Georgia wasn't paying me the slightest bit of attention. She was looking off across the room, and she was smiling. A big, relieved smile.

"There he is," she said, in the voice that meant Jared. "I wasn't sure he would come. Stay here," she continued, finally glancing at me. "I can't wait for you to meet him."

She took off across the room, and I was left to stand there

and really bask in the full extent of my hypocrisy. I was amazed that you could become a hypocrite without even meaning to—*just like that*. That it was so simple. That you could look into someone else's life and see the things they were doing with such clarity, even as you ignored those same things when you did them yourself.

The sad thing was, with a cocktail, it didn't sting nearly as much as I thought it should.

chapter fourteen

The six ways I was able to tell that the Cocky Arrogant Jackass Jared, also known (briefly) as Georgia's latest "boyfriend," was completely unworthy of a woman like Georgia and would inevitably crush her heart in some callous manner, which (surprise, surprise) happened sometime later that Friday night, long after I'd bailed and taken a cab home, were the following:

First, he was sullen and disrespectful when Georgia introduced him to me, because (as he claimed later during the dramatic *this is why I will never love you* portion of the evening) she was basically *claiming* him by towing him around her party like that and he was *independent, man,* and she should have respected him and not tried to *play him like that.*

Second, he made it very, very clear that his presence at the party—which had provided him with free food and an open bar, so wasn't exactly a great hardship—was a favor. A favor of such enormous proportions it was unlikely Georgia could ever repay it. He was therefore under no obligation to be polite to her, or even terribly nice, because hello—*he was there, wasn't he, what more did she want?*

Third, he was caught checking out the breasts and/or asses of at least four different women, none of whom were Georgia. And *caught* meant *both Georgia and I watched as young Jared drooled over a succession of cheesy, possibly augmented and almost certainly anorexic trophy wives of the partners, which Jared made no attempt to do subtly, and which he then acted all "What?" about.* Loser.

Fourth, he was happy to talk about his blond highlights and his many hair products, but sneered when Georgia mentioned her own beauty regime, and then made some ridiculously clichéd comment about women and bathroom time which was so clichéd that my inner raging feminist—usually quick to wave her fists in the air—couldn't even bring herself to respond. (Possibly she was drunk and looking for Prince Charming after all.)

Fifth, when Georgia left us to fetch him a drink, he felt compelled by the uncomfortable silence between us to ask me what I did. When I said I was a librarian he laughed. Loudly. Then he said, "No, for real." Then, when I assured him it was true and I had the librarian action figure to prove it—matronly figure, shushing action and all—he snorted and said, "Bet *that's* a real growth industry."

And finally, as the kiss of death, Georgia had to *explain*. Homophobic remark, asshole-ish story, snotty behavior? Georgia used all the excuses she could come up with: Jared didn't mean that, Jared has his own sense of humor, ha ha,

Jared likes to push people's buttons for fun, he's just tired tonight because he works so hard all the time, etc.

I ran through the list about sixty trillion times before it finally penetrated.

"I really thought he was different," Georgia moaned. This was an improvement over the wailing and the *what did I do, what's wrong with me* part. A breakthrough, really.

She hauled her comforter up around her neck and sniffled. She was sprawled out across her king-size bed, from which she moved only to visit the bathroom or let in the takeout Thai delivery guy.

I'd received the call a little before six—in the morning, I wish I was kidding—on Saturday. I staggered over with breakup CDs in hand and chocolate in my bag, and proceeded to hold her hand for most of the day. Amy Lee turned up after her office hours were finished.

"I don't want to be mean," Amy Lee said from her position slumped against the foot of the bed. "But enough with these guys, Georgia. This guy was a clown from the get-go and you know it."

If that was her new version of the speech, it sucked. I glared at her. She only shrugged, and set her mouth in a stubborn line.

"I can't help the way I feel!" Georgia cried. Very Tori Amos, with the arms flung out and the hair everywhere. I made a soothing noise, and patted her leg again.

Amy Lee just sighed, and crossed her arms over her chest. She didn't look at all soothing, or even sympathetic. She looked annoyed.

"Well, I can't!" Georgia threw at her, actually sitting up as she did so. I interpreted that as progress. "You fall in love with the person you fall in love with. You can't *control* that!"

"Maybe that's true," Amy Lee agreed, but she sounded impatient. "And you're saying that you were in love with this guy after what? Two weeks?"

"Almost four," Georgia snapped at her.

"Oh, *four* weeks." Amy Lee rolled her eyes. "My mistake."

"Hey—" Georgia started, moving as if to lunge in Amy Lee's direction, but Amy Lee raised her hands, palms out, as if to ward her off.

"Okay, relax," she ordered. "I told you, I'm not trying to be mean."

"Try harder," I suggested. She didn't even look at me, she was too busy staring at Georgia—no doubt willing her to refrain from throwing a punch.

"Then what are you trying to do?" Georgia asked. But she sat back.

"You hardly know this guy," Amy Lee said, in what she probably thought was a gentle tone. "You're never even in town, Georgia, so how much could you possibly have seen of him in four weeks?"

"Does that really matter?" Georgia demanded. "You want me to justify how I feel?"

"I want you to think about what you *really* feel," Amy

Lee countered. "You claim you're in love, but I'm sorry, I don't think that's true. Gus and I sat at a table in the Park Plaza and watched you the night you met him, and we were able to tell that he sucked from across the room."

Georgia's eyes slid to me, a betrayed sort of light in them. I had the intense urge to dissent, but thought better of it. At that moment, I didn't know which one of them I feared more, and seeing that expression on Georgia's face made me sick to my stomach.

"He seemed a lot like all the other ones," I said, shrugging. "I'm sorry."

"He's a carbon copy!" Amy Lee exclaimed. "And on some level, I know you know that, Georgia. So I'm wondering why you keep doing this to yourself." She opened her arms to indicate the rumpled bed, not to mention Georgia's puffy eyes and general state of disarray. "Aren't you sick of this yet? Because I think you deserve better, and I'm running out of ways to say that."

The silence, then, stretched out between the three of us. Aimee Mann crooned intelligent despair on the stereo and I snuck glances back and forth between the two of them, wondering what might happen next.

Eventually, Georgia sighed. It was as if a cloud moved away from the sun—her face cleared, and she tilted up her chin.

"You know what?" she said, a little unevenly. "I think I am sick of this."

I was so proud of her, I thought I might burst. If Georgia could stop the bad-boy madness, surely anything was possible.

"Okay then," Amy Lee said, her voice hushed.

Georgia smiled. It was a little watery, but it was there.

"Oh good," I said then, in a rush. "Because I'm dying to talk about Chris Starling. I think you should consider him."

"Are you kidding?" Amy Lee asked me. She looked disgusted.

Georgia blinked at me. "Consider him how?"

"Consider him as your next boyfriend," I said, in a ringing sort of tone.

Again, a long silence.

"I've changed my mind," Georgia said, scraping her hair back from her head and twisting it into a knot at the nape of her neck. "I think I'm actually sick of *you*, Gus. And Chris Starling. *Creepy* Chris Starling."

"He's not creepy at all!" I was outraged on his behalf. "He's totally cute!"

"See what I mean?" Georgia asked Amy Lee. "She's obsessed with Chris Starling."

"Creepy," Amy Lee said, "but an improvement on Nate Manning."

"Mark my words, Georgia," I said grandly, choosing to ignore Amy Lee. "You're going to marry that guy. He's—"

But I had to stop mid-prophecy, when she tried to smother me with one of her down pillows.

The next day I woke up early again, only this time it was from stress. Or a sense of impending doom. Or both—either way I was wide awake and kind of wishing Georgia had succeeded in smothering me.

At 2 p.m., we were all expected to assemble for a winter caroling party in further celebration of the holiday season. There were any number of reasons this was stressful. For one thing, Henry would be there, and I was somewhat worried that Georgia would be able to sniff out my second, sober, and thus far more serious betrayal of her on the winter air. Not to mention, I was worried about facing Henry after the phone incident. For another, Helen would also be at the party, no doubt prepared to lord her continuing relationship with Nate over me, knowing nothing about the Night of Seven Voice Mails.

And for even one more reason—what was a winter caroling party, exactly? Nobody knew. The invitation made a mysterious reference to *bells and bobtails*, which had given rise to my suspicion that horses might be involved, and possibly hayrides. It was out in some or other far-off suburb ending in -ham, so really, anything could happen. This was what happened when your friends tried to get creative with their holiday-making, and a simple drink near some mistletoe wouldn't do. The three girls throwing it had felt upstaged by a separate Christmas party last year, so, not to be outdone two years running, they'd shanghaied someone's mother's friend's house, and who knew what would come of it?

But I wasn't fooling myself. My real stress was Nate-shaped, and I didn't know what to do about it. My heart was jumpy whenever I thought about him, which I suspected was anticipation. I was looking forward to seeing him, and I knew this was destined to lead nowhere good. I hadn't seen him since he'd manhandled me at the party out in Winchester. I hadn't heard from him either, unless I counted the number of times I had replayed his messages.

One way or another, I decided, I had to sort out the Nate situation. Bells and bobtails be damned.

I tried not to think too much about it that whole morning and anyway, there were other things to brood about. Like what one wore to an outdoor party. In Boston. In *December*. Layers, obviously, but which layers? Exactly how fat was I willing to look to ward off possible hypothermia? I wrapped myself in a series of garments, and then rolled myself out the door and onto the T so that Amy Lee and Oscar could once again carpool us to suburban fun. It was a good thing New Year's was coming up soon—I wasn't sure how much more of the enforced gaiety I could take.

Especially when my friends were under the impression I was a bunny-boiler.

I stared out at the deceptively bright and sunny sky while Oscar drove out of the city. Amy Lee and Georgia took the car ride as an opportunity to lecture me extensively on the subject of my insanity.

According to my friends, I was prohibited from: talking to Nate, Helen, or Henry; speaking *about* Nate, Helen, or Henry; and engaging in any form of nonverbal communication to or about Nate, Helen, or Henry.

Although they said it in a lot more words than that.

"So what am I supposed to do?" I asked when they finished the initial tag-team lecture. "Pretend I don't see them? Ignore them if they talk to me? That's a great solution, and very mature."

"You can nod and smile, and then you can walk away," Georgia said. "Since you're so concerned with maturity all of a sudden."

"And I can't believe you're making it sound like this is going to be some hardship for you," Amy Lee chimed in. "Please try to remember that you don't *like* any of these people! Two of them betrayed you and the other one is Henry!"

I muttered something under my breath, and avoided looking anyone in the eye.

"I hope there's hot chocolate," Oscar contributed from behind the wheel. Apropos of nothing. "Everybody likes hot chocolate."

By the time we arrived at the party, I was about as gloomy as it was possible to get without *actually* curling up into the fetal position. There were a series of sleighs—horses, blankets, runners and all—arrayed along the country lane. Nearby, a series of Bostonians milled around in the fresh snow, looking either excited or dubious. Or a mixture of the two.

"I've always wanted to go on a sleigh ride," Georgia announced. She linked elbows with Oscar, and tugged him along with her toward the crowd. "Admit it, you have a yearning."

I watched Oscar deny it, and then looked at Amy Lee, who hung behind to keep glaring at me.

"I'm allowed to be in whatever mood I want to be in," I told her, feeling a little defensive.

"It's dashing through the snow on a one-horse open sleigh," Amy Lee retorted. "It's not a death march. You could lighten up a little bit."

"I'm fine," I said. I waited a beat. "And actually it looks like a *four-horse* open—"

"You're already freaking out, aren't you?" Amy Lee hissed at me. "No sign of any of them, and you're already a mess. Georgia's right. You flipped your lid with Nate and—"

"Okay, enough," I said, cutting her off. "You're the one making me crazy, Amy Lee. Why don't you stop monitoring my behavior? How am I supposed to feel with you *watching* me?"

"Fine," she said. "But any insanity in the sleigh, Gus, and I swear to God I'll feed you to the horses."

They were so worried about it, in fact, that the two of them flanked me as we waited for the whole party to arrive. Wherever I went, it was in a Georgia-and–Amy Lee sandwich. I would have been more upset about it, except for the fact that it provided a convenient buffer. I saw Nate and Helen arrive—apparently still together, if the hand-holding and outdoor snuggling were anything to go by. From a distance, I performed the nod and smile I'd been permitted. Inside, I was in turmoil. He hardly even glanced at me! What was he *doing*? Then Henry turned up not long after, crooked his mouth in my direction, and there was no need for nodding or smiling since I was suddenly too shy to look at him.

The last time I'd seen him, after all, he'd been mostly naked.

Don't get me wrong—I managed to see that he looked

way too delicious for a sleigh ride, and I squirreled away salient details about the way he wore his winter coat and jeans—and then I had to look away.

Georgia interpreted that as following the rules, and gave me an approving smile.

"Was that so hard?" she asked.

"I'm about three seconds away from going postal on both of you," I said. "But no, that wasn't hard."

After a moment, Amy Lee shook her head. "I have to go with Gus. That was pretty condescending."

"Definitely," Oscar agreed.

"Really?" Georgia looked crushed. "I was going for encouraging."

"And I'm the crazy one?" I demanded.

I let them bustle me along with them into a sleigh—the one not containing any of the people I wasn't allowed to talk to, of course—and then I relaxed into the randomness of the whole thing. The sun was already starting to fade by the time we set off, singing Christmas carols like loons into the coming winter night.

We sang until the stars appeared, and our cheeks were too frozen to sing anymore. I surprised myself by having a great time.

Afterward, we all crowded into the house, Oscar got his hot chocolate, and I came back to earth with a jarring thud. It was one thing to avoid Helen, Nate, and Henry while bundled up in a separate sleigh, singing about angels and mangers and walking in a winter wonderland. It was something else entirely while trapped in a house with them.

Not that they were chasing after me.

Helen smirked every time she looked at me, which rankled, but which I ignored because she was the one I cared the least about. Tonight, anyway. And besides, I knew things she didn't—things she would kill to know, in fact, about her supposed boyfriend. For his part, Nate shrugged a sort of apology in my direction, but stuck close to her side. I knew it was better that way, since Georgia and Amy Lee were watching me like a hawk, but the truth was, it felt . . . weird. I wanted to know what had happened. I wanted to know why he'd called that night, and not since. I was sure there was more to the story this time than *I can't be what you want* or whatever he'd said that night in the bar. I wanted—*needed*—explanations. I forced myself to stop looking at him.

I looked across the room instead, to where Henry lounged in the corner, propping himself up against the fireplace. Waiting. I knew he was waiting because whenever my gaze slid in his direction he met it, in a manner I could only describe as challenging. *I dare you to come over here*, that look said, right out there in the open for anyone to see.

It made me feel jittery. It made me feel as crazy as I was accused of being. It made me think I wanted to take that dare, and that was a whole different kind of crazy, the kind I'd thought had to do with Nate and had last time landed me naked and in the nearest bed with his roommate instead.

"I'm going to the bathroom," I announced. Amy Lee and Georgia exchanged a look. "Do I really need an escort?" I snapped. "Will I get to be alone on the toilet?"

They let me go.

The downstairs bathroom was occupied, so I climbed my way upstairs. The house was a beautiful old Victorian settled on the edge of a field. Stately and graceful, which was reflected in the furnishings. I found the bathroom and locked the door behind me.

Stately and graceful, I thought. *Two words that will never be used to describe me.*

When I came out, Henry straightened from the wall, and it was as if he filled the hallway.

My heart stopped beating, and then kicked back into gear.

I couldn't describe that look on his face, but it made my knees feel weak.

"Oh," I said. "Hi."

He smiled.

"So I've been thinking," he said in a casual, conversational sort of voice, completely at odds with the intent way he watched me. "No smart-ass remarks, please."

We stood facing each other in the hall. Behind him, I could hear the party noises float up from the floor below. The stairway was right around the corner from where he stood. I could make a break for it.

But I didn't move.

"I didn't say anything," I pointed out.

"And yet I could hear you." He eyed me. "Imagine that."

"Were you thinking about something in particular?" I asked. "Or was that just a general announcement? For reference?"

"What did I just say?" He shook his head at me. "Like three seconds ago?"

"I don't think I want to do this," I said, barely above a whisper. "Whatever this is."

"Oh, of course," he said, this time with more of an edge. "Because talking is scary. I keep forgetting how much you hate it."

"It's just complicated . . ." I began, and then stopped myself.

"I bet it is," he said. "You need to get over the Nate thing. I love the guy, but come on."

"You don't know anything about it!"

"I know Helen deserves him, and that's not a compliment. She's nuttier than he is."

I liked the way he said that—so matter-of-factly, as if Helen's nuttiness was obvious and there could be no rebuttal. As if Henry would certainly never be sucked into her games.

"But see, here's the thing," he said, forcing me to focus on him again. "I think what's going on between us qualifies as a pattern."

"What?" I frowned at him. "There were two isolated events. No us. No pattern."

"I think it's a pattern," he said. "Which must suck for you, since you think I'm some illiterate jackass of a spoiled rich boy."

I opened my mouth and then shut it with a snap. I felt my shoulders sink.

"Which sucks for me," he continued in a low voice, "be-

cause who wants to be into a girl who thinks he's a jackass? That got old in the fifth grade, believe it or not."

"Henry . . ." But I didn't know what to say. I knew suddenly that despite all of our sparring, I didn't want to be
responsible for hurting him, even in a small way.

"I don't know why," he said. "I just like you." His eyes
searched my face. "Obviously, this presents a problem. The
jackass issue. But then it occurred to me that you don't actually know anything about me."

"I've known you for years," I reminded him. "Almost a
decade, in fact."

He leaned against the wall. "What do I do for a living?"

"You're a lawyer," I shot back at once. Then, to be
obnoxious: "And you're a Farland." The trust fund was
implied.

He sighed. "What kind of law do I practice?" he asked.

I thought about it. I had a specific memory of Georgia,
ranting about *something*, years ago—but no, it was gone.

I shrugged.

"Exactly my point," he said. "You just know the basic
outline. You have no idea who I am."

"Why are you telling me this?" I burst out. I felt way too
emotional, and tried to rein it in. "What makes you think
I care?"

"I care," he shot back. "This is part of the adulthood
thing I believe we've touched on previously. I can't allow
myself to keep having romantic moments with someone
who hates me, Gus. Right? That's only logical."

"But I don't know you, so it's okay?"

"Something like that." He let his gaze drop, and his smirk reappeared.

"Listen." I had no idea where I was going, but I kept on, in the desperate hope something might occur to me as I floundered. "I handled the whole sex thing badly, I know that now. It was a rough time. And the last time just kind of—I don't—I mean, it was for all the wrong reasons . . ." I broke off, flustered.

"It was for the best reason," he contradicted me.

He reached across the space between us then, and traced a pattern along my jaw. I felt my body react to that—I sighed a little bit, and felt an ache spread through my limbs.

And then he was kissing me.

And it was hot. His mouth was clever and I couldn't seem to get close enough, to taste enough. He made a low sort of noise and pushed me back against the wall, angling his head so everything got deeper and hotter.

I had no idea what might have happened then, but there was a sudden shuffling noise in the hall behind him, and I jerked my head back and out of his grasp.

I was a little bit dizzy, so it took me a moment to blink and then look around him, behind him, expecting to see someone on a bathroom mission.

Amy Lee and Georgia stood there, a scant few feet away, gaping at us.

"Oh," I said brightly. "Hi, guys."

"You have to be kidding me," Amy Lee said flatly.

Henry turned, and then it was like a face-off. A face-off in a nightmare, except I was awake. My stomach cramped from the tension. I was afraid to look at Georgia, but I forced myself to do it anyway.

"Okay," I began, "I know that it must seem—"

"You're fucking him?" Georgia threw at me, scandalized. "Henry?" She didn't say "*my* Henry," but I heard it anyway.

"Not in a—I mean we only—um, I—" Language failed me. It had something to do with the way she'd said his name.

"How is that your business?" Henry asked her. He was very polite, but there was a bit of steel beneath.

Georgia's brows arched up, and then I watched her look at Henry for a long, long moment. Something passed between them, and then Georgia shrugged.

"It's not my business at all," she said, but she sounded almost respectful.

I actually thought, then, that maybe it would all be okay. Awkward and weird, but okay. I let myself breathe. I hadn't realized I was holding my breath in the first place.

"Fuck this," Amy Lee said then, in a strange, deliberate voice that made us all flinch. Everyone turned to look at her, and her flushed, angry face. "Fuck all of you."

"What?" Georgia looked as confused as I felt.

"Amy Lee—" I started.

"Shut up!" she ordered. She looked at Georgia for a long moment, and then she looked at me. I felt myself wilt. She didn't look at Henry at all.

"What's wrong with you?" Georgia demanded.

"I've had it with all of this crap, is what's wrong with me," Amy Lee snapped at her. "The two of you are exhausting and I can't take another minute of it."

"I didn't tell you because—"

But she didn't let me finish.

"I don't care why you didn't tell me," she said. "I don't care if Georgia spends the rest of her life prostrate on the bed, weeping over some loser. I promise you, I have better things to do with my time than keep up with these fucking soap operas."

"Hey!" Georgia sounded stung.

Amy Lee took a step back, and fired that angry look back and forth between Georgia and me again. I realized she was shaking slightly.

"I'm not in college anymore," she said. She wasn't snapping any longer, which, somehow, made it worse. "None of us are, but I'm the only one who seems to have noticed. I have a house. A dental practice. A marriage. We're talking about babies and college funds, and *you*—" She glared at me. "You're wearing my bridesmaid's dress to a party just to fuck with me while *you*—" She turned to Georgia.

"While I what?" Georgia snapped, daring her.

"While you go out of your way to live your entire life like it's the same Tori Amos album we listened to when we were all of twenty." She sucked in a deep breath. "You both need to grow the hell up, but I don't care if you do or not, because I'm not dealing with this shit anymore."

And then she backed up another step, while we all

just stood there and stared at her. There was a beat, and someone was breathing heavily—it might have been me, I couldn't tell—and then she turned, wrapped her arms around her middle, and took off down the stairs as if our friendship didn't lie in tatters behind her.

chapter fifteen

Every song on the radio was about heartbreak, it seemed, of one sort or another. What to do to keep him from leaving, how to get through those awful days right after she took off, the fantasies about the two of you getting back together, the sick realization that he might never love you again and maybe never did in the first place. It was breakup central all along the FM dial, and if the songs weren't enough, you could turn on the television to just about any prime-time show to *really* stick the knife in.

But no one seemed to talk much about what to do when your best friend broke up with you. There weren't whole artistic media devoted to the subject. There was Edie Brickell's "Circle of Friends," and that was about it.

I discovered—with no help in the form of a song—that what happened when your best friend broke up with you was a lot like what happened when you walked into your boyfriend's kitchen to find out that he wasn't your boyfriend anymore. Your world stopped with an audible crash as it splintered, but the *actual world* did not.

I did whatever was necessary to get through the moment.

Amy Lee disappeared down that hallway, and shortly thereafter, from the party. Georgia and I hardly looked at each other, not then and not afterward, when we sat in silence in Henry's Jeep as he once again chauffeured me across the state of Massachusetts. I turned to Georgia when we pulled up in front of her place, but she lifted a hand instead. She didn't exactly indicate that I should *talk* to the hand. It was more of a *stop, please* gesture. But it was still her hand in the air, aimed at me.

"I can't," she said in a thick voice I hardly recognized. "Okay, Gus? I just can't."

What, exactly, she couldn't do—talk to me, look at me, deal with what had happened—she didn't explain.

She just climbed out of the car and went inside. I watched the door close behind her and wondered—in an absent way, really, because I was about as numb as it was possible to be without actually turning into stone—if I would ever see her again.

Outside my apartment, I eyed Henry from across the gear shift.

"Want to come up?" I asked.

He smiled, and reached over. I noted that no matter what, he was always so very beautiful, which, for some reason, made me feel sad. Vaguely sad, anyway.

He picked up my hand in his and carried it to his mouth.

I think he kissed the back of it, but I couldn't be sure, I couldn't feel a thing.

"I don't think so," he said.

He was kind. But it was still *no*.

I knew that later, much later, I would probably spend whole days humiliated by that exchange, but it didn't matter then.

I just shrugged, and went inside.

Where I sat in the dark with the dog, and wondered when I would start crying, and whether I would survive it.

I got up in the morning and went to work, because even though I felt as if the world had received a serious wallop, possibly knocking it off its axis forever, there didn't seem to be any point to sitting in the house, brooding about it. I dressed without paying the slightest bit of attention to what I was putting on, which could have resulted in something sartorially exquisite. I didn't care enough to notice.

I hardly knew how I'd managed to get myself to work once I found myself on the wide front steps of the Museum. Once inside, I felt as if it were someone else performing my duties, going through my motions.

It was odd Minerva hadn't noticed, I thought as I walked back out to my desk from the bathroom to see that she was sitting there in my visitor's chair, awash in bright-colored scarves. For all her assorted manias and delusions, Minerva was usually pretty good at noticing emotional upheavals. (She ought to have been—she thrived on them.)

I studied her as she settled herself more comfortably in the chair next to my desk. Minerva favored bold colors and what she called her *bohemian flair*—thanks to a summer spent in Berkeley, California, at an impressionable age. Apparently, exposure to Berkeley led to a lifelong habit of draping oneself in tapestries, ropes of beads, and the occasional llama. (Okay, I was making that up. I wasn't actually sure it was *llama*. It could be anything hairy and particularly pungent in damp weather.) No wonder I had a phobia about California.

"Gus!" she exclaimed when she saw me walking toward her. "This new diet is *fabulous*—I can feel the fat simply *melting away!*"

She waved her hand in the general direction of her midsection, inviting me to agree and—preferably—to shriek at length that she looked *simply weak* with hunger so she could accept whatever cakes I then pressed her to consume.

I knew the routine.

This was, evidently, why Minerva had failed to notice my mood. This latest diet had something to do with eating shoots and leaves, if I'd heard her correctly, and had come recommended thirdhand from her longtime best friend and diet coconspirator, the horrifically named Dorcas Goodwin who was—for her sins—a middle school math teacher. (Yes. The woman was named *Dorcas* and taught vicious, sniggering thirteen-year-olds. I could only imagine the whispers in the halls, the name-calling in the notes passed in class.)

Their previous diet had involved a series of complicated

shakes and revolting powders for a very trying ten-day period.

"This one's all about *foraging*," she was telling me. "After all, it's how our ancestors lived for ages. *Ice* ages, Gus, and frankly I *just* can't imagine why we've rejected the hunter-gatherer lifestyle. There were no fat cavemen racing around the steppes, now were there?"

As if she had personally spent time on the prehistoric steppes, instead of reading Jean Auel novels like everyone else.

She was nothing if not frighteningly logical when you least expected it, if somewhat hazy on the details of the rise of agriculture. She was also obsessed with dieting. The fact that she remained a perfectly reasonable size ten on a five-six body, no matter how intense her exertions, never seemed to appease her. Once upon a time, when she was a slip of a girl (I'd heard the story too many times to repeat it without snideness), she'd dreamt of being a dancer, and she'd been a size six. That this had occurred when she was fifteen and largely without breasts never seemed to penetrate her diet-muddled brain.

"Minerva," I said then, because I had to stop her before she started raving about glycemic indexes and the importance of hydration. "You and Dorcas have been friends since you were kids, right?"

"Oh yes," she said, fastening her gaze on me. "It was practically preordained. You can't imagine what it was like to be so *creatively named* in the midst of all the Brendas and the Barbaras."

Until that moment, I don't think it had ever occurred to me that "Minerva" was a name that had been foisted upon a poor, defenseless child—that Minerva's parents were as much to blame (if there needed to be blame) for the odd duck of a woman before me as she was herself. Because what could anyone do, when thirteen and gawky and tragically named something like Minerva, but *choose* to *be Minerva*. It was sort of touching, when I thought about it.

"I can't imagine you as a Brenda," I told her.

She preened, pleased. "I wanted so terribly to change my name," she confessed. "I was jealous of the other girls, but in time, I grew into my name and now, of course . . ." She waved a languid hand. "Why did you ask?"

"Oh." I had to think about how to phrase the question I wanted to ask. I settled on: "How have you been friends with Dorcas for so long? How do you keep from fighting?"

"We don't do anything of the kind," Minerva said with a small laugh. "We fight all the time. She claims I'm attention-seeking and really, she's dreadfully immature behind all that ranting about *responsibility*. I expect we'll argue about it all the way to the grave."

"But do you ever have real fights?" I pressed her. "The kind of fight you're not certain your friendship will recover from?"

Not that what had happened with Amy Lee could be called a *fight*. In the strictest sense of the term, I would have had to participate in it, if it was a fight. Instead of just standing there while she told me off.

Minerva shifted her legs, and considered.

"You don't have to tell me the details," I assured her. Which was a waste of breath, of course. Minerva *existed* to over-share. She made a pensive sort of face.

"I don't recall the details," she said after a moment. "I know that we stopped talking for a while—you would think I'd remember everything that led to it. It was several months, I think. I was furious with her—I was determined we would never speak again, unless, of course, she offered a full apology."

"What did she do?"

"She was very unsupportive of me," Minerva revealed in hushed tones. "I wanted her to be on board with my decision to open a yoga studio, and she refused. She thought I was being led astray by a certain gentleman we knew at the time"—Minerva batted her lashes coyly—"and she *would not* accept my assurances that my love of yoga would transcend any possible relationship I was having with him." She sighed. "It was very unpleasant."

"Do you have a yoga studio I don't know about?" I asked, working hard to keep my tone even. I was trying as hard as I could to avoid imagining Minerva striking yoga poses, or writhing about on a mat trying to touch her knees to her nose. It was a struggle. And unless there was an attic in the Museum I didn't know about, Dorcas had been on the winning side of that argument.

"It didn't work out," Minerva said with a heavy sigh, as if she regretted the lost yoga studio nightly. "Though I do love the practice of yoga, and often wish . . . But that's neither here nor there. She was just so smug—it was unacceptable. We had a terrible argument, and then we didn't speak. You know Dorcas."

I did know Dorcas. She was one of those stereotypical New England Women of a Certain Age—the sort who would revel in describing herself as *no-nonsense*. She was always clomping in and out of the Museum in *sensible shoes*, while attempting to force Minerva to cut her hair into *something more appropriate for her years*, something like Dorcas's own serviceable, manageable bob.

Thinking about it, Dorcas and Minerva could only have met and become friends in childhood. At any other point in life, they each would have viewed the other as impossibly alien. Where Minerva changed her entire self-definition on a whim and the flick of a beaded necklace, Dorcas was *particular* about her position as a middle school teacher, her little house on the outskirts of Braintree, and her lifelong enthusiasm for breeding Cairn terriers. They shouldn't have been able to tolerate each other and so, naturally, they had been best friends for some forty years.

"How did you start speaking again?" I asked. "Did she apologize?"

"Did Dorcas *apologize*?" Minerva let out a peal of laughter. "Dorcas Goodwin, *apologize*? First she would need to know the meaning of the word, and believe me, Gus—she still doesn't."

"Then how . . . ?"

Minerva fingered the edge of one of her scarves, one in a hue I couldn't begin to describe.

"One day she simply called me, and carried on as if we'd spoken the day before, as usual." Minerva raised a shoulder. "And I missed her more than I wanted to hear any apology, since we usually speak *several* times a day, as you know, so I carried on the same way. The next thing I knew everything was back to normal. We never spoke of it."

"You had a huge fight that you never talked about." I tried to imagine it, and failed. In my experience, fights were inevitably followed by much longer State of the Relationship discussions which caused far more damage, and left much nastier scars. Which would fill me with trepidation under normal circumstances—but then, as I'd already worried, I wasn't sure this was a fight so much as a personal exodus on Amy Lee's part.

"After enough time passed, there wasn't much to talk about anyway," Minerva said. "Things worked out the way they should. Dorcas is my oldest friend. She's more important to me than anything I was angry about."

She tilted her head to the side then, and fixed me with a surprisingly perceptive gaze. I'd seen it once or twice before, and it always gave me pause. It suggested, among other things, that she knew I thought she was a madwoman. That she encouraged it.

I found I was holding my breath.

"And in any event," she said slowly, without looking away, "I think the important thing to remember is that all relationships benefit from a bit of breathing room. *Especially* friendships. It's only when you find yourself without the women who understand you that you realize there are very few women who will."

That night, I stood in my apartment in front of my answering machine with its big, red 0 and faced the fact that deep down, I'd expected Amy Lee to call. I didn't want to face it, but it was inescapable. No matter how many times I called my landline from my cell and vice versa, to make sure they were both in working order, there was nothing. Radio silence.

I hadn't expected her to apologize, necessarily, but I'd half-imagined some sort of *I was having a bad day, didn't mean to snap* conversation. That would make sense of the whole thing—because Amy Lee couldn't *really* tell Georgia and me to fuck off and *mean it*, could she? That had to be stress talking. Or maybe—who knew—she was having trouble with Oscar. Or with her dental practice. Once I thought about it, there could be a million reasons why she'd gone off like that. After all, Amy Lee was sort of famous for her temper. She had a short fuse, but the upside was she was usually over it just as quickly. I'd figured she'd spend Sunday ranting and Monday remorseful, and would call that night.

Georgia was a different story. I didn't know how she would react to the Henry thing, because there was no precedent for it. So while I hoped she would call, I could all too easily see why she wouldn't. I didn't like it, but I was the one who'd crossed the crush line. I would have to deal with the repercussions.

I stayed up much later than usual, pretending to be engrossed in a Sci-Fi Channel miniseries, while I deliberately didn't pay attention to my phones—landline and cell laid out on the coffee table, side by side with military precision. But no matter how much I pretended I wasn't listening for them, that I was fully engrossed in the *Battlestar Galactica* movie I'd seen at least seventy times before, they failed to ring.

On Thursday, I started to get angry. I sat at my desk and pretended to concentrate on work-related things, but really I was spiraling into a dark, breathless sort of rage.

Who had asked Amy Lee to step in and appoint herself the moral authority? The *grown-up*? Were we all supposed to forget the eight thousand ridiculous things she'd done in her lifetime, most of which I'd witnessed *without* the same response? Who was she to sit in judgment of other people?

Once I opened that floodgate, the rage poured on out.

It cast a wide net.

Whatever with Georgia and her *"I can't."* You'd think being sliced into pieces by our mutual friend might have produced a little bit of solidarity. *I* had raced directly to Georgia's side during the latest Stupid Boy crisis, at six in the freaking morning. *I* had been prepared to stay there for however long it took. Just because Amy Lee was suddenly too good for friends in need, it didn't mean I was. Just because Amy Lee would prefer to stay out in Somerville with her *house*, *practice*, and *husband*, that didn't mean I wasn't available should Georgia need me. Why was I being punished for Amy Lee's behavior?

Unless, of course, Georgia was mad about the Henry thing, and if she was? Then maybe I was the one who *couldn't*. I could see being upset. I'd lied, after all. I could stand to do some groveling for that. And in truth, I should have been up front about things as they happened instead of waiting to be caught. But it wasn't as if Georgia had had us camping out at Henry's door any time *recently*. As far as I knew, she'd been over her Henry crush going on five years now. Was she really going to end our friendship over a never-requited, never-consummated college-era crush?

I thought about Henry, too. Finally. And, at first, reluctantly.

I was humiliated for exactly twelve seconds and then I thought that *actually*, he could go to hell and take his *"I don't think so"* with him. What an ass. The man stood in a hallway and basically presented me with a point-by-point analysis of the reasons why it was okay for him to be into me and then, when I could have actually used him, he bailed on me. If that wasn't representative of my entire love life, I didn't know what was. I couldn't even call it a *love life*—it was just one pathetic relationship—or epic, fruitless crush, if I were to recall the embarrassments of my earlier twenties accurately—after another. I *aspired* to tragedy and heartbreak—my own relationships ended in whimpers and indifference.

Except for the only one I'd actually had recently, I reminded myself. I kept picturing that apologetic smile Nate had aimed my way at the caroling party. What did that mean? Was he apologizing *to* me or *for* Helen? Why had he called me *so many times* that night and then never again? Did he have any idea that it required nightly acts of near-Herculean will to keep from calling him again?

I didn't know what to make of Henry, or what he thought was the pattern between us. I didn't want to know. I was lost when it came to Amy Lee. In the woods over Georgia. The solution with Nate was simple: remind him how much he liked me and dislodge Helen's claws from him. Mess cleaned up, just like that. Jilted girlfriends were only considered psychotic losers when the boyfriend had *really* moved on, after all. And *really moved on* did not include seven voice mail messages in one night.

The rest of them could all go straight to hell, I thought self-righteously. They were far too messy to deal with, and I didn't know where to start. And in any case, I was *more than fine* without them.

chapter sixteen

The hyperactive holiday season in Boston, I discovered quickly, was not the greatest time of the year to be friendless.

My outrage faded to a slow burn as the days passed. After work every evening I'd wander around the city in much the same way I had years before, when I was eighteen and intoxicated by my sudden freedom. I'd fallen in love with Boston back then, and with Amy Lee and Georgia, all at the same time. The city was a monument to our friendship—there was hardly a corner in it we hadn't imprinted with one memory or another. Nights we'd hung out in the Bukowski Tavern, for example, toasting dead authors with over a hundred different beers. Running wild on Lansdowne Street in our clubbing phase. Celebrating Patriots' Day, or getting all kitted out in our Red Sox gear to root for the home team.

Helen was mixed up in there too, much as I'd prefer to deny it. The nights we spent trolling for cute boys when we were supposed to be studying. Shopping with Helen on

Newbury Street and marveling at her seemingly limitless credit card.

First Boston had been our playground, then it was our campus, and soon after that it was our home. I couldn't begin to imagine what it would be like on my own.

Okay, that was a little overdramatic. I had other friends. It was just that they were weekend and occasional friends. If I wanted to spend more time with the other members of my larger social group, I was going to have to expend a whole lot more effort. I was going to have to make a lot of phone calls, start accepting each and every invitation I received—do the things you were forced to do when you wanted to expand your circle. I hadn't had to do it in a very long time. The very *idea* of doing it filled me with a pervasive sense of *ick*. And, of course, even if I threw myself into it wholeheartedly, it would take ages to build up to the sort of friendships I had just (apparently) lost. You couldn't transform a coffee-once-a-month friend into a call-me-every-day-maybe-three-times-a-day friend just like that. It took time. Caution. Patience. And in my circumstances, it would also require explanations about why, exactly, Amy Lee and Georgia were out of my life. I couldn't face it.

And that was why, when I got home and allowed my nose to defrost, I called Nate.

I didn't want to spend even one more moment sitting around, wondering what he was doing and why he wasn't calling. None of those things seemed to matter any more. If he loved Helen, he wouldn't keep having those *moments* with me, when he looked at me in ways she would hate. When he reminded me that he could count on me. If he loved her, he wouldn't have called me seven times or turned up at my apartment that night.

There were all sorts of ways that someone could get trapped in a relationship that seemed like a good idea from the outside, but not so much from inside. Helen knew how to play games, so who knew what she'd used to entice him? And now he was stuck with her. He'd thrown me over so publicly and flagrantly—it had to be a matter of pride that his relationship with Helen last, right? It made sense. He was the one part of my incredibly messy life that could be cleared up with a simple, long overdue conversation.

With all of that in mind, it also made sense to call him.

I got his voice mail, which didn't surprise me—I didn't want him to pretend I was some random guy again. While I could see why he'd done it, it made me feel icky, the same way that old video for "Part-Time Lover" with Stevie Wonder did. It was all just gross. I was a fully grown woman, who was taking charge of her own destiny. Voice mail was much better. Voice mail, I could handle.

"Hey," I said. "It's me. I really want to talk to you about what's going on. We never talked about that night, and I think we should. I wish I hadn't missed all your calls. I feel like there's stuff we need to work out, don't you? Call me."

I was proud of myself when I hung up. Short and sweet. To the point. No hemming or hawing.

Go to hell, Amy Lee, I thought with extreme smugness. *I can too be a grown-up.*

A feeling that was confirmed, about an hour and a half

later, when my cell phone rang. Nate's name scrolled across my screen.

"I'm glad you called," I said, picking it up.

"I bet you are," Helen snapped at me.

I felt my stomach drop to the soles of my feet.

"Why are you calling me from Nate's phone?" I managed to ask.

"Why are you calling my boyfriend?" she countered.

"You have to be kidding me."

"You better leave Nate alone," Helen hissed. "Don't think I'm not wise to your little games, Gus. But you better remember that I'm not like you. I won't sit back and watch it happen, do you understand me?"

"Are you *threatening* me?" I was flabbergasted.

"I'll do whatever I have to do to babysit what's mine," Helen threw at me. "And if you think I'm going to—"

I heard Nate in the background then.

"What are you doing?" he demanded. "Is that my phone?"

"You want to tell me why you've been calling Gus?" Helen screamed at him. "She's on the phone right now! You can tell us both!"

I just sat there, listening with the part of me that wasn't frozen into place.

There was what sounded like a scuffle. Then Nate's voice on the phone.

"I'll call you later," he told me, as Helen shouted something (happily) incomprehensible in the background. Then he hung up.

And for the first time since she'd walked away from me

in that hallway out in the country, I entertained the possibility that Amy Lee might have a point.

My life was completely out of control. My best friends had stopped talking to me. I was, apparently, embroiled in a love triangle, except the only *embroiling* I'd been involved in recently had been with someone else entirely. Henry thought I was a nutcase, with good reason if I was honest with myself, and my mind kind of skittered away when it landed on *that* land mine. I suspected I had just made things a lot worse with Nate.

All of this, and I was turning thirty in less than a month.

I looked around at my apartment. At the dorm decor and the books all over the place as if a library had exploded nearby and I'd stockpiled the remains. The mismatched furniture I'd rescued from curbs and dumpsters across the city. I dreamed of showplace houses—hardwood floors and eat-in kitchens, but I figured that would happen . . . someday.

Nothing in my life indicated I was ready to put aside my childish things. I loved working at the Museum, but a steady, good job didn't exempt me from all the other ridiculousness in my life. I thought it was perfectly reasonable to talk shit about Henry. I was always willing to leap from zero to total dramatic outrage at the slightest provocation, because I always had before and it had, until recently, been fun. I spent entirely too many hours thinking of ways to push my friends' buttons, just for my own amusement. I behaved like a teenager on a WB show after sleeping with someone. I wanted my ex to *pay* for dumping me even as

I wanted him back, and I played absurd mind games with the woman he'd left me for. The one I was furious with for betraying our weird, twisted friendship though I had no qualms plotting to do the same if I could.

For all intents and purposes, I might as well be the same excitable twit I'd been when I was twenty-two.

Why was I such a *baby*?

I sat on the couch mulling these things over until light began to creep in the windows. I dozed then—but it was more of an exhausted coma than any restful, peaceful slumber.

I woke a few hours later, immediately cranky and with Linus panting directly into my face from about an inch away. I shoved his head away from me, and ignored the little dance he did when he realized I was awake.

"No," I told him. "Go lie down."

He ignored me, taking up one of his toys in his mouth and shaking it ferociously in my direction. Even my dog rejected my authority. Even he suspected I was failing miserably in the *grown-up* department.

I swung up to a seated position and scowled around the living room.

I was, I realized, going to have to do something about the way I lived. It was like that Rilke poem I'd taped to my walls in college: "*for here there is no place/that does not see you. You must change your life.*"

The phone rang again then, and I groaned as I fumbled around to look at the caller ID. But it wasn't Helen, ready for round two. It wasn't even Nate, the way I sort of expected it to be.

It was Georgia.

"Oh," I said into the receiver without bothering to say hello, "are we talking on the phone? Because I got the distinct impression you were giving me the silent treatment."

"I'm sorry," Georgia said in the same tone of voice. "Let me check my voice mail for all the calls you made to me— oh wait. You didn't make any."

"Which one of us threw up her hand—*very* daytime talk show, by the way—and said 'I can't'?" I demanded.

"I meant I couldn't talk about it *then*," Georgia said with a sigh.

"I'm telepathic this week," I told her. "But not last week, so I must have missed that. Sorry."

Georgia sighed again, more pointedly.

"Do you want to get some breakfast or not?" she demanded. "It's fine if you don't. We can just hang out on the telephone and be snotty to each other. We can talk about Henry. Totally your call."

I sighed even louder than she had.

"Fine," I said. "Give me forty-five minutes."

We met in a place near Georgia's condo. I found her sitting at a corner table of the small café, her hands cupped around a huge mug of coffee. She had her usually big and vibrant hair scraped back into a severe ponytail, and seemed to be practically vibrating with tension. I thought that boded ill.

"I can't even talk about how cold it is," I announced by way of greeting. I was also hoping to distract her. I began unwrapping myself from my layers and layers of winter wear. I draped my scarf, extra sweater, mittens, and hat on the back of my chair and sat. "I don't understand why I live here, when I happen to know there are places with no snow, ice, freezing rain, or nights that start at like 2 p.m."

"Because none of those places are Boston," Georgia said with a shrug.

I nodded at the simple truth of that, and ordered myself a bottomless latte from a passing waiter. Neither one of us spoke until it appeared before me. I didn't look at Georgia as I stirred in five packets of Splenda. When I did, she was shaking her head at me.

"What?" I asked.

"How can you put anything that sweet into your mouth?" she demanded. "Ugh. I think it would trigger my gag reflex." She put a hand to her throat. "I think it already has."

"I don't understand the whole *I can only drink black coffee* thing," I countered, eyeing her mug. "I bet those are the same people who will only read tedious, obscure novels because they think it makes them more intelligent. When really, they just read a boring book. Same with coffee. Why choke it down black and bitter when it can taste like dessert instead?"

"Maybe I just like the taste of it without a pound of sugar and six gallons of cream, because it's *coffee*, not *coffee ice cream*." She raised her lawyerly eyebrow at me.

"Maybe you do," I said, raising my own librarian eyebrows right back at her. "But that's just your *taste*. It doesn't make you a *better person*. I can't stand people who assign moral judgments to personal preferences."

Georgia considered me for a moment. "I think that's your way of talking about Henry," she said. "And we'll talk about that, believe me. And I guess we're going to have to talk about Amy Lee, too."

"I haven't heard from her," I said, watching her face. I was terrified I'd see pity or something there, which would indicate they'd talked to each other and were leaving me out. The way they had once, years ago, in a different fight I would have said I'd forgotten about. But she just pursed her lips slightly, and shook her head.

"Neither have I," she said. "That's a little extreme, even for her, but there's something I want to talk to you about first and if I don't do it right now I'm not going to do it at all."

"Oh God," I moaned, setting my mug down with a thud. "Are you breaking up with me too? Because I was much better with the silent treatment. I was perfectly content to convince myself that you were really busy, or held up in court, or buried in some document production somewhere without cell phone service—"

"I hooked up with Chris Starling," Georgia blurted out, cutting me off.

That hung there for a moment.

We stared at each other, and it was hard for me to imagine that I could look any more shocked than Georgia did.

"But I thought . . ." I shrugged helplessly.

"I know!" she groaned. "I don't know what happened to me! I was still upset about Jared, and I was so angry about the Amy Lee thing and your secret Henry thing, and we were in Scranton, Pennsylvania, and he smiled at me in that way he does and I thought *Gandalf eyes* and boom!"

"Boom?" I echoed.

"The next thing I knew we were half naked in his hotel room." Georgia let out a shaky breath. "I've become a cliché. I hooked up with the boss. If I'd done it at the office party, I could be the laughingstock of the office as well. Not like it matters. I can pretty much kiss my dreams of a partnership good-bye."

"Wait," I said, reeling. "How did you get from half naked to your partnership? What are you talking about? You have to tell me *what happened*!"

So she took a fortifying sip of her (dark and bitter) coffee, straightened in her seat, and told me.

Georgia had been out of her mind when she left for Scranton that Monday morning. She was emotionally unprepared to deal with a week in some city she wasn't sure she could find on a map. She was furious with Amy Lee, hurt that I had kept secrets from her, and all of that piled on top of the humiliating breakup with Jared.

"If you can even call it that," Georgia sniffed, "which I'm not sure you can, because that presupposes a 'relationship' and I'm not sure that mess qualified."

Neither did I, but it wasn't my place to say anything.

"Don't give me that look," Georgia said. "I'm the one who has to actually feel the way I do when I get crazy over inappropriate men. I knew Jared was another in a long line of complete assholes. Believe me, I knew."

"Back to Chris Starling?" I suggested. Diplomatically.

They had been taking depositions in Scranton, which, Georgia admitted, showed Chris Starling to his best advantage. He always unsettled the people he was deposing. It was the way he looked at people. As if he already knew their secrets and was personally disappointed in them when they failed to divulge those secrets when he asked.

Opposing counsel this time around was some hotshot type, all sleek with flashing white teeth Georgia just knew he'd like to sink into her jugular. Literally and figuratively.

"So basically he was the Jared type," I said.

"His clone, in fact," Georgia agreed. "Obviously, I was smitten."

"And now I'm confused. I thought this was a Chris Starling story."

"Just listen."

Georgia had locked eyes with Mr. Jugular, and they'd arranged to meet for illicit cocktails, all in secret, of course, since they were opposing counsel and had to maintain the appearance of propriety. Which, it turned out, suited Mr. Jugular just fine because while he'd certainly be up for whatever Georgia might have in mind—particularly in the bedroom, he made clear with his hand on her thigh—he needed to keep things extra quiet because he was, after all, engaged.

"Yuck," I said.

"Tell me about it," Georgia said.

Because he hadn't even *confessed* it—he'd just announced it. He evidently thought it would either be a turn-on for Georgia, or incidental information to file away in case Georgia got any *ideas*. At no point did it occur to Mr. Jugular that, upon hearing the news, Georgia might *not* sleep with him.

Which had really been the slap in the face.

"At what point did I become so obvious and easy that guys stopped trying to deceive me into bed with them?" she asked me. "At what point did I start wearing *that* sign around my neck?"

She had sat there for a long moment with Mr. Jugular's hand on her thigh. She was in a cheesy hotel bar in Scranton, Pennsylvania. It was a Monday night. And though the setting wasn't necessarily auspicious, Georgia felt her life shift right there and then.

"I can't even begin to stress how very much I'd like to tell you that it was like something out of a movie," she said now, "with a stirring song playing in the background and that light of battle in my eyes, but it was actually really quiet. There was Muzak. And this fucking guy. This *engaged* guy. And I realized that this was what my life was, who I was. This pathetic woman in a hotel bar, about to willingly sleep with some sleazy guy who couldn't even be bothered to conceal the fact that he had a fiancée." She shook her head. "That's how little he cared about me. And I could see with perfect clarity that it started right there and then. I could take this guy up to my room and we could have sex, it might even be good sex, and I could keep having sex with guys like him, and soon enough they'd be married guys. Guys with wives and kids. Guys with houses and whole other lives. Guys who wouldn't even bother to pretend at having a relationship with me. That would be who I was, and it all started right there in that bar with that guy."

She sat there for a moment, and I tried to read her expression, but she looked about as remote as I'd ever seen her.

"What did you do?" I whispered.

She looked up and met my gaze.

"It kills me that you have to ask," she said.

"I didn't mean—"

"Of course you didn't. Because how would you know?" She took a deep breath. "I got up and left. I wasn't even mean about it. I just said I had an earlier morning than I'd originally thought. And then I went up to my hotel room and sat on the ugly orange bedspread and cried. For about twelve hours."

"Oh, Georgia."

"It was fine," she said. "I'm fine. And it was kind of interesting to just . . . feel what I was feeling. I didn't have you or Amy Lee to call. There was nothing particularly dramatic about it. It was just me, and the person I was *this close* to becoming."

"Wow," I said.

One unfortunate side effect of choosing to reinvent herself while taking depositions in Scranton, Pennsylvania, was that Georgia had to face the catalyst for her reinvention across the table in the morning. In the way of men like Mr. Jugular since the dawn of time, he took sexual rejection badly. He used Georgia for target practice enough that at lunch, Chris Starling actually sat her down for a talk.

"He was in rare form," Georgia said. "Even for him. He took me to Burger King and while I was trying to enjoy my hamburger he looked up and said, 'This morning is, of course, why you can't sleep with opposing counsel.'" She imitated Chris Starling's dry tone perfectly.

I just shook my head, wordless.

Georgia snapped back at him. She had not slept with opposing counsel, she threw at him, and how dare he—

Good, Chris Starling said.

"He said it just like that?" I asked, enthralled. Georgia had made him sound so—fervent.

"Exactly like that," Georgia said, smiling slightly.

And it had altered everything. They'd finished lunch and returned to the depositions. Chris Starling had slapped Mr. Jugular down a few times. Georgia had played her part. It was all normal, except . . . it wasn't.

"All of a sudden," Georgia told me, "I was *aware*. I knew every time he took a breath. I could *feel* when he looked at me. It was crazy. I felt like I was wearing a corset, like I couldn't get enough air in my lungs, whenever he walked into a room."

"Wow," I breathed.

The days passed, until finally they were finished with the depositions. It was Thursday night, and they were due to fly out in the morning. Georgia once again found herself in the hotel bar, only this time, everything felt epic and terrifying instead of depressing and tired. They chatted about inane things, things Georgia couldn't even remember. Chris Starling pointed out that it was late, and that they had an early flight. He paid the check, and then they walked to the elevator. It took a long time to come, and they'd seemingly run out of things to say. Georgia felt as if she might burst—into tears, into laughter, into pieces, she wasn't sure. The elevator finally arrived, they got in, and the door closed, leaving them all alone inside. They stared at each other. Georgia made some crack, something about having nothing to say, because she couldn't bear the silence for another second.

Which was when Chris Starling pulled out his big gun— that smile.

Georgia felt something melt inside of her, and it was like he'd been waiting for it. Without saying a word, he reached across the distance between them, pulled Georgia to him, and kissed her.

"Just like that?" I was whispering. I practically had to fan my face.

"Exactly like that," Georgia whispered back.

And it turned out that Chris Starling could kiss. So well that the next thing she knew they were in his room, rolling around on his bed, and half naked. Georgia had come to in a moment of clarity.

"What does that mean?" I asked.

"It means I sat up with as much dignity as you can when you have to refasten your bra and find your shirt," Georgia said dryly. "And then I told him that I was tired of being treated like Sally, the Sheraton Whore."

"Oh, no." I put my face in my hands, and then peeked at her. " 'Sally, the Sheraton Whore?' "

"Oh, yes."

"Well . . . what happened? What did he do?"

"He sat there in understandable shock as I gathered up my tattered dignity and stormed away," Georgia said. "I can't blame him, really."

"He didn't chase after you?" I frowned. "Maybe I don't like him very much after all."

"He didn't chase after me," Georgia said. "The next morning, on the oh-so-awkward taxi ride to the airport, he said exactly one thing to me. Guess what that was?"

"I can't possibly."

"He said, and I quote, 'If you're Sally the Sheraton Whore, what does that make me?'"

I thought about that for a moment.

"Huh," I said. "Ouch."

She let out a sigh, and took a deep pull of her coffee.

"Well?" I demanded. "What happened next?"

"We flew to New York, got stuck for hours in JFK while they deiced the runways or something equally irritating since it's *December* in the *Northeast* and you'd think they'd be *prepared*, and got home late last night. I believe Chris and I exchanged three entire sentences. When I got home I cried some more, pretended to sleep, and then called you." Georgia gave me a thin smile. "It's been quite a week, and just so we're clear, I wasn't giving you the silent treatment. Not deliberately."

"Okay," I said. "That's a lot. And your partnership dreams are involved how?"

"Hello. My boss has seen my breasts." Georgia made a face. "And while they're obviously smoking hot, I also in-

sulted the man and ran away. I just shot my career trajec-
tory in the foot."

"Oh." I thought about it. "Not necessarily."

"But most likely," Georgia said. She shook it off, and
smiled at me. "But it's your turn. Tell me the Henry story,
you lying bitch, and it better be good."

chapter seventeen

"Well," Georgia said when I finished telling her the tangled history of Henry and me, up to and including his rejection of me after the caroling party.

And then she fell silent, her attention on the French toast she'd ordered.

"Well?" I echoed after a moment, not at all interested in my omelet. "That's all I get?"

"I'm trying to decide whether or not I should forgive you," Georgia said, eyeing me. "Not for keeping it a secret, or even for the whole Henry-is-evil thing, because whatever. Shit happens. But because you have had *intimate* and *personal* contact with that man's hot body, and you kept it from me when you know *perfectly well* there was a time when even *proximity* to Henry Farland was enough to keep me going for weeks."

"I didn't know how to tell you," I said, suddenly fascinated with the cheese-and-tomato omelet. "There was this whole angry denial thing going on, and I thought you'd hate me. If that helps."

"It really doesn't." She shook her head. "I loved him so much it actually hurt me, like it was some separate, tumor-ish thing."

"I know you did," I said quietly. "I remember."

It was horrifying, because really, how did this make me any different from Helen? The point of the divide between women like Helen and women like me was that women like me weren't supposed to do the kinds of things women like Helen did without blinking. Crushes—particularly long-term epic crushes like the one Georgia had had on Henry—were sacrosanct. I might as well have slept with her college boyfriend, given the amount of emotional energy she'd put into Henry once upon a time. It didn't matter that it had been completely unrequited. Betraying that required the same level of self-absorption on my part.

"Henry Farland was the *archetype* for all the Jareds," Georgia said dryly. "Beautiful, lethal, completely amoral . . . I haven't forgotten, even if you did."

"You must hate me," I said in a small voice.

"The part of me that will always be nineteen years old and struck dumb by her first sight of Henry when he sauntered into that party, all tan and beautiful?" Georgia shook her head. "*She* hates you. She might even have cried a little bit. The good news is that she's been crying over Henry for about a decade now, and she hates *him*, too."

"I would hate me." It was true. I was all about bringing the hate. "I'm really sorry, Georgia."

"I should hate you," she agreed, "but I'm running out of best friends this month." She settled back into her chair. "You're off the hook. Henry ruined his own myth for me years ago."

"When did he do that?" I asked. It could have been the barely-legal stripper he'd dated that one time. The infamous rumor campaign he'd instituted against poor Felicia, the girlfriend who'd had the temerity to leave him when he was twenty-three. Or his ability to be snide under any circumstances, particularly when it hurt. I hadn't realized that something had happened to make Georgia get over him. I thought time had simply passed.

"The whole time he was in law school I was able to keep the crush intact," Georgia said, with a faraway look in her eyes. "You know, because I figured he would go into corporate law, make a ton of money to match the ton of money he already had, and I would yearn forevermore."

"He's a lawyer just like you," I said brightly. "Yearn away."

"He's a lawyer, but he's not like me," Georgia said, almost sadly. "He spends the bulk of his time trying to shut down my clients. He works for a pittance and usually out of the kindness of his heart, like he's the personal version of the ACLU. I can't stand him."

It was funny when perception changed. It was almost as if I could feel my vision shatter, and then alter so much it was as if the way I'd seen before had never been. It had happened to me once before, quite violently, in Henry's kitchen that night, and I had the inkling it was happening again in that café with Georgia.

I had to blink a few times. No wonder he'd said I didn't know him at all. There was a caricature called Henry that I carried around in my head, but he had no relation whatsoever to the real one. The real one was a complete stranger to me—although I was pretty sure I'd glimpsed him for the first time in that hallway the day of the sleigh ride.

"You look shell-shocked," Georgia said, with a grin. "Don't worry, Gus. I really do forgive you. Hell, with that body? I'm jealous. I wouldn't touch his wussy do-gooder ass with a ten-foot pole, mind you, but I'd encourage you even if he *was* the devil."

"Speaking of which, I don't get why you went along with the whole 'he's Satan' thing," I said, frowning at her. "When you knew he was practically the Mother Teresa of the legal community."

"First of all," Georgia said, "I am always available to mock, vilify, and tease. Why? Because it's fun. Whatever certain dentists of my acquaintance might think." She sniffed. "And anyway, I adored Henry from afar for years, which he knew and did nothing about. What am I, radioactive? He had it coming."

She forked in a mouthful of her French toast and eyed me as she chewed.

"What?"

"You and Henry," she said. "Are you . . . ?"

"I can't even think about Henry," I said. "I wouldn't know where to begin, anyway. Stuff just keeps happening, and he's off-limits—"

"If you mean because of me, he's really not. You can have him."

That didn't make me feel any better. I blinked. "And anyway, there's the Nate thing," I said instead of thinking about Henry any further.

"Jesus Christ. Not again. Not *still*."

"It's not what you think," I assured her.

"Oh, good. Because I think you're chasing around after a guy who treated you like shit." She pursed her lips. "A subject I happen to know something about."

"Well, okay, yes," I admitted. "It might resemble that kind of thing. But the truth is—"

"The ugly truth about Nate is that he cheated on you and only left you when you caught him *in the act*," Georgia said. "Has it ever occurred to you to wonder what his plan was? I mean, what if you hadn't caught him? Was he just going to keep seeing both of you?"

I gaped at her for a moment. Then shook it off. "You don't have all the information," I hastened to tell her. "It's not that cut-and-dried."

So I told her everything. About what he'd said to me on Janis Joplin night. Those strange, yearning moments at the Park Plaza. The Night of Seven Voice Mails. About when he pretended I was a guy so Helen wouldn't suspect anything. About last night's ridiculousness.

"Wait a minute," Georgia said. "Is this seventh grade? She called you from *his* phone?"

"I keep trying to tell you people that she's the crazy one here," I pointed out. "Not me."

"I don't know if she's crazy," Georgia said with a sniff. "I've hated that bitch since the nineties. Since I laid eyes on her in our hallway freshman year and saw exactly what kind of girl she was. But it's obviously crossed her mind that if she could steal Nate from you, he's the kind of man who can be stolen."

"I think maybe he's just trapped," I told her. "You know what Helen's like. You know how convincing she seems to be to men, for whatever reason."

Georgia sighed. "I think you want him to be trapped, because that way, there's an excuse for how he's stringing you along." She held up her hand when I started to argue. "Believe me, Gus, I know about this kind of thing. I'm the *poster girl* for this kind of thing. You spend fifty percent of your time making excuses for some guy's shitty behavior and the other fifty percent of your time fantasizing about how great things could be *if only*."

"Nate isn't Jared!" The moment I said it, I wished I hadn't. Georgia's eyebrows rose, and I felt myself flush. "I just mean, the situations are different," I said quickly. "I knew Nate for years before we started dating. We were together for almost four months. Okay? I'm not trying to be all Amy Lee about it."

"It's okay." Her voice was brisk.

"I didn't mean—"

"It's seriously fine," Georgia said. "Jared was a loser and I was overdramatic. End of story."

When it came to Amy Lee herself, however, Georgia was less forgiving.

"Sure she had some points," she said, stabbing at her plate with her fork. "She was probably right, in fact."

I let out a breath.

"I thought so too," I confessed.

"But that's how she expresses herself to her two best friends in the world?" Georgia continued. "That's how she takes us aside and lets us know that she has some concerns? By talking down to both of us, in front of someone else, at a party?" She shook her head. "She's always thought she was better than us. This is the same thing as that time she was all up on her high horse about how everything was so much different for her when she met Oscar because she had a *good-looking* boyfriend. Please. As if the men we liked were trolls?"

"Okay, sure," I said, remembering what was definitely not Amy Lee's finest hour. "That was so long ago, though. She seemed a little too serious this time."

"Of course she was serious," Georgia said, and then sighed, and I saw sadness flood her face. "The fact is, Amy Lee had the good fortune to trip over her husband at the age of twenty-three." She made a face. "She gets the *option* to have adult choices."

"This is a little unsettling." I stared at her. "I prepared myself the whole way over here for you to tell me that I'm the asshole in this scenario."

"I have a very serious bone to pick with Amy Lee," Georgia replied. "And believe me, I plan to pick it. But I don't think you did anything wrong. Sneaky and behind my back, yes, but I can sort of see why you'd feel you had to. I had the killer crush for so long, of course you were afraid I'd go ballistic."

"I miss her," I confessed. "I'm not used to her *hating* me, Georgia. I'm used to talking to her three times a day."

"She doesn't hate us," Georgia said.

"She told us to fuck off."

"She doesn't hate us," she repeated, but it sounded more wistful this time. She shook her head, and then met my eyes as if together, if we concentrated, we could make it true. "She's confused, obviously, but she doesn't *hate* us, Gus. How could she?"

That question haunted me later that night, when I was once again in prone position on my couch, glowering at the ceiling.

Amy Lee had always been different from Georgia and me. We'd gone to BU for any number of reasons, most of them ridiculous (I had fantasies of my life in Boston, Georgia thought the TA she'd met on her tour was hot) whereas Amy Lee had *plans*. She'd enrolled at BU as part of the Goldman School of Dental Medicine's seven-year plan. Three years of regular arts and sciences classes, then four years of dental school. While we floated from this to that, and Georgia even changed her major twice, Amy Lee remained focused.

She'd always found us a little bit exasperating, now that I thought about it. For a long time I thought Georgia and I provided Amy Lee with a bit of much-needed chaos and levity in her otherwise extremely goal-oriented world. There had been a time she'd loved us for that. I didn't want to admit that time might have ended. No matter how much I wanted to make her apologize for that scene in front of Henry, I wanted her friendship more.

I just didn't know what to do about it.

Because it was one thing to not call her, to share in the silent treatment, not-talking thing. It was something else entirely to risk calling her only to find myself screened to voice mail, or fobbed off on Beatrice, the receptionist. In this day and age, as Helen had already demonstrated to me, the only way to force someone into a confrontation they might not want was to show up in a place they couldn't possibly avoid you (unless they were willing to climb up their own fire escape). There was too much technology to hide behind, otherwise. Until I picked up the phone, I was *not talking* to Amy Lee as much as she was not talking to me. Once I made a call, she might decide to blow it off, and then she was *actively* ignoring me and there was no getting around that.

I thought that someday soon I might be in a different place emotionally, where I could handle that possibility, but I wasn't there yet.

Not yet.

Tonight I just missed her.

It actually came in handy that it was the Christmas season, I thought a few days later. I could mope through my job, or my nightly rounds of the stores in my vain hopes for in-spired gifts, but at least the fact that I *had* to come up with

gifts meant that I was moping while out and about in public. I made the usual last-minute selections for my parents,
and agonized over what to get my sister and her husband.
Only the kids were easy—and anyway, it was fun to shop
in toy stores around Christmastime. The looks of abject
horror on the faces of all the parents were sort of funny if
you knew you weren't responsible for Santa's choices come
dawn on Christmas morning. And besides, I could only
descend so far into self-pity while surrounded by screaming infants, with Salvation Army bells ringing insistently
in my ears.

It was this logic that got me to the last holiday party on
the last Thursday before Christmas.

First, though, I'd tried to rustle up reinforcements.

"I'm happy to report that I am completely unavailable,"
Georgia told me that morning, in a very alarming and
perky sort of voice. "As I am currently sitting in the lovely
Seattle-Tacoma Airport, enjoying the local ambience. But
you have fun."

"Is he right there?" I asked in an excited whisper.

"I'll have to get back to you with those figures," she sing-
songed. "I'll call you when we land in Boston, whenever
that might be—there's apparently some storm."

"It's almost Christmas," I said. "Of course there's a
storm."

"We'll talk soon," she promised, and hung up.

I spent the rest of my day neatening up my work area in
preparation for Christmas vacation. It was one of the major
perks of working for Minerva. She and Dorcas removed

themselves from wintry Boston every Christmas. One year it was the Bahamas, another year it was St. Barts. This year they were hitting Cancún. They were usually gone until after New Year's. All I had to do was deliver them (and Minerva's numerous trunks—yes, *trunks*) to the airport the following afternoon and I was free.

First, however, there was the evening to get through, and the last of the holiday parties. I debated not going. After all, if Georgia wasn't going to be there, what would be the point? I didn't know if Amy Lee would show up—and I couldn't decide which would be worse. If she didn't, I would be left friendless, which could prove challenging indeed should Nate or Helen turn up. If she did show up, well, that could turn out to be a very different sort of challenge.

And I wasn't kidding anyone, least of all myself—I wanted to go. I wanted to see what had happened between Nate and Helen. I wanted to see Nate. I wanted to look him in the eyes and figure everything out once and for all. I didn't want to do it without backup, of course, but it seemed that I was out of luck. I didn't have backup—but I had a boatload of cosmetics.

I dressed in my best holiday finery—my favorite high-octane jeans and the sparkly top I saved for such occasions—and spent a long time making my eyes look deep and inviting. I tried not to think about the fact that it was Helen who'd taught me how to do those things—until it occurred to me that should I succeed at getting Nate back, it would all be very ironic. And then, when I was done, and had put on my absolutely insane stiletto boots—boots that practically begged the icy Boston sidewalks to knock me on my foolish ass, the ones I'd saved up to buy and loved more than the rest of my wardrobe put together—I sank down on my couch and let myself mope for a few minutes.

Strangely, it was thinking of Helen that got me back up on my feet.

The fact was, women like Helen achieved *that girl* status because they got away with things other women didn't. And the reason they got away with things was because they dared to do what they wanted to do. I, for example, would never pick up a boyfriend's messages or harangue another woman in his life. Not because I was above such things, but because deep inside I would be worried that the boyfriend in question preferred the other woman. Helen would never allow such a worry to penetrate her consciousness. Helen would always saunter through life as if everyone and everything she brushed against adored her. I had watched her do exactly that for years.

I sat a little bit straighter on the couch.

There was a divide between Helen's sort of woman and mine. As an example, my kind of woman didn't like to venture out alone. I preferred to march through life with my friends, in a pack, because we made our fun wherever we went (until recently), and because it was infinitely more comfortable that way. Helen, meanwhile, didn't know the first thing about packs of friends. She went wherever she wanted, spurred on by her own bravado (also known as a healthy dose of arrogance, in my not even remotely humble opinion) and her knowledge that her legs really did look amazing in those shoes. I didn't care what people thought of me so long as my core group thought well of me and shared my experiences. Helen didn't care what anyone thought of her.

Helen wouldn't even have these thoughts, I knew. Helen would just fluff her hair and go.

Except, I reminded myself, Helen had sat right in this very apartment and tried to pretend that she wasn't worried about her boyfriend and another woman. That woman being me. Helen was obviously deeply concerned about what happened between Nate and me. She even seemed to care what I thought of her. Not enough to get in the way of what she wanted to do, of course, but she'd certainly tried to talk to me afterwards. In her own inimitable way, naturally, but she'd tried. I'd bet she really believed she'd been reaching out to me.

What all of this meant, I thought, was that Helen wasn't the fearless, confident goddess I'd admired ever since I was eighteen. She *chose* to present herself that way. She *chose* her saunter and her air of entitlement. Maybe she was faking it to make it just like everyone else. Maybe she was just as worried and insecure as I was—she just didn't let it get in the way of doing what she wanted to do.

And if Helen could do it, so, by God, could I. I was going to get up, go out there, march into that party, and have a good time. Even if killed me.

I surged to my feet and pulled my good winter coat from the closet. I inhaled the sweet tang of my perfume and the crisp scent of my shampoo that hung around me like a cloud. I felt my hips sway, accommodating the high, dangerous heels. I felt good.

I locked my apartment behind me and set off down the hall toward *the best party I would ever attend*, because I was going on *my terms* and *my*—

"What," came the back-curling, querulous voice from behind me, "is that *racket*?"

Irwin.

Talk about bringing my power walk to a screeching halt.

I pivoted around and glared at him. He stood in his doorway, scowling at me, his tatty bathrobe around him like a nasty blue cloak.

"I'm walking down the hall." I stated the obvious.

"Are those your *shoes*? Making that ungodly noise?"

Sure enough, out came the notebook and the pen, and he began scribbling.

I felt my chin jut out, which was never a good sign.

I opened my mouth to get good and petty, and then stopped.

This, right in front of me, was a golden opportunity to act like a grown-up for a change. Storming about, assigning nicknames, leaping through windows to get away from the guy—none of that was particularly mature behavior, and more to the point, it didn't work.

"I'm really sorry," I said. This was so surprising for Irwin that he stopped writing and looked up at me, his mouth a perfect, astonished "o."

"Excuse me?" he asked.

"I'm sorry my shoes are so noisy," I said calmly. Pleasantly. "But I'm not sure how I can go about walking down the hall without making *some* noise."

"Er, no," Irwin said in a completely different voice. The hand holding the notebook dropped down to his side as he watched me—a bit as if he expected me to turn into Sydney Bristow, haul off, and kick him back through his door.

"There's too much hardwood," I continued. "They should really put down some kind of carpeting, but I don't think the owner cares. And why should he? He lives out in Western Mass."

"Of course, you're right," Irwin said. He peered at the floor. "It gets so slippery with all the slush and snow, too."

"It takes them forever to get around to mopping," I commiserated with a sigh. "And I know my dog doesn't help."

Irwin tutted at me. "It's the owner who needs to be more on top of things."

I gave him a big, conspiratorial sort of smile.

I didn't think he would go for it, but he did—his lips curved up. I thought it looked a little rusty. I wouldn't have been at all surprised to discover it was the first he'd smiled in months. Maybe years.

"I think I might write the owner a letter tonight," Irwin said, puffing out his chest.

"I think you should," I told him, and it was more smiles all around.

And when I sauntered out into the frozen night in my noisy stilettos, I didn't just feel like a goddess.

I felt like a grown-up.

chapter eighteen

A grown-up feeling I got over pretty quickly once I arrived at the party, which was held in an apartment in Cambridge packed full of holiday merriment and a whole lot of people to match. I could do just about anything with my friends at my back—saunter around in a royal blueberry gown, for example. But I wasn't much for sauntering when I was alone.

It didn't matter that Harry Connick Jr. was crooning in the background, or that a group of people I knew from college were in all likelihood together in a pack somewhere— probably the kitchen. High school had felt that way too—I'd known that my whole junior high class must be *somewhere*, but I'd still felt exposed the moment I walked through the door.

Exposed as well as vulnerable, disliked, and ignored, all of which were my own thing and only in my own head, I knew. That didn't change the fact that I felt that way. I eased my way along the edges of the living room, helped myself to a drink, and tried to blend in with the decorations on the Christmas tree until the bad teenage feelings went away.

I had great plans to surgically excise the quaking, complaining teenager within someday. If I could just get rid of her and her thousands upon thousands of issues—*Do I look fat? Am I ugly? Will anyone ever love me? Will I always be alone? Is she fatter than me? How ugly am I? Are they making fun of me?*—I was convinced I would immediately become the sort of casual and laid back *adult* person who was forever smiling and was genuinely unconcerned with the size and/or shape of her body.

I wasn't holding my breath.

However, I was not dressed to hide my head in shame. I had a rule about stilettos, and it was this: I didn't wear them unless I planned to kick ass in them. Stilettos were for striding and sauntering, never skulking.

I straightened up from the wall and tossed my head back. I reminded myself that I had a mission. I made my way through the crowd, smiling at the faces I recognized—the faces I would have to think about cultivating further, if I was truly as friendless as I felt—and kept my eyes peeled. It took about six seconds of reconnaissance work to locate Nate and Helen in the kitchen. I settled myself near the bar set up in the living room and then I waited. About ten minutes later, Nate wandered out on a refill run, as I'd known he would.

His eyes met mine and he smiled.

"Gus!" he said, as if he was delighted to see me. I felt relief trickle across my skin, and smiled back.

"I'm glad you're here," I told him. "I really wanted to talk to you."

"Things got a little out of control," he replied. He shook his head. "You know how she can be." The look in his eyes invited me in, to join in the conspiratorial laugh at Helen's expense. I don't know why I didn't.

"That night," I said instead, getting right to the point. "All those messages. What did you want to talk about?"

"I still want to talk about it," he said, still smiling. "But I'm not sure this is the place, you know? I don't want to be interrupted. It's too bad you weren't around that night."

My stomach twisted in remorse. He had been *so close*. He had been *right outside* while I was playing out revenge fantasies with his roommate. I couldn't believe that was it for us. I had to believe there'd be a second chance. I had to—or all of it meant nothing. We were just something he could end whenever he felt like it.

"You can give me the CliffsNotes version," I suggested. "So I know what we're dealing with."

Nate opened his mouth to respond, but closed it again when Henry came up beside him, smirk at the ready.

"A librarian encouraging the use of CliffsNotes?" Henry mocked me. "I'm shocked to the core."

I had to take a moment to let the impact of seeing him ease a little bit. I was always so surprised by how blue his eyes were, and how easily he held himself. It was easy to get caught up in the way he looked at me, particularly when it occurred to me that he wasn't off-limits any longer. It made my knees feel a little wobbly. I had to shake it off, and focus.

"Another beer?" Nate asked Henry, for all the world as if Henry hadn't just interrupted an important conversation. I was still reeling from realizations I wasn't ready to investigate too closely, so I decided to concentrate on one thing at a time. First I had to figure out what had happened with Nate. It had consumed me for too long to give up now. Only when I did that could I think about what a Henry who wasn't off-limits might mean.

"Nate and I were sort of talking," I told him. I didn't like the look that came across his face then, nor the tightness around his mouth.

"A trip down memory lane?" he asked. I wasn't at all fooled by the light tone. "I can think of a few fantastic moments to add to that."

"Except no one asked you for your contribution," I snapped at him.

"I have a great memory," he snapped right back. "I bet I can remember every single time you—"

"Told you to shut up?" I finished for him. "Here's another one to add to the collection. Shut up, Henry!"

My voice had gone up at the end there, which I noticed only because I could hear it echoing in my ears. Henry and I glared at each other. He looked like he wanted to personally kill me.

"What's up with the two of you?" Nate asked, reminding me that he was there. I jerked my attention away from Henry to see Nate studying us, his dark eyes flicking from Henry's face to mine and then back again.

"Nothing," I said, trying desperately to sound blasé. "Henry's just being his usual obnoxious self."

"While Gus has taken it to a whole new level," Henry replied.

"And I'm about to take it somewhere else," Helen snapped from Nate's elbow, where it seemed to me she appeared in a flash of smoke, but that could have been the hysteria flooding my brain.

"Baby!" Nate said in the same tone of delight he'd used before. On me.

The *exact same* tone.

"Don't you 'baby' me!" Helen snapped. "What the hell are you doing?"

With her ire focused on Nate, I had a moment to breathe and take in the scene. The bizarre love triangle that was really more of a love rectangle. Henry looked furious—and it was all directed at me. Helen was ripping Nate a new one. I thought I should feel something about one or both of these things, but all I could think about was the fact that Nate had used *the exact same tone* with me.

Has it ever occurred to you to wonder what his plan was? Georgia had asked. *Was he just going to keep seeing both of you?*

The answer hit me then, like an unexpected wave of icy cold water across the bow. I actually took a step back.

Right in front of me, Nate was appeasing Helen. I recognized the tilt of his head, the encouraging smile, the twinkle in his dark eyes that told her she was the only one who *got* him. I recognized it because I'd seen them before. Directed at me instead of her. I recognized that easy, conspiratorial, *intimate* voice, too. I'd heard it on my voice mail.

This was what Nate did.

I was just a puppet on a string.

And the worst part was that everyone knew it—had always known it—except me. Henry was right there, watching it. Watching me.

It was why he'd let me in the house that night.

The truth of it made my stomach lurch again, this time dangerously. I had to get away. I looked around wildly, and—

"Oh, no, you don't!" I heard Helen snap, and then I felt her fingers on my arm.

"Let go of me," I said when I half-turned to glare at the offending hand. She must have leapt across Nate to grab me, but I couldn't bear to look in his direction just then. Much less in Henry's. Helen let go, but she stepped closer to me.

"We need to talk," she said, those anime eyes dark.

"I don't think so," I said, and broke for the front door.

I made it through the crowd, threw the door open, and was halfway down the stairs inside the apartment building before I realized I would need my coat. Because it was December and bitterly cold. I turned back—and practically tripped over Helen.

"What the hell are you doing?" I yelped. "Are you *following* me?"

She looked at me for a long moment, breathing hard from what I assumed was the mad dash she'd made across the apartment in my wake, and then it was as if something swept over her body. She seemed to shiver a little bit, and it took me a moment to understand that she was furious.

She made that fact even more clear by tilting back her head and letting out a frustrated scream.

I practically leapt out of my skin.

Seriously—she screamed. And this was no fishwife screech, either. It was a full-on banshee howl.

I was in shock. Her voice echoed off the walls, and I expected the neighbors to leap out from behind their doors, possibly brandishing weapons.

Unfortunately, no one intervened.

"I can't take this anymore!" she cried, her hands rising up in the international sign for total exasperation. "I have *had it* with you!"

Needless to say, I was taken aback. *She* was sick of *me*?!

"It's always *Gus this* and *Gus that*," Helen fumed. "Gus is so cool! Gus is so smart! Gus is so *funny!*" She glared at me. "Henry thinks you're hilarious. Nate wants to know why I can't have a sense of humor about my clothes, like you did with that disgusting bridesmaid's dress."

"Thanks for reminding me," I snapped at her.

She shrugged, her mouth pulled low in the corners. "I've tried everything I know how to do, and you're still mean to me."

I had to fight to remain calm.

"Helen, I hate to point this out, but when you started dating Nate? He was already dating me. Forgive me if I wasn't inspired to hold hands and declare us *best friends forever.*" Not that I wanted to think too hard about Nate just then.

"You don't know what it's like to be the outsider," Helen retorted. "You have Amy Lee and Georgia, and the three of you have gone out of your way to leave me out since college. You think I don't see the looks? The rolled eyes? I know what you think of me."

"And again," I said, still fighting my temper. "You claimed to be a friend of mine and then you stole my boyfriend. You *stalked* me. You completely lied about the conversation we had so you could play more head games. What do you expect me to think of you?"

"That's just your excuse." She crossed her arms over her chest and narrowed her eyes at me. "You've been making fun of me since the day we met."

"Hardly," I retorted. "You were the one who thought she was cooler than everyone else."

"*You* thought I was cooler than everyone else," Helen retorted. "And God help me if I didn't live up to it!"

"If your stealing Nate was designed to make me think less of you," I threw back at her, "congratulations. I don't think you're cool anymore."

"You know what?" Helen let her hands drop to her sides. "I don't know why I bother. I can never win. I'm the one who always calls you and begs for the scraps of your attention, and meanwhile I'm lucky if you bother to call me of your own volition more than once a year."

My mouth fell open, because she was right. That's not how I would have described our relationship, of course, but still.

"You never gave me any indication that you'd be interested in my calling you more often," I said, feeling defensive.

"Of course not," Helen scoffed. "Because I'm not a person. I don't have feelings like anyone else. Whatever. Girls like you always play these stupid games."

"Girls like me?" I didn't like that at all. There weren't any *girls like me*. There was *that girl*, sure, but no *girls like me*.

"Oh yes," Helen said. Her eyes darkened. "In boarding school it was Jessie Unger. Everyone loved Jessie and she hated my guts. It didn't matter what I did, she still hated me. She and her friends called me names and made up rumors about me." Her gaze sharpened on me. "You think I don't know what Georgia and Amy Lee say about me?"

"Did you steal Jessie Unger's boyfriend too?" I asked pointedly.

Helen made a noise in the back of her throat.

"Boys are easier to get along with than girls," she said. "They don't judge you, or whisper about you behind your back while they're nice to your face. They either like you or they don't."

"You flirt with them, Helen! That's why they like you!"

"Like you don't flirt." She shook her head. "Oh, please. You try to entice men with your *I'm so smart and funny* thing, but that's not flirting? What is?"

Any leash I had on my temper snapped with that one. And unfortunately for Helen, I had a lot of ammunition.

"Hmm, let me think—" I pretended to think for all of six seconds. "How about wailing about possibly getting stung by a bee *in December* so other people's boyfriends fawn all over you and *carry you* back to the car?"

"I can't help it if I'm allergic," Helen snapped.

"Or how about the way you have to *lean so close* to every male who crosses your path? You have to *lean in*, and then *gaze at him*, and then look away while *moistening your lip.*" I acted it out for her, with a complimentary flip of the hair, as I had done many times before for the amusement of my friends. "What the hell is *that*?"

"I can't believe you *study* me!" Helen cried. "And like you're one to talk. 'Oh Henry! You're so evil!'" She mimicked me in a high, grating falsetto. "'Every girl in Boston fawns all over you, but I'll make myself different by hating you! Evil, nasty Henry! *Notice me*, Henry!'"

I actually saw a haze of red before my eyes, and had to blink to clear it. I also took a few deep breaths.

"Fine," I told her. I didn't want to touch anything she'd said with a ten-foot pole. Or, for that matter, a large steel girder. "Maybe we're both in glass houses here."

Helen seemed to deflate a little herself. She looked away, and I watched her catch herself just as she went to do that lip thing.

"See?" I said, pointing. "You lick your lip! You do it on purpose!"

"Um, hi, I'm not flirting with *you*, Gus. "

"You flirt with everyone, *Helen*. You've been doing it since you were eighteen."

"Anyway, it's automatic," she said, but she didn't do it again.

We stood there for a moment, and the wretched absurdity of the situation rose up and threatened to choke me.

Here Helen and I were, standing on a staircase, fighting over a guy I might have just realized wasn't worth it. If I didn't escape this situation that I'd helped make, I might be the first person in the history of the world to *actually* implode. I felt it coming, boiling up inside me like the stomach flu.

And with it, the unwelcome thought that none of this had ever been about Nate. Not really.

"Okay," I said briskly. "This has been unpleasant and I guess I'm going to go—"

"Did you sleep with him?" she asked, cutting me off.

I was convinced I hadn't heard that right.

"What?"

"I want to know if you slept with him that night," she said, shifting on her feet a little bit so that she suddenly looked stiff and almost wooden. "Why else would he call you so many times?"

She didn't look at me. It was the anti-Helen. No flirtatiousness or *leaning*. Just words.

I stared at her. "Is this a joke?"

She pursed her lips slightly. "I have to know."

"And you can't ask him?" I asked. The evil part of me started to enjoy herself. "It must suck, not being able to trust your boyfriend."

Helen just watched me, saying nothing.

Maybe Helen was right. Maybe there really was a *girl like me*. Because the urge to mess with her almost overcame me. Why shouldn't she get to feel the way I felt? Why shouldn't she taste a little bit of her own medicine? Her performance in my apartment the day after the Park Plaza came to mind. How would she like it if I pulled that on her? Why shouldn't I play her game?

Because he just wasn't worth it, I told myself. Reluctantly. I could tell her I'd slept with him, and embroil myself in who knew how much further drama with the two of them, or I could tell her the truth and wash my hands of them both right there and then. I could continue being an immature brat or I could grow up, for once.

It was a harder call than it should have been.

"No," I said, without realizing that was what I'd decided. "We didn't sleep together. I never even saw him that night. He just left me messages." I held her gaze and remembered something she'd said to me once. "I'm not like you."

She didn't like the last part, but still she looked relieved. And why shouldn't she? I'd just given her my boyfriend. *Her* boyfriend. I wasn't sure, suddenly, that he had ever been mine.

She knew it, too. Her eyes were calculating as they swept over me, no doubt looking for my angle.

I didn't know it myself.

"Merry Christmas, Helen," I told her softly, and then I went to find my coat.

chapter nineteen

For the first time in years, since I'd left for school when I was eighteen, I was *delighted* to escape to my childhood home for the holidays. Everything in Boston had gotten way too out of control, and the best way to deal with that was to relax into the embrace of my mother's decidedly anti-Atkins, anti-Food Pyramid holiday cooking.

Which I did with such dedication that I thought about very little else for days, except, occasionally, my expanding waistline. Happily, that was what sweats were for.

Things I was not thinking about included:

Nate Manning, and his conspiratorial smiles. The ones that reeled you in and ruined you, because you thought they were something special.

Amy Lee's deafening, spine-crushing silence.

Helen Fairchild, who had said things I found I just couldn't dismiss, much as I tried. I could dismiss a lot of her *that girl* behavior, but I couldn't dismiss the fact that despite it, we'd remained some form of friends for over a decade.

The way Henry had looked at me at that last party, as if I was a deep disappointment to him. As if he'd never known he was supposed to be off-limits in the first place. Which made me ache.

My emotional immaturity, particularly as pointed out by Amy Lee.

Nate, Helen, Henry, and me; my rectangle of ridiculousness.

And finally, the fact that my family clearly thought I was "going through something," if their overly careful manner around me was any indication. It reminded me of my actual teenage years. (On the upside, they'd all seemed to enjoy their presents, which was a point in my favor, I thought.)

After a few days, the joys of ingesting cookies by the handful in between three square meals a day paled somewhat, and I headed back into Boston. I might have been imagining my father's sigh of relief when he left me at my place, but I wasn't entirely sure. He could just as easily have been cursing the snow as my unpleasant attitude.

I picked up Linus from the kennel that same day, and despite his tremendous joy at seeing me again—which he expressed in the form of big, slurpy kisses and a lot of protest barking—my apartment seemed lonelier than before. I kicked my duffel bag into the bedroom and then returned to look around at the exact same things I'd been looking at for the past decade. I sat in my living room and glowered at the posters on the wall for a good long while, and then, just like that, I decided I'd had enough.

Unless I planned to move, which I didn't, it was time to stop brooding and start living up to my conception of myself.

I didn't even unpack my bag, I just set about the most intense spring-cleaning my apartment had ever undergone. I pulled down all the posters, sorted all the books, and hauled everything collegiate, untouched, ridiculous, or otherwise embarrassing out of the apartment in garbage bags.

It was brutal, and there were many painful moments. In the depths of my closet, for example, I located the baggy flannel shirt my post-grunge college crush had left in my possession. It was right next to a selection of old mix tapes from high school, piled high in a dusty brown bag, all of them so old the song lists had faded away. I got rid of both the shirt and the bag, but it hurt more than I wanted to admit.

It was mid-afternoon on my second day of Total Life Reorganization—which had involved, that morning, the purchase of actual bookshelves I planned to hang on the wall as opposed to the rickety mishmash of bookcases I'd picked up here and there over the years—when there was a knock on my door.

My heart raced a little bit, but I had, thankfully, gotten it under control by the time I opened the door. Which was a good thing, since the person standing there was Irwin.

"Oh," I said, blinking at him. Partly because I was feeling a touch crazed, and partly because Irwin wasn't wearing his trademark robe, preferring to rock the holiday appliqué sweater and a pair of elastic-waisted jeans. "I must be making a lot of noise. I'm sorry."

"No, no," he said, blinking right back at me and the

chaos that must have been clearly visible behind me. "Are you moving out?"

He restrained his probable joy at this prospect, which made it possible for me to be polite.

"Just cleaning out the college-era stuff," I said, not pausing to consider the possibility that Irwin might not be as fascinated by this process as I was. "Which is pretty much my entire apartment and everything I own. All I have to do is get this ratty furniture out of here, and figure out how to get my new bookshelves on the wall, and I'll be good to go. Don't worry, I shouldn't make too much noise after dark."

Irwin stood there, the gold menorah on his dark blue sweater practically glowing in the hallway. He opened his mouth, then closed it. Then opened it again, then shifted his weight from foot to foot, and I was starting to think we would stand there forever when he finally spat it out.

"Why don't I help you?" he asked, and then turned bright red.

He didn't *blush a little.* He *turned crimson.* It was somewhat alarming.

The old Gus would have screamed *no way,* slammed the door, and mocked the man mercilessly with her friends.

The new Gus decided that the man just wanted to be neighborly, and maybe even friendly. If our shared history was anything to go by, he didn't interact with others often, and if his continuing blush was any further indication, this was a big deal for him.

The new Gus also wanted the damn furniture out of her apartment, and she couldn't do it alone, superhero fantasies or no. She also had few options for mocking calls to friends, since Amy Lee was off the list and Georgia had all her calls forwarded to voice mail.

"That would be really nice of you," I told Irwin with a big smile and let him inside.

With Irwin's help (his name, I discovered, was Steve, but I was never going to be able to think of him as a *Steve*), I removed all the mismatched curbside furniture I'd collected since college and left it on the curb for the next owner to locate. There was a sense of closure in that—from the curb my furniture came, and to the curb it was returned. I was confident that Boston's student population would help themselves to it all before nightfall.

Irwin/Steve turned out to be handy with power tools, and before I knew it, the walls in my living room and bedroom were lined with matching, uniform bookshelves—the kind that weren't made of crappy plywood, and which housed my books without taking up floor space. It turned out that my apartment was significantly more spacious than I'd realized—since I hadn't *seen* parts of the floor since I'd moved in.

It also turned out that Irwin/Steve was significantly nicer than I'd imagined. He was a freelance writer of nonfiction articles who lived on caffeine and deadlines, which explained his rage over my numerous interruptions to his routine. He was also the owner of a pickup truck, so the next day my new friend and I took a trip to the Pottery Barn near

Copley Square and I blew a huge chunk of my savings on an overstuffed love seat, chair, and ottoman, all in a deep burgundy color with plentiful pillows. This was furniture that made me happy just looking at it. Irwin helped me haul my new, grown-up furniture back to the apartment, and I ordered us a pizza to celebrate.

After he left that night to work on another article with a looming deadline, I sat in the quiet of my new, improved home, and liked what I saw around me.

In a few short days, my apartment had been transformed from a sad and pathetic dorm room into a cozy, comfortable place that I wasn't sure I wanted to leave. I needed a few accents, to be sure, but my home was *homey* for the first time. A place to read and relax, and, I was sure, grow up. You would have to, in such an environment. The apartment itself demanded it.

And if I could effect that kind of change in my apartment—the *pit of dormitory despair* as Amy Lee had once called it—I figured it couldn't be too difficult to work a little spring-cleaning on myself. A new year was coming, I was turning thirty in just two days, and it was high time I introduced the new, improved Gus to the world. I was fuzzy on the details, but I knew the basic outline. I knew how I *wanted* to be, it was simply a question of *being* who I wanted to be.

I thought I had had it all figured out before. I'd had *the plan* perfectly clear in my head. I wasn't going to cross over into thirty without the triple crown in hand: serious boyfriend, career, and great friends. But then Nate hadn't acted according to the plan. And I didn't know what had happened to my friends. I didn't know if anything was fixable, either. But I had the career, sure, so score one for me.

It was time to accept that maybe, just maybe, I didn't have to have it all figured out by the time I turned thirty. Maybe I could just work on me, and see what else fell into place.

I was pretty sure that was otherwise known as *living*.

"I haven't heard a peep out of Amy Lee and I'm guessing we're not going to," Georgia barked down the phone line late that night, without the slightest preamble. "Because as we've discussed, she's better than us and therefore not required to behave the way she wants other people to behave."

"Maybe she doesn't know what to say," I suggested, as an alternative view.

I was lounging on my new love seat, enjoying the feel of the fabric and the view of my new bookshelves. Some people lusted after cars, which had never made sense to me. For me, bookshelves could inspire whole spontaneous sonnets, so maybe it was an *each to her own* scenario.

Anyway, just being near them made me feel optimistic and charitable.

"Whatever," Georgia said. She was clearly nowhere near any bookshelves. "The point of this phone call is that I rented a car and I'm picking you up tomorrow morning at ten-fifteen. And don't you dare do that thing you do, with all that *oh I'm* almost *packed* nonsense, okay?"

Our friend Lorraine, who was famous for over-the-top

parties ever since a memorable graduation extravaganza back in school, had taken over the entirety of a sprawling cliff-top mansion of a hotel that commanded nearly panoramic views of the bay below. According to Lorraine's e-mail, *The place is unbelievably high class—in the summer you practically have to be a Kennedy to get a room in the Hill House—but this is the off-season, people! We're gonna just PRETEND to be Kennedys!* Perhaps because she was feeling thirty approach, Lorraine had decided the time had come to be famous for a new extravagant party.

Everyone we knew was going.

"Ten-*fifteen*," I told Georgia, with extra emphasis on the *fifteen*. "I hate it when you show up early. You know that's as rude, if not ruder, than being late, right?"

"Just be ready," Georgia ordered. "These are dark days, Gus. Don't force me to take out my mood on you."

That was why I didn't tell her that we had a problem, which I had opened my mouth to do. I didn't want to have the fight in advance. I just wanted to bask in the glow of what felt like a brand-new apartment and thus a brand-new life.

Everything else—Amy Lee, Nate, Helen, even my assorted misconceptions about Henry—was just so much detritus.

I'd taken the actual detritus of my life and placed it on the curb.

I could do it emotionally, too.

All I had to do was start cleaning out the corners, and work from there.

*   *   *

"What the hell happened in here?" Georgia demanded the next morning. She'd arrived—as I'd expected—a few minutes before ten. Now she was standing just inside the doorway, actually gaping at the apartment as if she'd never seen it before.

Which, of course, she hadn't.

"I had a sudden attack of adulthood." I finished off my coffee and grinned at her. "It's good, right?"

"I think I'm in love with your couch," she said with a lustful sigh. "Yum." She walked over and sank into it, and sighed again, with pleasure. "I can't believe how great this place looks! It's so . . ."

"Grown up?" I fished.

"Exactly." She grinned. "Way to go, Gus! I didn't think you had it in you!"

I was still feeling the buzz. I'd had no idea what a difference it could make to truly love the place where you lived. Who knew happiness was as easy as spring-cleaning?

"Are you ready?" Georgia asked around a yawn. "We have the open road to conquer, or anyway, the Mid-Cape Highway, so let's get a move on."

I smiled. "About that. We have a small, slight problem."

Her eyes narrowed. "Don't try me."

I waved my hand at the dog.

"The kennel was booked through New Year's," I said, unperturbed. "I had to pick Linus up when I got back from New Hampshire, because they were above capacity."

Georgia looked over to where Linus was stretched across the passageway between the living room and kitchen, his shaggy tail pounding out a staccato beat against the floor.

He sprang to his feet the moment he realized we were looking at him, and came trotting over, all licks and wriggles.

Georgia dislodged Linus from her thigh, and then she looked at me.

"You want me to share a hotel room with this animal," she said.

I opened my mouth to deliver the perfect retort, but she held up a hand.

"Don't say it," she said.

"You have no idea what I was going to say."

"That I've shared a hotel room with far more offensive animals?" Georgia snorted when I tried to look innocent. "Yeah, that's what I thought."

"He's actually in a really obedient phase lately," I lied. "It's going to be fun, I bet."

Georgia looked heavenward, and then heaved a sigh.

"If I ever find out that this was deliberate, I will make the rest of your life an exercise in misery," she promised me.

"That was a very impressive threat, Georgia," I retorted. "But you might want to consider doing something with your hair before you try it out again. No one takes Raggedy Ann seriously."

Georgia reached up and tugged at one of her wild curls, which had escaped the bun she was sporting.

"Truly," she said, "this hair is the bane of my existence. It's always betraying me. That threat should have had you rolling around on the floor. Maybe even crying. It was that good."

"Whatever, Raggedy Ann," I said, swinging my bag to my shoulder. "Let's go."

chapter twenty

Linus stretched himself across the entirety of the back-
seat, and Georgia swung behind the wheel of what looked
to be a Matchbox toy car. I was amazed she could fold her
legs into the driver's seat at all.

"Where did you get this thing?" I asked. "And why not a
Tonka truck, if you were in that sort of mood?"

"This was the only economy car I could get on New
Year's eve," Georgia told me. "You're lucky we're not taking
the bus. Blame Amy Lee—we were supposed to road-trip
with her, remember?"

We didn't speak again until we'd loaded ourselves up
with Starbucks goodies—lattes all around and several
items from the baked goods case, because it was clearly
that kind of morning. Georgia drove us out of the city, and
once we started south on I-93 toward the southeast, Route
25, and the Cape, she adjusted her sunglasses against the
winter glare and cleared her throat.

It was so formal, it knocked me right out of my zoned

contemplation of the barren winter scenery, which I was busy melodramatically comparing to my emotional life. I turned to look at her.

"There's an update," I said with a happy sigh, reading her expression. "I knew it!"

I settled back against my seat, and listened.

Things with Chris Starling had been, as expected, awkward.

I don't see any reason to hash things out, he'd told her when they'd next seen each other at the office. Right after the Sheraton Whore incident. *What happened in Scranton should stay there. We're both professionals.*

"And he wasn't kidding," she told me, her voice gloomy. "All of a sudden he turned into Mr. Senior Associate. He stopped calling me by my first name, it was all Ms. this and Ms. that. He had his secretary call me instead of doing it himself." She shook her head. "Basically he stopped annoying me, and the moment he did—the moment he became the lawyer I wished he'd been that whole time—I hated it."

They'd been doing a round of very unpleasant depositions out in Seattle. Georgia only got two days to go back home to her family, which was tense because, as I could imagine all too well, her mother was unimpressed with any *career* that had so far left Georgia single, without prospects, and unable to spend a longer Christmas with her family as a loving daughter should.

She'd had to leave her mother's house to return to Seattle, where Chris Starling continued to behave as if he were a run-of-the-mill corporate attorney. It was like out of the frying pan, into the fire. Although significantly chillier.

"You know what his eyes are like," Georgia said. "Now imagine them completely blank and without that . . . Chris Starling spark. It was like he suddenly had zombie eyes."

"Oh my God," I whispered, delighted. "I know you *finally* woke up and realized he was a cutie, but is that what I think it is? Because from over here it sounds like the short, fat, balding guy managed to get to you!"

Georgia actually blushed, which was all the confirmation I needed, because I wasn't sure I'd ever seen *that* before.

"He is not short and fat, or even balding," she said. "*Maybe* he has a receding hairline."

"You're preaching to the choir, Georgia."

"I don't know what I feel," she said. "It's way too soon to be throwing big, scary words around and you have to let me finish the story, okay?"

"Please," I said, gesturing for her to continue.

It was in rainy, dark Seattle, outside a hotel near the Pike Place Market, that Georgia finally lost it. They were returning from another round of depositions, and were both quite obviously chilled to the bone. Georgia—very naturally—suggested they grab some of Seattle's famous coffee. The original Starbucks was within walking distance of the hotel lobby. She figured they could ease the chill between them as well as the outside chill from the Seattle winter.

I wouldn't want there to be any further misunderstandings, Chris Starling said in that monotone he'd been using, with a cold sort of glare to match.

Which had infuriated Georgia so much that she'd lost it right there, standing outside in the endless rain.

"What do you mean, you lost it?" I asked. Because it was hard to picture.

"I mean I completely lost it," Georgia said. "Flipped my wig. Went nuts. Whatever you want to call it."

"You screamed at him?"

"Mostly," she said, "I burst into tears."

Had she known that tears were the secret to cracking Chris's disinterested exterior, Georgia might have tried it earlier. Because the moment she broke down, his whole Mr. Distant Boss thing crumbled. *Oh no*, he said, horrified, *please don't, Georgia.* He kissed her, and so suddenly they were kissing while Georgia was still sort of crying, and it was raining, so then it was funny, too, and they couldn't seem to *stop* kissing, and when they ended up in a hotel room this time, they stayed there all night.

"So . . . ?" I asked, after a long beat.

"So . . . wow," she said, and flashed me a wicked sort of grin.

"Wow," I echoed, happily.

They had done a lot of talking, in between more exciting things, and it turned out that Chris had had a thing for Georgia for a long time.

"Which, now that I think about it," I said, "duh."

"I know!" Georgia cried. "I'm such an idiot."

Chris was older, at forty-two, and knew exactly what he wanted from life—he had the impending divorce to show him the folly of hanging on to the things he *didn't* want. He told Georgia very frankly that he and his ex had been the perfect corporate couple. She was a consultant and more cutthroat than he was. They'd planned a perfect life: no kids, nice cars, sleek condos and a weekend house in Vermont. The only trouble was, Chris hated it. He wanted a different life from the one he'd trained for, he discovered. He was tired of being married to his job, with a wife married to hers. He wanted to take it easier. Maybe see the person he was supposed to be living with. Maybe quit Waterbury and work somewhere with better hours. Maybe see about the kids it turned out he wanted after all. He wasn't sure about any of those details, he just knew he wanted out of the rat race.

Only trouble was, he had this thing about hard-as-nails career women. Particularly mouthy ones with wild, unprofessional hair and Amazonian bodies.

"So?" I demanded when she lapsed off into reverent silence yet again. "What happened? Are you going to live happily ever after *the way I predicted* or what?"

"Well," Georgia said, straightening slightly in her seat. "That's the thing."

It turned out that Chris Starling was the cautious type.

This is great, he had told her just last night, *but what happens between us on the road is completely outside reality. It's wonderful, but I think you need to think about what it would mean for it to be a part of your reality here in Boston. I'm not exactly your type.*

So they agreed that Georgia would go off to the big New Year's party, where she would be forced to contend with Jared—the last of his type, we could all only hope. Chris didn't want to hear from her until she'd looked around her real life and imagined him in it. If she thought he might fit, despite the fact he was about as removed from her normal sort of boyfriend as could be, well, she could call him and they'd talk about it. But no need to rush into anything. If she was confused, that was fine. He wasn't any twenty-five-year-old jackass, filled with ultimatums and drama. She could take her time.

"That's almost cruel," I said then. "Doesn't that make you want to call him *right now*?"

"You don't even know."

"I *like* him!"

"So do I," Georgia breathed. "I just want to get to this stupid party, see dumbass Jared, kick myself, and call the man I think I should have been into about a year ago. Then, if there's time, I want to drink a lot of champagne."

"Don't kick yourself too hard," I said, moving my suddenly overheated feet away from the Matchbox vent. "It's not like it would have done you any good a year ago because there was a whole wife issue."

"Well, there isn't one now," Georgia said. "And not to get all defensive here, since Amy Lee isn't even in the car to make fun of me for feeling too much too soon, but I have no idea what I feel for him. It's weird and big and messy, but I've never been so excited about someone before. Not someone I could actually *talk* to, who made me laugh and *cared* about me. So this is all new."

"You have to call him as soon as possible!" I squealed a little bit in vicarious excitement.

"Oh hell yes," Georgia said, her smile taking over her face. "Why do you think I'm driving so fast?"

She wasn't messing around. But there was only so much even Georgia could do about the holiday traffic that inched across the Cape Cod Canal. To say nothing of the glut of cars that moved like molasses up the Mid-Cape Highway toward Provincetown. It was afternoon by the time we made it to our destination: a pretty seaside village stretched along the elbow portion of the flexed arm that was the Cape Cod peninsula.

We were still of one mind—locate Jared, note the many differences between Jared and Chris Starling, bask in Georgia's awakening to the wonderfulness of Chris Starling, call him as planned and in so doing sort out Georgia's heretofore painful love life.

If there was time, I might even deal with some issues of my own, but I was putting all that on the back burner. Duty to friendship called. Also, I was repressing.

First, though, we had to check into the hotel. And, not inconsiderably, sneak Linus inside.

To give our friend Lorraine credit, the place was as beautiful as she'd claimed. Pictures of the main building in the height of summer graced the walls—blue hydrangeas and holly bushes beneath the Cape Cod bright blue skies. It was all much starker this time of year, of course. The winds howled in from the bay and stalked around the corners of the house, but inside the fires were lit and the rooms were pretty and bright. Sparkling lights glowed on evergreen trees both indoors and out. It was impossible not to warm to the place.

"We're totally getting booted out of here," Georgia hissed out of the side of her mouth. "Have you looked at that concierge?"

She marched across the lobby to the reception desk, leaving me to stand by a collection of evergreen branches while she sorted out our reservations. I looked at the concierge in question—he looked as if maybe he performed in a bouncer capacity as well. He had arms like whole meat lockers. There was no way we would be sneaking Linus past a bruiser like him. I swallowed.

Then I reminded myself that Georgia was a top attorney, and dealt with the criminal element every day—or anyway, while deposing them all over the country—and therefore probably had a wily criminal mind of her own. Just to keep up. At which point I was forced to remind myself that Georgia was the woman who once forgot the entire concept of caller ID, called a guy she was dating one hundred and fifty seven times in one day (which was not as much of an exaggeration as you might imagine), and was then *surprised* when he ordered her never to call him again. Before he picked up and moved to Jacksonville, Florida.

Put Georgia's idiocy together with my klutziness and the very *fact* of Linus—and, oh yeah, we'd be sleeping in the car.

"All right," Georgia said, walking back over to me. "Our room is on the fourth floor. Tragically, it's still next door to certain dentists the way we requested back when we still liked her, but that's going to be the least of our problems. Let's go check it out."

"What about . . . ?" I indicated the outside with my eyebrows, where, if I looked closely, I could just see the outline of Linus's shaggy head smashed against the front window of the car. Then I looked back at Georgia and tried to indicate *Linus* with my eyes.

"I think we should check out the room and then look for alternate entrances," Georgia said. She looked around. "There's no way we're getting anything past the front desk."

So we hoisted up our bags and smiled widely at the woman behind the reception desk—perhaps too widely, judging from the confusion on her face—and trudged up the staircase. Old stately manors, apparently, were big on elegance and bay views, but short on elevators.

By the time we reached the fourth floor, I was winded and Georgia was gasping for air. We stopped at the top and sucked in oxygen.

"This is what happens when you work ninety hours a week and have no life because you sold your soul to a corporate law firm," Georgia said, and then had to pause to breathe deep. She eyed me. "Looks like the much-ballyhooed life of the mind isn't doing a whole lot for you, either."

"You're fat, greedy, and soulless," I threw back at her. "I'm just fat."

"I'm ready to take my fat, greedy, and soulless ass to bed," Georgia retorted, wiping stray red tendrils back from her face. "Can we find this room?"

It was done up in blues and creams, and it was lovely. We threw our bags onto the two full-size beds and then headed straight back out. As Georgia had suspected, there was another entrance around the side of the big house. Once we got Linus inside, we could just whisk him up the stairs and into the room with no one the wiser.

Linus, all kinds of grumpy after being cooped up in the car, expressed his ire by dawdling across the lawn as I tugged on his leash and hissed at him to hurry. He didn't even deign to look up at me, he just continued to sniff the bare earth and placidly cock a leg every few feet.

"Hurry up!" Georgia whispered—loudly—from the door she was propping open.

I shivered, shooting nervous glances toward the front entrance through which, at any moment, I expected to see the muscle-man concierge come running with assorted other staff members to apprehend me.

Finally, Linus let me haul him indoors, and Georgia eased the door closed behind us. We grinned at each other as if we'd just completed a covert operation to save the world rather than sneak a mutt into a hotel, and then we started up the stairs in a rush.

"See?" I was definitely feeling smug. "You should have more faith in us. We rule!"

"Hey," she protested from the step behind me, "in case you haven't noticed, we have a history of making bad situations terribly and horrifically worse."

"We're all grown up now," I said, even more smug. "You should give us a little more credit."

Which, naturally, is when it happened.

Georgia, too busy laughing to watch where she was going, tripped over her own feet and crashed into me.

"Ouch!" I cried, and threw my hands out to catch the banister.

But to do that, I had to drop Linus's leash.

Linus trotted up another step or two, and then paused. He turned.

Our eyes met.

He noticed that no one was holding his leash. He cocked his head to the side.

For the space of one heartbeat, and then another, I stared at my dog. He stared back.

"Good boy," I murmured, pulling myself upright, never breaking eye contact. "Good, sweet boy. Stay, Linus!"

I swear to God, he smirked at me.

And then he bolted.

"Shit!" I yelped, and threw myself after him.

Everything sped up.

"Linus!" I hissed, tearing after him. He ignored me completely. He galloped up to the third-floor landing and then took off along the hall. I could tell that he was having a merry old time—his tail was waving happily in the air and every now and again he would toss a coy little glance behind him to make sure I stayed close—and out of reach. I was sucking in gulps of air and cursing under my breath.

"I knew I should have gotten a gerbil," I snarled.

We skidded after him into a small sitting room, tastefully done up in cranberry hues. Georgia crashed into me from behind, tossing me forward into the room.

"Ow!" she cried, grabbing her elbow.

"Block the doorway!" I commanded, righting myself and crouching low. "Whatever you do, don't let him get past you!"

"What if someone comes?" she hissed.

I couldn't answer her because all of my attention was focused on Linus. It had obviously just occurred to him that he might be trapped.

He turned to face me, and assumed what I called his vulture position. His body tensed, and his head lowered, as he watched me approach with his canny eyes.

"Sit down," I told him.

Yeah, right.

"The next time you get a dog," Georgia complained behind me, "you might consider actually *training* the damn thing."

For a moment, I thought Linus might back down. His ears flicked from front to back, and his head cocked just slightly to the right.

"Good boy," I crooned approvingly. "Sit down, Linus."

I eased a little bit closer, reached out and down with my hand—

And he took off.

Georgia squealed and jumped at him, smacking into the doorjamb while Linus zoomed through her legs.

"You suck!" I threw at her as she collapsed into a heap in

the doorway. I vaulted over her crumpled body and hurled myself down the hall after my dog.

This was the end of the line, I knew.

He was headed straight for the main staircase, which would deliver him directly into the main lobby and deliver us directly out on our collective ear. If I was going to save this situation—and I had to—it had to happen *then*.

I pumped my arms and legs like some kind of marathon runner and then, just as Linus turned the corner toward the top stair, I dived.

I lunged forward in an all-out dive. My fingers stretched wide—I felt the canvas leash with the tips of them—but Linus danced just out of reach—

SMACK!

I hit the ground in a belly flop and skidded a few feet. I slid directly into what took me a moment to recognize as someone's feet. I blinked. Familiar-looking black boots with a four-inch heel, polished to gleam. And under the right foot—pinned and immovable—was Linus's leash. I seized it in both hands, too full of adrenaline and relief to care about the many ways in which I hurt. I would deal with that later.

I thanked the powers that be, and then looked up, ready to kiss the feet in front of me. I was already lying there in position, prostrate and everything.

"Hello, Gus." Amy Lee peered down at me, and let out a little sigh. "I thought that was you."

chapter twenty-one

"Oh, terrific!" Georgia said from behind me. Her sarcasm preceded her by about three feet, like a kind of bad smell. It made Amy Lee recoil in the same way. "Look, Gus! Amy Lee is here to judge us!"

She came to a stop next to me, which meant her sharp-toed boots were mere centimeters from my face. That made two sets of dangerous heels within easy stomping distance. I decided it would probably behoove me to get up.

"Was I interrupting something?" Amy Lee asked in her snottiest voice. "Because it just looked like the usual immature crap to me."

"Merry Christmas and a happy new year to you!" I sing-songed, grabbing Linus's leash from under Amy Lee's foot and restraining myself from trying to fling her down the stairs. Because violence was better imagined than actual, I reminded myself. *Actual violence* led to prison terms.

For his part, Linus seemed completely unaffected by his dash across the hotel. In fact, he—oblivious to the group dynamics—was delighted to see Amy Lee and kept trying to lick her hands.

"Forced holiday cheer will definitely divert everyone's attention," Georgia snapped at me. "Good call."

And then the three of us just . . . stood there on the landing, not quite looking at each other. I had a dramatic moment wherein I imagined our history hung there in the air between us, but I suspected it was just the pine smell from the evergreens downstairs in the lobby.

"I think things kick off around 4 p.m.," Amy Lee said eventually, still not looking anywhere in particular. "Lorraine insists on black tie. I have to get changed."

"So do we," I said, unnecessarily, since both Georgia and I were sweaty and in jeans.

"We all received the same invitation, I'm pretty sure," Georgia said, her tone scathing. I looked at her, trying to communicate a gentler form of *shut the hell up* with my eyes. She only pursed her lips a little bit, but she didn't say anything else.

Amy Lee let out a long-suffering sort of sigh, and turned away.

Thus began the truly awkward climb up the stairs to our adjoining rooms on the next floor. We all trudged along in a deeply uncomfortable silence broken only by Linus, who was panting happily. He seemed perfectly content to stay on his leash *now*, I noticed.

Outside our rooms, Georgia unlocked our door while Amy Lee unlocked hers. I stared at the carpet. Still, no one spoke. Georgia threw open the door and stormed inside. I followed her, and set about unfastening Linus's leash.

We could hear Amy Lee's door slam, and then, once again, there was only silence.

"Well!" I said into the oppressive quiet before Georgia's storm of temper. "That was awkward."

"She has to be fucking kidding me!" Georgia exploded.

"She's obviously still mad about whatever she's mad about," I said, trying to sound soothing. "So let her be mad. She'll talk to us when she's ready."

It wasn't that I wasn't mad myself, not to mention hurt that one of my best friends was still acting like she hated me, but I was more concerned with damage control. This wasn't an afternoon sleigh-ride party that we could all storm away from. This was a hotel out in the country and we'd all be staying the night. It was also a national holiday. I figured my hurt feelings took a distant second to keeping Georgia from throttling Amy Lee before the clock struck midnight.

"That stuck-up, self-righteous—"

Georgia couldn't even finish, she just whirled around and stomped over to the door that joined our room to Amy Lee and Oscar's. She balled her hands into fists and started pounding. She was no fragile flower, either, so she made quite a racket with all of her Amazon strength behind each blow.

"Could you please—" I rubbed at my temples. "What do you think this is going to do, exactly?"

"I think it's going to open the door," Georgia snapped. "And then I think me and Miss Holier-than-Thou are going to talk about this bullshit."

"You're trying to beat down the door so you can *talk*," I pointed out, mildly. "Where have I heard that before? Oh, yes, from violent, crazed—"

"Either help me or shut up, Gus!" Georgia barked.

I chose the second option, and waited.

It didn't take long before the door flew open and Amy Lee stood there, practically hyperventilating with rage.

"Have you lost your *mind*?" she hurled at Georgia.

"How *dare* you sit in judgment of me?" Georgia threw right back. "Whenever you needed a friend, I was there for you—I was *always* there for you! And in return for over *ten years* of friendship I get what? You telling me to fuck off in some random party? Have *you* lost your mind?"

"I held your hand through the first four hundred heartbreaks, Georgia," Amy Lee snapped. "Which for a *normal person* would end sometime, like after the *fifteenth identical situation*—except not you. You just keep going and going—you're like the Energizer Bunny of stupid, pointless relationships!"

I thought Georgia might actually faint from her fury, which I swore I could hear sizzle along her skin, and so bodily placed myself between the two of them.

"Everyone needs to calm down!" I announced—okay, it was closer to a shout.

"It must be pretty bad if *Gus* has to step in and be the adult," Amy Lee said, with a little snort of extremely obnoxious laughter.

I reminded myself to take a deep breath. While I was doing so—and thus not throttling Amy Lee myself—Georgia recovered enough to leap to my defense.

"Are you the model of adult behavior, Amy Lee?" Georgia demanded from behind me. "Because I think you'll find that *sniggering* at people is usually frowned upon *on the playground.*"

"I should have known that the two of you would just gang together and *wallow* like it's senior year of college again," Amy Lee spat.

"Have I lost *my* mind?" I asked no one in particular. "Why the hell are we talking about *college*? The last I checked that ended when we graduated *seven years ago!*"

"Some of us graduated," Amy Lee retorted.

"You see, Gus?" Georgia asked acidly. "Amy Lee is just better than we are. She works harder now, just as she did then, which is hard to imagine, I know, since she's so fucking perfect. She's *just better.*"

"I don't know about better," Amy Lee snapped. "But let's see—I don't lie about who I'm sleeping with, nor do I thrash around in my bed like some fucking opera heroine for whole days."

"You condescending—"

"The two of you can't even come to a New Year's eve party without turning it into a circus!" Amy Lee continued, talking over Georgia.

"You really are full of yourself, Amy Lee," I told her, because the hell with deep breaths, I wanted to slap her. "If we're such a trial for you, I'm surprised you kept us around as your best friends in the entire world for over ten years. So I guess that makes you the real psycho here, doesn't it?"

I wasn't even yelling, or particularly snide. In fact I was the calmest voice in the room. And yet, it was like I'd slapped her the way I'd briefly imagined.

Amy Lee seemed to crumple in front of me. Her face sort of folded in on itself, and it took me a long, horrified moment to realize that she was crying.

Amy Lee never cried.

She didn't cry when her heart was trampled by her high school love, when she broke her finger, or when her body betrayed her once a month. Or even at her own wedding. No tears for Amy Lee—that was the rule. She was all about stoicism and grim determination. Once, long ago, she'd gotten a little misty-eyed during a particularly intense conversation over tarot cards and cheap red wine, but we'd been all of nineteen then and she blamed the wine.

So it took me a while to realize that what she was doing was sobbing. I might have thought she was convulsing, except I saw the tears. I didn't have to look over at Georgia to see that she was as floored by this as me—I could feel her hand digging into my arm, where she was holding on to me for dear life.

"I am *not* psycho!" Amy Lee said, between gulps of air and more floods of tears. "I just *feel* psycho!" She took both of her hands and placed them on her belly. "I'm fucking *pregnant!*"

If it was possible to get more still and more silent, we did. It was as if Georgia and I turned to stone right there in the doorway. Amy Lee sobbed some more and backed into her room, where she sat on the edge of the bed and held her face in her hands.

"Oh my God," I said, hardly breathing. "Are you serious?"

"Like I would joke about the fact that I'm going to be someone's *parent*," Amy Lee snapped, obviously recovered. Sure enough, she sat up again and wiped her eyes. "Georgia still has issues with her mother and she's about to turn thirty—"

"About to? Hello? In *April*, thanks, and let's not rush it!" Georgia yelped. She let go of my arm when I glared at her. "Sorry, Gus."

"And you know what?" Amy Lee asked, still somewhat emotional if her shaky voice was anything to go by. "I can't believe neither one of you noticed! I *told* you Oscar and I were going to start trying!"

"You said it that one time," I said, stung. "And then you never mentioned it again!"

"I haven't touched alcohol in months!" Amy Lee cried. "Is there a bigger sign than that?"

"You told me you were taking on the designated-driver role to be fair to Oscar," I reminded her. "I'm sorry that I took what you said at face value. And who cares, anyway?" I took a step into the room. "How far along are you?"

"And why didn't you just *tell* us?" Georgia demanded, finally roused from stone for a reason other than defending her age. "You're a walking hormone bomb, for God's sake. No wonder you wanted to kill us."

We both inched into the room, and sank down on either side of her on the bed.

"Can I . . . ?" I asked in a whisper, and held out my hand. She wiped at her eyes again, and nodded, and I laid my palm across her belly, where there was a slight rounding. The sort of thing that would suggest a weekend with Toll House cookies on a figure like mine, but meant something else entirely on tiny little Amy Lee. I let out a breath, awed.

Georgia, wide-eyed, leaned in and placed her hand next to mine. Amy Lee took a ragged breath, and let it out into the sudden stillness of the room around us.

"I'm about three months along," she said in a quiet voice. "You're not supposed to say anything until then, because so many things can happen."

"Nothing is happening to my godchild," I declared, and I could feel my eyes begin to well up as I began to think of the ramifications of that. I had thought everything would change when Amy Lee got married, but Oscar had added to the life we were used to living together. I had no idea what a baby would do.

"Hi, baby," Georgia whispered at Amy Lee's belly, and then leaned over to place a soft kiss there.

We all laughed a little bit, and when Georgia sat up again she was glassy-eyed too.

"You're going to set me off," Amy Lee wailed.

"I'm already set off," I replied, and sniffled.

"We don't cry!" Amy Lee said. "*I* don't cry!"

"I think we're allowed to take a small break from being completely and totally kick-ass, here," Georgia said, wiping at her nose. "It's not every day we get to meet the next generation."

We were all laughing and weeping, sometimes at once, when the door swung open, and Oscar appeared with bags on each arm.

"Oh, Jesus," he said, looking alarmed. He dropped the bags where he stood. "What now?"

chapter twenty-two

Georgia and I had a little bit of time to whisper to each other as we got ready, but mostly we just made faces and shrugged as we tripped over ourselves and Linus to and from the bathroom. Amy Lee was pregnant. She and Oscar were going to be *someone's parents* in just a few months. It was going to take a bit more time to process.

When we'd finally squeezed ourselves into our black-tie appropriate gowns (no royal blue taffeta, thank you), located our wraps, adjusted our control-top pantyhose (maybe that was just me—I swore by control top because it alone tamed the belly, even as I loathed it for that restricted, uncomfortable feeling), and lectured the dog on the importance of being quiet (again, that was probably just me), we assembled in the hallway. It was a very different group from the angry one we'd been before. For one thing, Oscar was there, looking very James Bond-ish in his tuxedo. Amy Lee smiled at me, I smiled back gratefully, and I felt more emotional about that than I thought I should as Amy Lee led the way downstairs.

There was something about wearing formal clothes that encouraged you to behave, I thought as we made our way down toward the lobby, where the other guests were beginning to converge. I was still concentrating on everything that had happened with Amy Lee—because while part of me felt giddy and a little bit weepy with relief that the worst was over, there was still a large part of me that simmered with unresolved anger. She had been horrible—unjustifiably so, I thought— but then, what was the point of talking about it? Hashing things out would only prolong the nastiness. It seemed that she wanted to use being pregnant as an all-purpose excuse for everything that had happened between the three of us, and though it went against the grain, I wanted to let her.

I remembered Minerva's story about her fight with Dorcas then. It had seemed so foreign to me—the idea that you could move forward without a painful airing of grievances on both sides. But maybe Minerva had it right—maybe it wasn't necessary to pick apart pain. Maybe some things just weren't worth fighting about. Some friends weren't friends anymore, but family—and there were different rules for family. It didn't make sense to sit down with family and detail all the reasons they'd upset you—for many reasons, not least among them the fact that they could whip out a checklist of your transgressions themselves. And after you'd both picked apart the carcasses, why would you want to be friends again? Maybe the important thing was to recognize that everyone felt wronged and slighted—but the point worth concentrating on was that everyone loved each other. If we worked from that premise, we should be fine. Or anyway, I hoped we would.

"What's that face about?" Georgia asked from beside me. She looked particularly regal with her hair in an updo. "You look entirely too pensive. Don't tell me you're already having the post-holiday blues. It's not even midnight yet."

"I'm not," I said immediately.

"Every year right around your birthday you get depressed," Georgia reminded me. "It's like clockwork."

"Okay, maybe I am, a little." I shrugged. "Next weekend will be my first free weekend in a long time."

"Next weekend I plan to lie on my couch and revel in the brand new year, enjoying the fact that you will be a decrepit thirty while I remain a young and vital twenty-nine," Georgia said with a blinding smile. "I have it all planned."

"Really? Because I plan to lie on my fabulous new couch and think about how, as the older and wiser one, I will *choose* to forgive you your transgressions even though you really don't deserve it," I said with the same smile. "You poor little lost soul."

"Yikes," Georgia muttered. "That's horrifying."

Forgiveness and acceptance, I thought as we found a spot near the largest tree in the lobby. Although I'd been kidding with Georgia, I was pretty sure those were the keys to relationships. Everything else was just ego and hurt feelings.

I had to remind myself of my commitment to adulthood—sternly—when I looked across the glittering lobby to see Nate,

Helen, and Henry standing together near a selection of robust poinsettias. Nate and Helen were holding hands, exactly the way they had long ago at the party at Henry's house. She was dressed to accentuate her fragility and big, sad eyes, and the only difference in my reaction was that *this* time I could see how skillfully she'd achieved her goal. It was still annoying.

Although—if I thought about it—not *personally* annoying. So. Progress.

Nate and Henry were both dressed in tuxedos, although all comparison ended there. I thought Nate looked like the surly sort of waiter you debated not tipping at all and then over-tipped because you were intimidated. Henry, meanwhile, looked divine. It was as if he'd been hiding his light underneath the bushel of regular clothes, and only now, in black tie, could his true glory shine forth upon the masses. And shine he did.

The thought that I might have ruined any chances of ever touching him again was a sudden, searing misery that threatened to drown me.

Oscar followed my gaze across the room and sighed.

"I had the most depressing conversation with Henry when I was checking in," he said. "He claims his reputation as male slut was totally exaggerated. The guy was my hero, but he says it was all made up."

"Mostly by me," Georgia said happily, and raised her eyebrows at me. "If any girl strayed within a foot of him, I assumed they were sleeping together. I might have told every other living human being in Boston that they were, too. Mea culpa." She didn't sound in the least repentant.

"I think I might burst into tears," Oscar said.

I had to take a moment to deal with the actual reality of Henry: force for good and no more of a floozy hound than anyone else. The inkling I'd had in the café with Georgia turned into more of a tidal wave.

"You're not still staring at them?" Amy Lee demanded, shaking her head at me. She thought I was still tied in knots about Nate, I realized when I saw the look on her face. What a difference a few unpleasant weeks made.

"I am," I replied, meeting her eyes. Daring her. "But not for the reasons you think. I don't really care what Nate and Helen do. I was more interested in ogling Henry."

"But—" Amy Lee looked at Georgia.

Georgia waved a careless hand in the air. "Over it."

Amy Lee opened her mouth, and then shut it again with a faint snapping sound.

"You should be free to ogle whoever you want," Amy Lee said after a moment. Magnanimously. "It just might take me a few minutes to stop with the knee-jerk name-calling, that's all."

"I'm on record as always liking the guy," Oscar reminded me. "Still do. Although he's off the hero list."

"I don't see why we have to stop calling him names," Georgia said with a sniff. "Just because Gus *likes* him now, forever breaking the heart of the nineteen-year-old girl I once was, that doesn't change the fact that *I* think he's bleeding-heart liberal scum."

I didn't have the chance to answer that as it deserved, because the doors to the banquet hall were opened and we all started to file inside for the cocktail portion of the evening. Henry moved away from Nate and Helen for a moment, and our eyes caught from across the lobby. I expected him to ignore me—and maybe it was time I learned to stop with the expectations, especially where Henry was concerned.

Because instead of ignoring me, his eyes grew a little bit more blue as he looked at me, and then he nodded his head. Just once.

It wasn't exactly friendly, but it wasn't a bitch slap, either.

It was as if the moment I'd stopped running after Nate, I'd finally realized I'd been running away from Henry the whole time. And I didn't think I wanted to run any longer.

I wanted more than a nod.

"Wake up, space cadet!" Georgia ordered, grabbing me by the arm and steering me toward the nearest bar. "If you fall on your face because you're daydreaming about *my* epic crush, I guarantee I won't catch you."

"And I'll probably laugh at you," Amy Lee said in agreement.

"I'm so glad we're all in love again," I said, making my voice warble with emotion that I was only partially faking. "It makes me feel so warm inside."

The party got rowdy, fast.

First of all, we'd been attending parties with these people for years now, so there was a kind of party shorthand. There was no awkwardness over initial drinks as the night swung into gear. Oh, no. The first round of cocktails had hardly begun and there was already a din that rattled through the hotel. It was as comfortable as any of our usual weekends, just in party clothes.

Second, it was New Year's eve, which added a manic energy to the whole shebang. People weren't as placid as they normally were. You got the sense that everyone was *personally invested* in having a good time. Which promised that the night would be fun, on the one hand. And on the other, it was slightly alarming.

And then, third, there was a whole lot of drama swirling around in the banquet hall when it came time for the sit-down dinner Lorraine insisted upon, because she threw every party as if it were the wedding reception she worried she'd never experience.

"Please tell me my eyes are deceiving me," Georgia said into my ear as we looked for our assigned table. "Please tell me that is not my ex-*whatever* all over that incredibly skanky twig with the blown-out hair."

I looked over and sure enough, horrible Jared was lounging about at the very table we'd been searching for, all but licking the neck of a very familiar-looking female.

"Her name is Ashley," I told Georgia, remembering her from the Park Plaza and the elevator she'd exited with Henry. "I don't know if this helps or hinders, but I think she's deeply stupid."

"Water finds its own level," Georgia snapped. "Which doesn't explain why *I* felt the need to go wading."

Jared broke from his escapades when we arrived at the table. Georgia and I made a big show of arranging our purses and wraps on our respective chairs, as Amy Lee and Oscar sank into their seats. Jared leaned back into his chair and waited until Georgia was forced—by virtue of running out of options—to look at him.

"Hi, Jared," she said mildly, as if the last time she'd seen him had not been their nasty breakup and she had not, in fact, wept over him.

"Georgia," Jared murmured. He flicked a look my way. "That your date?"

"As a matter of fact, yes," I snapped. "Is that yours?"

My tone made all sorts of rude assumptions. Ashley didn't notice. Jared didn't care. He just smirked at Georgia. His expression was very easy to read: Georgia was a pathetic bitch, and he wanted to hurt her.

Then he turned his attention back to Ashley and started whispering in her ear.

"Whatever," Ashley said, far too loudly. "I want a drink!"

Jared stood up, and pulled her after him. He threw a look back at Georgia, all *How you like me now?* as if he had Kate Moss on his arm.

We all let out a breath when he was gone.

"What a little shit!" Amy Lee snapped. "Someone needs to take him down a peg!"

"And you know what?" Georgia had a sort of dazed look on her face. "That person doesn't have to be me."

"You're absolutely right," I agreed with a nod.

"Even two weeks ago, this all would have hurt," Georgia continued in the same musing tone. "A lot. It would have required some serious retail therapy and a whole lot of moping. But tonight? I just don't care. I don't *have* to care. It's not even about Chris. I mean, it is. Thanks to him, I finally get that all of this was always totally beneath me. No wonder he wanted me to figure this out on my own— because there's no way anyone could have told me that I would be watching that loser and feeling sorry for *him*. Dumbass." She shook her head slightly, as if clearing it. "Somebody order me a drink—I have to go make a phone call."

I felt like cheering as she turned around and strode out of the party, but I decided that would be inappropriate, so I just grinned instead.

"I'm not sure I know what she was talking about," Amy Lee said from her seat. "But I know empowering when I see it. Go Georgia."

"Hell, yeah," Oscar agreed. "Although that guy could use a punch in the nose, definitely."

"He's not worth it," I said, waving a dismissive hand.

We all basked for a moment, letting the celebration swirl around us. Then Amy Lee frowned.

"Did she say Chris?" she asked. "As in Chris *Starling*?!"

I smiled.

"What have you people been *doing*?" she demanded.

chapter twenty-three

Later in the evening, the band had kicked into its seventies section and I decided to take a break from my groove thing to see what damage I'd done to my makeup. I had the sinking feeling it was the "shock and awe" kind of damage, but only a mirror would be able to tell me for sure.

Over near the doors to the lobby, I turned to look back at the crowd. It was hard to believe the holiday season was over. It seemed as if it had just been summer a few moments ago, and now it was New Year's. True, I'd been mucking about in high drama for a while, which did tend to make the time pass quickly.

As a way to avoid really thinking too much about the last half of the last year of being in my twenties, freaking out over Nate had worked like a charm.

I laughed a little bit at that, and then looked around the party until I spotted him. Helen was close to his side, as expected. Nate stood, rocked back on his heels as if he were wearing ski boots, laughing at something one of our college friends was saying. His dark hair still fell enticingly over his forehead, and the roses in his cheeks were in full bloom. I knew that if I wanted to, I could jump back into it with him. I could expect the secret smiles, and maybe one of those nights he would move from messages into reality. But where would that leave me?

Nate had been the perfect plan. Getting together with him at that Fourth of July party had eased my panic. It didn't matter that I was turning thirty or that I lived in a crappy apartment completely overrun with dog hair and books. With Nate, I had a serious boyfriend and *that* meant I was still in the game. It meant I wasn't *on the shelf* or whatever other horrible spinster term I wanted to use.

Which might have been fine, except that for Nate, I was just a placeholder. It didn't matter why he'd wanted Helen more than me, it just mattered that he did. He'd run after her the night I'd walked in on them, not me. He'd stayed with her, rather than talk things over with me. He'd gotten angry with me when she seemed angry at him. And everything else was just the game he played. At worst, he was manipulative and calculating, but I wasn't sure his behavior was that thought out.

The good news was, I didn't have to care about him any more. I didn't have to worry about his motivations. He had been right a long time ago, proving that when people said things you didn't want to hear about themselves, you should listen: he wasn't who I wanted him to be.

I didn't have to care about that, either.

I was free.

*   *   *

I found the bathroom, and had just finished mopping up the worst of the mascara issue when the door slapped open and in walked Helen.

"We really have to stop meeting like this," I said lightly, straightening. "But if you're here to fight with me, I have to tell you, I think we should institute a time-out on national holidays."

"You're just as funny as ever," Helen said, and came to stand next to me. There was silence as Helen fluffed her hair and straightened her dress. I finished reapplying my lipstick and tossed the tube back into my clutch.

Then we just looked at each other's reflections in the mirror. We looked like strange inverse images of each other. Helen was dark, in a pale blue dress, her tiny bones appearing almost birdlike. I was much fairer, in a rich green dress, and my skin looked almost like peaches in the forgiving light. The fact that we'd dated the same man, when we had so little in common and shouldn't have appealed to the same taste, should have been funny. It occurred to me that maybe, someday, it might be.

"I didn't want to tell you this," Helen said, ruining the moment, "but I kind of did like the fact that I stole Nate from you. Specifically you, I mean. As like karmic retribution. Is that bad?"

"The fact that you thought there was some karmic retribution there is troubling," I told her, shaking my head. "Or anyway, it's not like hearing that makes me want to rush out and make us some friendship bracelets, but then, it's not like I was planning on doing that anyway." I turned so I was looking at her instead of her reflection. "But that's okay, isn't it? We don't have to sing 'Kumbaya' and hold hands."

"I hated the Brownies," Helen confessed. "Didn't you? Those ugly uniforms, like we were little Jawas. And all the mothers were mean."

"I liked the Brownies," I said, frowning as I remembered. "I just couldn't sit still during the ceremonies, and I didn't make it very far in the Girl Scouts."

"Girl Scouts." Helen shook her head. "I made my mother sell the stupid cookies. She was way better at it."

She turned back to face the mirror again, so I did the same. We both futzed about with our hair, and then met eyes again through our reflections. I thought that probably meant something—that we could only *really* look at each other through a looking glass. Literally.

I didn't know where that thought came from, but I could feel that it was true. It had something to do with the two of us, seemingly so different, standing there side by side. There was no wall between us. But we both wanted to think there was.

"I was up at my mom's place in Bar Harbor over Christmas," Helen said. "I drove out past Acadia. Do you remember?"

"Your quarter-life crisis on Cadillac Mountain," I said, almost smiling. "Of course I remember."

"I don't know why you told me the truth about you and Nate before Christmas," she said then, not looking over at me, her voice oddly stiff. "But I feel like I owe you one. I just thought you should know that if I can repay the favor, I will."

"I'm glad you and Nate are good," I said then, because while that wasn't precisely true, I wasn't upset about it, either. She could have him.

Helen slid me an *oh please* look.

"Seriously," I said. "I don't think I was ever really that into him, if you want to know the truth. He just fit into the plan. And I thought *he* was into *me*."

"Uh-huh," Helen said. She smoothed her dress over her narrow hips, and gave me a sideways look. "And he was never that into you. But I'm glad we're friends again now, and can talk about it." She smiled for a moment. "Anyway," she said. "I think I'm going to go dance—it's almost midnight."

She wiggled her fingers at me, grabbed her clutch, and left—the idea that we were *friends again now* hanging behind her like perfume.

In her world, maybe we really were friends. Despite all the mess of the past weeks. Or as if the past weeks didn't matter. It wasn't as if she had any basis of comparison.

But I knew we could never be friends, not really. Not according to my definition of the term. She'd stolen my boyfriend, and that wasn't something you got over. I might forgive it. Maybe. But I'd never forget it. She was never going to be like family to me. She would never be *necessary* to me.

The thing was, it wasn't as if I'd been a particularly good friend to her, either. She had been right—I didn't call her often, and though in the past I'd defended her to Georgia and Amy Lee, it had always been a sort of half-assed defense. All, *I know she's annoying but I find her kind of amusing.* Of course Helen had picked up on that. She was many things, but she wasn't stupid.

It would have seemed laughably impossible even a week ago, but tonight was New Year's and everything felt different. Someday, I thought, there might be another dawn for me and Helen on Cadillac Mountain.

Stranger things had happened.

"Hey," Nate said.

I smiled my thanks at the bartender and then looked at Nate.

"Happy new year," I said, and moved to slide past him.

"Listen," he said, with that smile of his cranked to full gear. "This might sound crazy—you know she can be a lunatic—but is there something going on between you and Henry?" He laughed before I could answer. "I told her she was out of her mind, of course. I know how you feel about him."

"By 'her' you mean Helen, right?" I took a sip of my wine. "That would be your girlfriend? Who you talk about this way to your ex-girlfriend?"

Nate's smile dimmed. "You and Henry don't make any sense," he said. "You know that, don't you? The guy spends his entire life looking for new bimbos to score with. A girl like you can't possibly be with him."

I was clearly supposed to jump all over the *girl like you* part, so instead I asked, "Why do you care who I'm with?"

"You're not, are you?"

I wanted to tell him I was with Henry more than I could remember wanting anything else. Anything besides actually being with Henry, that was. I sighed.

"I'm not with anyone, although I can't understand how that could interest you even—"

Nate was all smiles when he cut me off.

"I knew I could still count on you, Gus," he said. "Promise me you won't do that to yourself. Promise me you won't go there."

It was unimaginable to me that I could ever have wanted this guy, so desperately, for so long. Maybe my desperate pursuit of him after that night hadn't been about him after all. Maybe it was about the other huge event that had occurred that night, the one I'd been avoiding ever since. The one that, had I looked at it clearly, would have changed everything for me.

But Henry had been the unthinkable. He had been off-limits.

In any event, midnight was fast coming, and the New Year was about to dawn. I had much better things to do than entertain this conversation.

"Gus," Nate said. "Not Henry, okay? Not my *roommate*. Show a little respect."

I just shook my head and left him there.

We all screamed the countdown, the ball dropped in New York City, and the band began to play "Auld Lang Syne."

I hugged Amy Lee and Oscar, and Georgia did a little jig with me before dashing from the room yet again, to make another phone call. Couples were hugging each other in the center of the dance floor, and off to the side I saw Helen perform one of her come-hither looks on Nate.

Henry, standing near them, caught my eye again.

I smiled.

He held the look for a long moment before he turned away.

That was that, then. It was a new year. I would find him in it, somewhere. I was sure of it.

In the meantime, I had exactly one day left of my twenties.

It had been a long, weird year. The entire Nate debacle, from its giddy beginning in July to its extended bitter end. The Henry thing. Or *things*, to be precise. Helen. Amy Lee's blowup and the new life she had in front of her. Georgia turning over a new leaf and actually letting herself see what Chris Starling had to offer.

A year ago I'd decided that I would cap off my twenties in style, but really, all I'd done was cram the essence of them into one final year. The second half of one final year, in point of fact. The truth was that I'd been spending years running away from myself. I hid myself in drama, silliness, stupidity, banality. So afraid to grow up. So afraid to involve myself in relationships where I might be expected to give the same love I got—instead of sixth-grade shenanigans. I bored myself with all the *when I grow up* nonsense, but I was worried it would never happen even as I longed for it.

This time, though, I thought I'd actually learned something.

This time, I thought I really might be ready.

Maybe being an adult wasn't crossing some arbitrary age line into wisdom. Maybe it was like anything else—training wheels and mistakes, trial and error, and now and again that feeling that you might have wings.

I liked the idea of it enough to let it move me to my feet, and then out to the dance floor where my friends were waiting. We didn't have wings, but we could dance.

chapter twenty-four

I turned thirty without noticing, while I slept an exhausted sleep that tried to make up for the New Year's festivities as well as the emotional hangover from the Amy Lee upset. When I woke in the morning on January second, I was bleary-eyed, in dire need of caffeine, annoyed with my rambunctious dog, and, apparently, thirty.

Talk about anticlimactic.

Georgia, Amy Lee, and I had stayed up half the night after the party ended, giggling as if there'd never been any rift between us. Oscar had sacked out earlier in their room, with Linus curled up beside him. The next day, we ate breakfast overlooking the stormy bay outside the windows, and then piled back into our cars to join the traffic jam headed back toward Boston.

Once in my apartment, which still delighted me in all its bookshelved goodness, I passed out fully clothed across my bed, woke briefly around 11 p.m. to throw off my jeans and crawl under the covers, and slept away the last of my twenties in a dreamless sort of coma.

Linus barked at me from the door to the living room, completely unconcerned with my advanced age and lack of epic dreams. He just wanted to pee.

Outside, the snow had started to fall sometime before I woke, so the city streets were quieter than usual. Linus romped around in circles, barking happily at the snow-flakes. I caught a few flakes on my tongue on the off-chance I was being secretly filmed, because that was what cute girl-movie heroines did, and then headed back indoors.

My parents had left a singing message on my machine while I was out, which, not for the first time, caused me to wonder exactly where I'd come up with the singing voice I'd had way back when I dreamed of Broadway. My sister would probably leave another song later in the day, but at least I knew she *tried* to sound bad.

"What are we doing to celebrate?" Georgia demanded when she called. By that point I'd retreated to the couch, and was watching some action flick involving Bruce Willis and many dubbed-for-profanity scenes on cable.

"I'm not sure we're doing anything," I replied around a yawn. "It's snowing and it turns out, I don't think I care."

"Yeah, whatever," Georgia said. "I'll be over around eight."

She arrived at seven-thirty, bearing drinks and accompa-nied by Chris Starling—who seemed perfectly at ease in my living room and with Georgia, I was pleased to see. Even more exciting, though, was the fact that Georgia seemed just as laid-back around Chris. I'd never seen her relaxed around a new guy. Ever.

"That seems to be going well," I murmured to Georgia in the kitchen, while Chris poked around in my books.

"We'll see," Georgia murmured back, sounding totally noncommittal, but she was practically radiant.

Amy Lee and Oscar turned up about fifteen minutes later, also with drinks, although in their case the drink was sparkling cider.

"I'm quitting alcohol, too," Oscar told me. "In sympathy."

"That's really sweet of you!" I told him, containing the *aw.*

"It's called survival," Oscar retorted, and only grinned when Amy Lee made a face at him. Then they were caught up in meeting Chris Starling, making noise about the re-decoration, and ordering pizza delivery.

"I can't *believe* this place!" Amy Lee said. She jerked her chin toward Chris Starling and mouthed: *So cute!* "I thought you were going to do the dormitory thing for the rest of our lives. This is just amazing!"

"There's more to do," I said, grinning. I mouthed: *SO cute TOGETHER!* "But it's definitely a good start."

"And Irritating Irwin helped you?" she asked, lowering her voice to a whisper, as if she thought he might be pressed up to his wall with a glass tumbler.

"He was great," I said. "I couldn't have done any of this without him."

"Does he have a crush on you?" Amy Lee asked, narrowing her eyes at the far wall.

"Not that I know of." It not only hadn't seemed that way to me at the time, it sketched me out to consider it, since that would somewhat take away from the new friendship I'd thought I'd made.

"I bet he does," she said, settling into the armchair. "Don't you think, Georgia?"

"Absolutely." Georgia waved her hands around the living room. "Exhibit A."

"Wait a minute," Oscar said. "How is the room an exhibit?"

"Why would he help Gus out if he didn't have an ulterior motive?" Amy Lee asked, sounding perfectly reasonable.

"Because guys can't just be nice," Oscar said, rolling his eyes at Chris Starling. "They have to have ulterior motives."

"They don't *have to*," Georgia said. "They just *do*."

"Help me out, here," Oscar begged Chris.

"I'm with them," Chris replied, leaning back with his hand resting comfortably on Georgia's leg, as if it belonged there.

"You're killing me," Oscar told him.

"I might carry a bag of groceries, but put up shelves and move furniture?" Chris shook his head. "Not unless I thought I had an in."

"He's just a nice guy who doesn't get out much!" I protested. "You all have evil minds!"

"Except me," Oscar said.

"And Gus, apparently," Georgia said, eyeing me. "I didn't know turning thirty meant you'd go all *marshmallow-centered.*"

I was saved from answering that by the buzzer for the door, and the immediate heart attack Linus underwent upon hearing it. He barked. He howled. He hurled himself against the front door as if he thought we were under siege.

Because of this, delivery people did not come to my apartment door more than once.

"It's the pizza," I said, "and you should be grateful, Georgia, because I had a withering comeback planned."

"I'm trembling with fear," Georgia assured me.

"And anyway," I told them, grinning as I got to my feet, "you should all consider getting over the Irwin thing, because he's coming over at eight-thirty."

I slipped into the hallway, and headed for the front door below, flicking a glance at Irwin/Steve's door as I passed it. I didn't think he had a crush on me—and I also didn't care to rip apart his motivations. If our sudden friendship was going to blow up in my face, I didn't think there was much I could do about it in advance. It occurred to me that this mind-set was a significant step away from the norm for me.

Maybe I really was growing up.

I hurled open the door to the outside and froze as the snow whirled around me in a cloud, but not because I was cold.

It was Henry.

"You're not the pizza man," I pointed out.

Unnecessarily.

He stepped inside, and let the heavy door fall shut behind him as he brushed the snow off. He didn't look like *GQ* tonight, he looked a little wild and significantly snow-covered. His jeans and parka were caked in it. But his cheeks were flushed with the cold and the color made his eyes seem as impossible as summer.

"I like the snow," he said with a hint of his usual smirk. "So I went for a walk. But then it turned out that I was here."

"What a coincidence," I said.

"Not really," he said. "I talked to Helen. She told me a few things." He looked particularly intent. "She seems to think you've moved on from the Nate ordeal."

This, then, was my favor. She moved fast.

"And then Nate talked to me," Henry continued. "The whole way back from the Cape, in fact. He explained in excruciating detail how and why you and I could never be together, and how he'd explained this to you, too, but you seemed—how did he put it?" Henry smiled slightly. "Unconvinced."

"Nate and Helen talk a lot."

"They do. I'm hoping they'll move in together and leave me in peace."

"Today's my birthday," I felt compelled to tell him. The foyer was small and damp, with a cold draft, but I didn't feel the chill. I wasn't sure I was breathing. "I'm thirty. An adult. I have big, extremely adult plans."

He fought a grin.

"What does that mean? A mortgage?"

"Please. I just redecorated my apartment. I'm in no position to buy a seat cushion, much less something requiring a *mortgage*."

"So only partially adult plans, then."

"I thought you were mad at me," I said in a voice that started off strong but ended closer to a whisper.

"That's because I was," he replied easily. He pulled off his heavy ski gloves, one by one. "Do you realize that you always think the worst of me? Is that deliberate or what? You take anything I do or say and twist it into something ugly."

I opened my mouth to snap back that he was the one who did the ugly things, no twisting necessary, but stopped myself.

All of the things I had been angry at Henry for could be looked at in a totally different way. He'd let me into the house because he thought I should know what Nate was doing—and in so doing, he'd violated the Guy Code, which was no small thing. (Or so Oscar assured me.) And sure, he'd rejected me that night after the sleigh-ride party, but maybe (just maybe) he hadn't wanted to repeat our first encounter—where I was an emotional wreck and accused him of taking advantage of that after the fact.

Maybe evil, satanic Henry was just something I'd made up, to cover the fact I'd been dating the wrong friend.

"I don't actually know why I do that," I said eventually, and then I smiled at him. He seemed almost surprised for a moment, and then his eyes brightened.

"Maybe, going forward, you can take a breath and consider things before flying off the handle," he said. "Just a suggestion."

"Are we going forward?" I asked, searching his face, terrified I'd see the usual mocking expression. But his eyes were clear and completely serious.

"That's the only explanation I can come up with," he said, almost apologetically, though he was smiling. "Even when I'm avoiding you, here you are."

I felt something swell in me then. It wasn't desperate, or triumphant, or any of the things I was used to feeling around men. This was quiet and thrilling, and new. It felt like it might spill out from me, and fill whole rooms.

It felt like gladness.

"I have people over," I told him, still in that hushed tone. "It's a party."

"Which I'm crashing," he said at once, reverting to the stiff and formal tone I suddenly realized meant he was uncomfortable. "Okay. Well—"

"I'm just telling you so you're prepared," I interrupted him. "Because I'm asking you up again."

"Oh," Henry said. It took a moment to penetrate and then he said it again, in a different tone.

He swallowed, and it astonished me that someone so gorgeous could be as nervous as that little motion suggested.

"Yeah," I said, smiling at him. "*Oh.* It's Amy Lee and Georgia and their men, so it might turn ugly for you. I'm assuming you can handle it."

"As you know," Henry said with a lazy grin, "I can handle ugly. I live for it, in fact."

Halfway up the stairs, I reached over to grab his hand, and curled my fingers around his like they belonged there.

He smiled down at me, and held on like he'd never let go.

Which, in that moment, I believed.

about the author

MEGAN CRANE: *Frenemies* came about because of the movie *Mean Girls*. Seriously. I went to see it with my boyfriend, who squirmed through the entire thing and couldn't believe how nasty all the girls were to one another.

Oh please, I thought. *They toned it down for nationwide distribution. The reality was* much *worse.*

Which got me thinking. I love my women friends. I literally wouldn't have a clue who I was today if it weren't for the friendship, guidance, and support of the women I know. My mother, my sister, my grandmothers, my aunts, my cousins, my friends, my coworkers. They've all helped me create this creature I like to call *me*. (They also make me laugh so hard it makes my stomach hurt, which I believe to be a key ingredient in lifetime friend-

ships.) But as *Mean Girls* made me consider, the women I love are only half of the story.

What about the other women? The ones that we don't get, who seem to inhabit some other universe with alien social rules. The ones we think are really amazing and we're so close to them and then they stab us in the back without blinking an eye . . . or whatever, that could be my issues talking.

As women, we're attuned to the undercurrents of inter-actions. I've been as angry and hurt by a rolled eye as men I know have been from a fist to the face. Everyone knows *that girl*. Everyone's had a best friend break up with her.

I wanted to write a book about all that crazy girl stuff.

Let me know what you think.

You can find me at www.megancrane.com. Or www .welcometothe5spot.blogspot.com. Or just e-mail me at megan@megancrane.com and tell me all about *that girl* in your life!

Thanks for reading!

Meg

5 Reasons to Suspect Your Friends Have Turned Into Grown-ups

(or Maybe Just Turned on You):

 Your best friend gives you a very long lecture concerning china settings, table placement, and the importance of "couple friends," but what it boils down to is that you're single and thus not invited to her dinner party.

2 Nights out now require consultations with date planners/significant others, and extensive plans involving concrete destinations. "Let's go out" is no longer sufficient.

3 Speaking of which, when your friends discuss drinking, they're actually talking about proper hydration for maximum health benefits. Not last night's shenanigans.

 When she plans to stay with him forever, buy a house, have kids, celebrate anniversaries, etc., it turns out that she's unwilling to have those historically graphic conversations about his sexual prowess. It also means you should stop asking.

 It's not that she's screening her calls. It's that her secretarial staff has strict instructions to do so on her behalf.